FREEDOM'S LONELY CRY

BOOK 2 *of the* ESSIE LASSITER TRILOGY

SAM POLAKOFF

FREEDOM'S LONELY CRY
BOOK 2 of the ESSIE LASSITER TRILOGY

Published by Komodo Dragon, LLC
Forest Hill, Maryland

Book design by GKS Creative

Cover image used under license from Alamy

ISBN (print): 978-1-7338898-8-9
ISBN (e-book): 978-1-7338898-9-6

Library of Congress Control Number: 2026904718

FIRST EDITION
Printed in the United States of America

www.sampolakoff.com

ALSO BY SAM POLAKOFF

The Diary of Essie Lassiter

An Inch from Oblivion

Escaping Mercy

Shaman

Hiatus

A Christmas Tale (for children)

This novel is dedicated to my father, Jay Mitchell Polakoff

1936–2025

PROCLAMATION

This book is a work of historical fiction meant for entertainment only. Historical accuracy was neither the goal nor the intention. This novel contains a combination of real and imagined characters. Some scenes were based on actual occurrences, and the author imagined others to enhance the reader's enjoyment.

8 JULY 1776

On a humid summer's morn in New York, General George Washington gathered his troops. Sitting high atop a magnificent white steed, he unfurled the parchment from his blue coat and read the Declaration of Independence for all to hear. His men responded with cheers. The loyal patriots, who listened on the periphery, joined in. Following the recitation, a dozen patriots in Battery Park lassoed the towering statue of King George III with chains and brought it to the ground. Later, the Continental army melted down the British symbol of monarchist rule and produced forty-two thousand musket balls.

1776

CHAPTER 1

Cromwell, Maryland

Essie grew more worried with each tremor rippling through her womb. The unexpected activity on a Thursday afternoon stymied the house of worship's normal serenity. As the church's lone harpist, Essie willingly fulfilled the pastor's request to play Handel's new composition at Sunday morning's service. After she perfected the music, she sat with Penny, who kept her company and was deep into a Fielding novel. The clock struck twelve bells. Her stomach roared. Penny, eager to have a little brother or sister, lovingly chastised her.

"You are with child and mustn't ignore the needs of the womb. You should always carry an apple or a crumpet."

As a midwife and a nurse, Essie didn't need to be reminded of such basic advice. Despite her awareness amid the busyness of her days, she often disregarded her stomach's rumblings. Guilt befell Essie as she looked down at her belly. The developing bulge amazed her. The town seamstress had been most gracious in expediting the delivery of larger clothes to accommodate a figure changing as fast as the town itself.

Everyone took a side, Essie thought. While the Declaration of Independence brought the colonies to the precipice of a formal union, it also drew a sharp divide among its citizens. There was little common ground, and neighbors who were formerly congenial turned surly and withdrawn. Essie sighed. The thought of unrest in the face of a promising future disturbed her.

Pastor Vinson emerged with cornbread baked by a parishioner. He was a bachelor, and the ladies of Cromwell adored the elderly clergyman. Essie gracefully accepted the cornbread and applied a thin layer of strawberry preserves that Pastor Vinson kept in the church's small cupboard. The food was delectable.

"I hadn't realized how hungry I was until I began eating," Essie declared to the beaming clergyman, who reveled in helping others.

Famished, Essie consumed the pastor's cornbread like a hungry wolf attacking a rodent in the woods.

"When will Aquila return home?" Pastor Vinson inquired.

Essie wiped a crumb from her mouth. The pastor pointed to her chin with a sheepish expression. Essie blushed as she dabbed a handkerchief to her face, removing the residue of strawberry jam.

"Forgive my rudeness. The way I am eating, one would think I hadn't done so in days," Essie replied. Then she recalled the question he'd put forth. Essie was prone to prattling on.

"The last I heard, Aquila was in Brooklyn with General Washington. I have had no word of his return."

"I do hope Father is all right," Penny said.

Her father's absence was difficult for a girl approaching fifteen. Penny and Essie had formed an even tighter bond since the hospital room wedding a few short months ago. Essie was merely thirteen years older than her stepdaughter and only six years younger than her husband. The relationship between Essie and her stepdaughter felt more sisterly than parental. They told each other everything.

Essie took one last bite of the cornbread and gripped her stomach. Doubling over in pain, she crumpled to the floor.

"My God, Essie, are you all right? Did the cornbread make you ill?" Pastor Vinson asked. The older man kneeled beside Essie, unsure of what to do. Finally, he yelled, "Penny, quickly, run to the hospital and bring Dr. Clarke or Dr. Van der Beek at once!"

The young girl fled the church, and Pastor Vinson held Essie's hand, tenderly patting it. "Stay put. I may have some sarsaparilla in the cabinet."

She lay still, doubled over in pain. Before the pastor returned, Essie reached down between her legs and was horrified to find her hand awash in crimson.

CHAPTER 2

Brooklyn, New York

A bayonet rifled through his innards, leaving the fallen soldier gutted. Colonel Aquila Wright noted the death of Jeremiah Barnes with dismay. Aquila had lost the most prized infantryman in his regiment. The damn British, he thought. *What will it take to see them pack up and leave America to flourish?* The regiment had counted Barnes among the elite. These were the men who were the bravest, the ones Aquila assessed would afford the American side the best chance to prevail. From a distance, atop his horse, Aquila noted Barnes writhing in pain on the ground. He blanched at the sight of the man's intestines and the volume of spilled blood from the open wound. Barnes was from Aquila's hometown of Cromwell. Aquila knew the family well. He vowed to personally write a letter of condolence to Barnes' parents. But first, Aquila faced a decision he detested. One born of war that forced men to perform acts of treachery in the name of mercy. Aquila would need to ride toward Barnes and place a bullet in his skull. Once the battle subsided, the field medic would assess who he could save. For Jeremiah Barnes, no hope of recovery remained. Even if the battle ended forthwith, the wound was too severe.

Aquila waved his right arm to the Second Regiment, ordering them to attack with fervor. Once he could determine a proper path, Aquila would make his way toward Barnes and perform his act of mercy. Aquila watched as the second wave made its way forward with muskets and pistols at the ready. A cannon blast diverted his attention. He cocked his head hard left and saw six of his men falling backward.

The British cannonball struck its target! Aquila shook his head in despair. They were taking heavy losses. Patriots had their own cannon, but the enemy outnumbered them by a ratio of four to one. The prospect of victory was bleak. Aquila turned back to see if he could make his way to Barnes but was aghast to see a British officer charging forward with his men. Aquila sighed heavily as the front hooves of the British officer's horse trampled the remains of Jeremiah Barnes.

CHAPTER 3

Cromwell, Maryland

Through bleary eyes, Essie saw the lanky figure of Dr. Timothy Clarke duck under the doorframe leading to the church's back room. His baby face peered down at her as she fought the weight of her heavy eyelids. Timothy sounded as if he were speaking from the rear of a cave. His words echoed through her brain, making comprehension difficult.

"Pastor, I need you to pick up Essie's feet while I support her head and shoulders. We will move her to the cart outside."

Essie floated through the sanctuary like a gull by the seashore. The church's wooden rafters were but a blur as her body danced effortlessly on a cloud of air.

"Be careful down these stairs," Timothy instructed as Pastor Vinson moved backward down the steps leading to the street. "I've got a mattress in the cart. We shall place her upon it for the short ride to the hospital."

After she was in the cart and the wooden tailgate secured, Essie gazed at the billowy clouds and languished in the cool breeze of the north wind.

"I shall gather Penny, and we will meet you there," proclaimed the distressed voice of the old clergyman. Pastor Vinson had become Essie's surrogate father since she had arrived in Cromwell from England three years prior. He had saved her time and again.

Timothy mounted the carriage, and Essie soon heard the *clip-clop* of hooves pounding a path down Main Street to the hospital. Essie could hear Timothy's baritone voice call out to passersby, "Clear the way! Medical emergency."

Dr. Henrik Van der Beek was waiting for them outside the hospital entrance. Essie could hear Henrik's frantic steps rushing toward the back of the cart.

"How is she?" Henrik asked anxiously.

Timothy wiped his arm across his forehead. He was drenched in sweat. "She has lost a lot of blood. The baby . . ." And he stopped speaking for fear of further upset.

The tailgate lowered, and Henrik climbed in. He placed his hand on her head, displaying the love they all felt for Essie. With great care, he hoisted her shoulders and helped Timothy move her from the cart to the street. As they carried her toward the hospital entrance, Essie could make out the big, bold lettering on the sign that bore her name:

THE ESTHER WRIGHT HOSPITAL

"Let's bring her into the main operating theater," Timothy said.

Essie grabbed hold of Henrik as they laid her on the surgical table. "Save my baby," she pleaded.

Henrik's face betrayed his words. He replied in his Dutch-accented voice, "We will do all we can."

Essie again fought the urge to sleep. As a midwife, she wanted to help the doctors as best she could. Her voice was stilted. Her thoughts remained unspoken. Still, she heard pieces of the doctors' conversation as they worked to save her.

"We could cauterize the area," Henrik suggested. "I could heat a metal rod in the fire pit behind the hospital."

Timothy shook his head. "No, if we do that, Essie will never bear children. I know she wouldn't want that."

"It may be out of her hands," Henrik replied. "Her life is in danger."

Timothy again relieved his face of perspiration. "Once the placental fluids have passed, we can elevate her lower half to quell the blood loss and then apply a botanical solution. This will give Essie her best chance to live while saving her reproductive abilities."

Henrik remained unconvinced. "Till sunset. If your treatment does not yield results by then, we will have to cauterize to save her life."

"Agreed," replied Timothy.

No longer able to fight the urge to sleep, Essie drifted away on a turbulent sea reminiscent of her long journey from England. The currents took her up, then down, and caused a wave of nausea. Essie wanted to have Aquila's child and to be by his side until they both grew old. Now, these desires were in peril. She gripped the sides of the table with both hands, praying she would live to see tomorrow.

CHAPTER 4

New York, New York

As ordered, Aquila appeared promptly at 7:00 a.m. General Washington used the top floor of the Madison Hotel as his temporary quarters. Once Fort Lee was complete, they would move there or to Harlem Heights. Aquila saluted, stood at attention, and awaited permission to ease his posture. General Washington rose from behind a weathered pine desk and extended his hand. Aquila took it, and his grip unwavering, George Washington locked eyes with Aquila. His steely-eyed determination softened, Aquila thought, as the leader of the Continental army spoke.

"I received a dispatch during the night. It was from Mrs. Greene in Cromwell. It's addressed to you. Believing it to be a military report, I opened it and read it. You have my sincere apologies."

Washington handed him the dispatch. The apology shocked Aquila. Why should Washington feel compelled to offer regret for opening a simple dispatch? Responsible leadership demanded that he do so.

Aquila unfurled the rolled parchment and read the letter from his dear friend, Celia Greene.

Dear Aquila,

I pray this letter finds you safe and in good health. Essie has lost her baby. This, I assure you, was an act of nature, unforeseen and unpreventable. Melancholy has reared its ugly head, but fear not. Between Penny, Hazel, and me, we are tending to her body and spirit. Essie requested that I not inform you of this unfortunate occurrence, but, as your friend, I believe you should know.

Celia

PS: If you see Charles, please extend my undying love.

Distraught, Aquila wished to conceal his emotions from General Washington. Try as he might, his hand trembled, and the dispatch fell to the floor. Washington approached and placed his right hand on Aquila's shoulder.

"Martha had four children from her first marriage. We have none of our own. I cannot imagine how you must feel."

Aquila gathered himself and embraced his commanding officer. "Thank you, Your Excellency. It is hard news to bear. I appreciate your support."

"A leave would certainly be in order," replied the general.

Aquila hesitated, unsure whether he should accept Washington's gracious offer or stay the course. Finally, he stated, "Essie is in good hands. She has her friends Celia and Hazel, and of course, our daughter, Penny, to look after her."

"Very well. I am not at liberty to discuss the matter, but soon I may require you to take on a new post, one that could result in returning home to Maryland and points farther south."

"Yes, sir. Whatever you require of me, I shall do."

Aquila was ready to retreat from Washington's headquarters. He exhaled and thanked God his beloved was all right. The melancholy would fade. Treasured friends like Hazel and Celia knew how to pull Essie through the dark. He turned to leave.

"Aquila, before you go, I understand you are intending to resign from the Congress."

"Yes, General. It has been the greatest honor of my life, and I hopefully will serve again one day in the future, but one must choose how to allocate time. I have concluded I can serve our country more effectively by assisting you in the field."

"And Charles Greene feels the same way?"

"Yes, that is accurate."

"I commend your and Colonel Greene's courage in making the difficult decision. Doing the right thing is not always the easiest path."

Aquila was about to reply when his nose twitched. "Sir, do you smell that?"

"I do," Washington replied as he hurried to the hotel's open window.

Aquila joined the general by the window. The consequences of war were bearing down on the Continental army. Across the street, four buildings were ablaze. A strong wind spurred the flames. People streamed into the street, screaming, choking, and clutching their loved ones and prized possessions.

Springing into action, Aquila declared, "Your Excellency, I will alert the troops at once!"

"Save the artillery. Let's rendezvous at dusk across the river at Fort Lee."

Barreling down the hotel stairwell, Aquila burst onto the street, aghast to witness every building on the opposite side of the street on fire. He shielded his eyes to avoid the smoke's evil-fingered touch. The strong wind would make the fire uncontainable. Upon seeing a lieutenant from his regiment choking, he draped his arm around the young man and brought him to safety behind the Madison. They sat on the ground, and Aquila took the measure of the distressed man. His face had blackened from smoke and falling debris, but Aquila found no overt burns.

"Catch your breath, Lieutenant. I need you to alert the men. Get everyone to the storehouse. I need you to move everything across the river to Fort Lee."

Coughing, the young soldier found his strength and rose, replying, "Yes, sir."

"I shall meet you at the storehouse forthwith. There we will round up every boat and barge we can to move men and materials."

On the street, orange embers flittered downward, landing on other buildings of wooden construction. Aquila quaked with horror as the embers settled and burned, giving birth to new flames and more devastation.

A woman fled a burning structure, running toward him. He heard her plea. "My boy. My boy is still inside."

"Where?"

"In the manager's quarters at the rear of the first floor. My husband runs the hotel. He left early this morning on an errand. My boy is still inside. The smoke was so thick. I tried, but—" She choked on inhaled smoke. "I couldn't find him. Please help!"

Aquila noted the hotel across from the Madison. Fire consumed the building. Aquila raised his right arm to shield his eyes from the smoke while trying to find an opening. Not seeing one, he measured the odds of success, judging them slim and none.

"Is there a door at the building's rear?"

"No, just a window."

"Wait here."

Aquila ran through the narrow passageway between the burning hotel and its neighboring building, which had just caught fire. He found his way to the hotel's rear face and saw the window to the manager's residence. A young boy, perhaps four or five years old, was trying to raise the window from a smoke-filled room.

"Stand back and cover your eyes," Aquila commanded of the boy.

Then he took his elbow, protected by the blue coat he wore, and thrust it into the window. After taking off the coat, he employed it to push away the broken glass from the ledge.

"Come to the window. Stand on anything you can and raise your arms toward me."

The boy did as he was told. Aquila placed his muscular hands under the boy's outstretched arms and pulled him to safety. He shook off his coat to release any remaining shards of glass and wrapped the boy underneath the heavy blue cloth. Clutching the bundle to his breast, Aquila ran through the alley onto the main street and delivered the child to his mother.

"Make your way to the river. Catch a ferry to safety," Aquila instructed. Then he turned northward and jogged through the frantic crowd to the storage area.

Who could have started this? he wondered.

New York City was burning. There was no hope of saving it. Aquila came to a sudden halt. Running through the inferno, his uniform clung to his body. Beads of sweat stung his eyes, and plumes of dark smoke whipped up by the wind made it difficult to breathe. He clutched his chest and felt his knees buckle as he dropped to one knee and gazed at the firestorm enveloping the stronghold the Continental army needed to maintain if independence was to be secured. He rose to continue his journey to help save the armaments, and a drop of perspiration ran down his cheek. The tiny bead of moisture escaping his eye was a tear, one that reduced his tenor to the same rubble as New York City. Was he crying for the lost city and the people who would lose so much? No, Aquila reasoned. He was grieving for his unborn child, who would never live to see the new nation so many had sacrificed so much for. Aquila had saved a young boy but regretted being denied the opportunity to rescue his own child. Had he been home, perhaps Essie would not have endured the loss. Had he been there, he could have picked her up and carried her all the way to the hospital she founded. There, Dr. Clarke or Dr. Van der Beek might have reversed the fatal course of events. Exhaling, Aquila shed a tear for his beloved Essie. What she must have endured!

Alone in a sea of displaced people, Aquila ran to his destination. Saving the republic was a step toward returning to Cromwell. Once home, he vowed he would wrap his arms around Essie and Penny and never let go.

CHAPTER 5

London, England

Lord George Germain hoisted the ale, reveling in each sympathetic sip. His secretary and chief aide, Bartlett Connington, sat across the table with his quill, awaiting the next instruction. The pub catered to soldiers, mainly the military crème de la crème of London. Germain wasn't sure why he continued to frequent the establishment. He asserted his right, disregarding customer animosity. It had been seventeen years since the Battle of Minden, but he feared he might never live down his transgression.

Germain ran his index finger the length of his long-pointed nose, a feature he was reticent to embrace. People had mocked him since he was a mere lad playing on the streets of London. His so-called friends at Trinity College were unmerciful. Yet it was Germain who now turned his nose to those who disrespected his authority. They resented his success.

His head itched. He resisted the urge to scratch. *The damned wigs. So uncomfortable.* Germain took another drink of ale and addressed Connington.

"These fools sneer at me, but it is I who shall have the last laugh. They revere Howe, Clinton, and Cornwallis." He pounded the oak table with his fist, causing the ale to splash over the side of the stein. "I will set the fools straight. These field generals in America will rue the day they mocked the strategic instincts of Lord George Germain."

Connington quivered in fear, unsure of whether to respond. Finally, in a shaky voice, he said, "You are the secretary of state for America. It seems the decisions are yours to make."

Germain smirked. “That’s what Lord North said when he appointed me to this position. And let us not forget that Lord North, as the prime minister, answers only to King George, who has restored my good name to the rolls of the Privy Council.”

A drunken officer sneered at Germain from the next table. “Hey Sackville, you sack of dung, you have no right to drink in a military pub. Refusing orders in the field is an unpardonable sin. Leave, you insubordinate leech.”

Germain turned his head toward the drunken man. Far less inebriated than his antagonist, Germain had control over his mind, body, and actions. He would do nothing rash. He expected such garish behavior from uninformed louts. Before he could respond, Connington took up his defense. “What is your name, sir? You are speaking to Lord George Germain, the secretary of state for America.”

“I know who the bugger is. Changing his name and assuming a hereditary title doesn’t change what he did at the Battle of Minden.”

“I will see to your court martial,” Germain scolded.

“Well, you ought to be familiar with that,” the drunken officer mocked.

Germain did a slow burn. After refusing the order to charge the French in the Battle of Minden, his superiors discharged him and sent him home to England. Later, he was court-martialed at his own request, seeking to clear his good name. While found guilty and removed from King George II’s Privy Council, he was later quietly reinstated when King George III came to power.

Germain drew in a deep breath. “Have your drink and sleep it off. You are of no consequence to me or the kingdom you profess to serve.”

Germain rose, turned his back on the drunkard, and left the pub, more determined than ever to halt the American Revolution.

CHAPTER 6

Fort Lee, New Jersey

Aquila huddled with his men in the nascent fort in the northernmost part of New Jersey. They were safe for now. General Washington had ordered them to stay put until he returned from New York. With the loss of Manhattan to fire, holding their positions at Fort Washington, White Plains, and Harlem Heights was essential to the Continental army's odds of success. Aquila instructed his men to help complete the construction, uncertain of their stay's duration at Fort Lee. While the work continued, Aquila took stock of the armaments General Washington had ordered him to save. Aquila lamented that three cannons and a cache of Pennsylvania rifles were left behind in the haste to flee the burning city. Still, they salvaged what they could.

Aquila was restless. Eight days was a long time to remain idle when a war was raging. Perhaps the patriots needed his help to hold the remaining forts in New York City. Should he send a dispatch to General Washington offering his help? No, he concluded. Aquila wished to be seen as obedient in all matters regarding military strategy. As the senior officer stationed at Fort Lee, Aquila recognized the importance of maintaining a foothold in northern New Jersey. This was especially prudent should they lose the battles at Fort Washington and Harlem Heights. The patriots suffered heavy losses in the New York City fire and the battle of Long Island. British warships brought more men and armaments downriver from Canada. Aquila worried that America's lonely cry for freedom was falling on the Lord's deaf ears. How, he questioned, could a merciful God allow so much death and destruction in the fight for what is just?

Bracing himself for a prolonged pause from battle, Aquila left the armament storage shed and went to check on the construction progress.

"Colonel Wright," called a young infantryman on horseback. "I have an urgent dispatch from General Washington."

With his senses heightened, Aquila grabbed the rolled parchment from the soldier and read:

Aquila,

I have recommended, and Congress has agreed, that to win this war, we will need a navy. The British ability to inflict damage by sea is daunting, to say the least. We must meet this advantage with the greatest effort possible. I assigned General Benedict Arnold the task of building our sea force, and I am ordering you and your men to the camp at the southern end of Lake Champlain. You are to aid General Arnold in procuring materials and overseeing construction. Your men will assist boat builders and craftsmen in felling trees and patrolling the shores in reconnaissance.

This is a critical mission. As you know, the British have a stout navy. Ours contains the sole captured ship from the failed invasion of Montreal; a 12-gun schooner named the Royal Savage. We must construct the rest with haste. I entrust to you this task of strategic importance, and I thank you for your dedication to your country.

Yours truly,

General George Washington

Washington was entrusting him with an important task—serving under the leadership of the heroic General Arnold. For sure, Washington was relying on Aquila's vast construction experience in Cromwell, having built grist mills and Maryland's first hospital. His enthusiasm sparked to new heights, Aquila sent his chief aide to round up the troops. They were off to Lake Champlain.

CHAPTER 7

London, England

The dank, musky odor in his Whitehall office bothered Lord Germain's nose. High-esteem cabinet members had nicer working quarters. After Lord Germain told Prime Minister North that he was displeased with his office, North informed him that the entire Whitehall building shared the same temperate conditions and that nobody had targeted him with a conspiracy. Germain sneezed and blew his elongated nose with the ever-present white muckender. He deserved better. He was, in his own humble opinion, misunderstood. His intellect was superior to most of the imbeciles Britain called leaders and heroes. Still, the Battle of Minden continued to haunt him. The recent mockery at the pub was not an isolated occurrence. Thank God that Lord North saw enough in him to provide domain over the feckless generals he had in the field. Clinton, Burgoyne, Howe, and Cornwallis were good enough as field generals, but strategists they were not. Carleton was more interested in being governor of Quebec.

The only one he trusted was Preston G. Willard. He was older and more experienced and had the battle scars to prove it. Willard had seen it all. No one knew how to tamp down the enemy like Willard. France knew all too well, having succumbed to many defeats in the Seven Years' War. The only man to offer a sympathetic ear after the debacle in Minden was Willard. He was anything but a prototypical British military leader. He could think for himself and voiced his opinions even when they flew in the face of conventional wisdom. Knowing he needed to suppress the rebellion once and for all, Germain could think of no one better to lead the effort.

"It's freezing in here," complained Lord Germain to his meek assistant.

Undismayed, Connington threw another log onto the fire.

The office at the far reaches of Whitehall always disappointed. Too cold in the winter. Hot and muggy in the summer. Once the American campaign was complete and the rebels returned to the fold, Germain would petition Lord North for better quarters.

"Where is Willard?" he bellowed.

"The general should be here any moment, sir."

Germain huffed and blew his nose. Then he heard the thunderous footsteps of an enormous man. When he looked up from the interminable pile of documents on his desk, he spotted the menacing figure of the man many regarded as the greatest military mind in recent British history. General Preston G. Willard towered in the doorway. His head was only a few feet from the top of the doorframe, and the man's girth crowded the entry. Germain wiped his nose, then scrutinized Willard's determined brown eyes and questioned whether a soul existed within. Germain chuckled to himself. Finally, Willard spoke, and Germain could see his mouth for the first time. The bushy gray mustache and beard shrouded it.

"You summoned me, Lord Germain," the giant man stated in a voice marred by the pains of war and decades of grog.

"Yes, General. I wish to review the current state of the American affair and then deploy you to New York."

"In what capacity, Lord?"

"Why, as commander in chief, naturally."

"As you know, I will serve in whatever capacity required of the crown, but you already have many able-bodied generals in the colonies. Howe, Clinton, and even Cornwallis and Carleton could assume the mantle."

"True enough," Germain sneered. "None of them has your record of military acclaim nor the ability to adjust strategy on the fly." Germain stood and began pacing back and forth, a lifelong habit he embraced when needing to articulate a plan or ponder in times of strife. "We control New York City and recently ousted the rebels from their camp in Fort Lee, New Jersey."

Willard looked down at Germain.

The secretary of state for the American Department understood why subordinates and enemies alike feared this imposing figure. Without saying a word, he instilled command. When he spoke, no one dared question his words. Not even Germain.

"We are not engaged in a prizefight. This is war. Class and decorum have nothing to do with it. In my view, it has already dragged on too long," Willard stated.

Germain gathered his courage. He did not wish to show timidity in front of General Willard. He was sure Willard could sense his anxiety. Despite the cold air in his dungeon of an office, Germain broke out into a sweat and wiped it with the same muckender he had used to blow his nose.

"The colonial rebellion must cease forthwith. The sacrifice of New York City by fire was a viable strategy to rid the city and its waterways of the rebel forces. Under British control, the city could be reconstructed to function as a stronghold aimed at dividing the northern colonies from their southern counterparts, thereby implementing a divide-and-conquer tactic." Germain stopped and blew his nose. The air in his office never failed to aggravate him. "You are to rendezvous with Generals Burgoyne and Carleton and move troops south from Montreal. Battalions led by Generals Clinton, Howe, and Cornwallis are to isolate the American forces from joining in or around New York City. Simultaneously, I believe it is prudent to attack the Massachusetts colony. Securing Massachusetts and New York City will cripple the rebels and enable a swift conclusion to the war. Your leadership is of particular importance." Germain sneezed. Again removing the linen cloth, he wiped the tip of his nose and continued. "Many have advised that the Richelieu River terminating at Lake Champlain negates our naval strength. I beg to differ. You must act to preserve the integrity of our naval advantage in the Hudson. I trust you will employ the shipbuilding strategy we spoke of when we last met."

"You needn't worry. I know exactly how to proceed," Willard said confidently.

"Your bravery and leadership in the Seven Years' War are unparalleled. The capture of Canada established what should have been a stronghold for our forces to prevail in America. The current leadership on the ground does not have the military prowess to end this infernal conflict." Handing Willard a sheath of documents, he continued. "These are your orders. You leave on the next ship out.

General Willard, I assure you, you will receive a handsome reward if you end this war quickly."

Willard departed, and Germain paced in contemplation. This was the only logical move to make. The field generals in command posts scorned Germain. Germain would not endorse leaders lacking respect. Willard was a brute, but he would honor authority. He would secure victory and make Germain look brilliant.

Germain shuffled through the stack of documents enveloping his worn and weathered desk. He placed a small leather pouch to his nose and sniffed the fine tobacco imported from the Maryland Colony. Taking a pinch, he placed it inside his pipe and tamped it down before using his burning candle to ignite a small piece of rolled parchment to light the pipe. Germain treasured the sweet smell of the tobacco. He waved his hand back and forth to clear the smoke from his eyes. Oddly, the pipe afforded Germain a sense of scholarly intellect. In his musty office in Whitehall, alone, he fantasized he was at the London Gentlemen's Club, the most private of such places, being announced in a collegial manner for ending the American Revolution with nothing more than his brain and his thumb. Satisfied, he sat back in his creaky wooden chair and watched the smoke spiral toward the ceiling.

CHAPTER 8

Cromwell, Maryland

Both legs, saw below the knees . . . now! Before it's too late." Essie heard Timothy's directive to his colleague, Henrik, and their young charge, Dr. John Robinson. Despite her experience as a midwife and less-than-eager surgical nurse in the throes of war, Essie detested the horror of poking through men's insides. It was all so needless. War. Amputations. Death. Political disdain was the root of it all. As long as men had egos and their associated pigheaded pride, the prospect of war was safe. Women were much more reasonable. And smarter. Essie sat in a rocker in the hospital lobby and wondered how she could make a difference. In America, people longed for the freedoms put forth in the Declaration of Independence. The freedom to live, love, and pray as one saw fit while respecting the choices of one's neighbor, even if those choices differed greatly. England, on the other hand, espoused none of these principles. In Essie's opinion, the proximate cause of the American Revolution was a combination of ego, pride, and greed. The king wanted to rule the world. His subjects would comply with the monarchy's preservation of historical norms, even its whimsical view of the future.

A light sweat broke out across the bridge of Essie's nose. Her stomach cramped. She had advised many a woman on the aftermath of losing a child during pregnancy. This was the first time she had experienced it herself. She caressed her abdomen with her hand and closed her eyes, willing the discomfort to pass. Her legs felt as if she had fallen and landed in a sea of sharp-edged pinecones. Suddenly, a cool cloth pressed against her forehead and dabbed at her nose.

"Hazel, the hospital is so busy. I thought you might be pressed into nursing duties."

Hazel had assumed most of Essie's responsibilities as the hospital administrator.

Her best friend threw her a warm smile. "I am nursing someone in need right now."

Since befriending Hazel on the treacherous journey across the sea to America, they had become inseparable. "Can I get you some peppermint tea to calm your stomach and your mind?"

"Yes, but only if you will join me."

"Of course. I'll return shortly, and we can talk. You appear troubled."

Essie closed her eyes and rocked gently. The doors of the hospital swung open every few minutes with another emergency. She wanted to rise and help ease the pain of the sick and wounded, but she had nary the strength. She could only call for nurses or doctors and try to comfort the distressed newcomers. The *clip-clop* of approaching horses thundered through her brain, a constant reminder that theirs was the only hospital within a hundred miles. Injured soldiers often reached Cromwell, nearly expired from travel and lack of proper medical care en route. There had to be a better way.

Hazel returned with a small tray, the kind used for patient meals. On top sat two bone-colored clay mugs filled with steaming tea. The scent of peppermint relaxed Essie as Hazel sat down beside her in a hardback chair, and they both inhaled the pleasing aroma.

Essie ceased rocking and sat up straight. Her sweat had given way to chills, and the hot tea revived her.

"Now, tell me what's on your mind?" Hazel inquired.

Essie sighed. "It's a jumbled mess, if you must know. My mind races from losing the baby to reuniting with Aquila to trying to be a mother to a teenage girl. And all the while, I sit helpless here in the lobby while you and others are rushing about in attempts to aid the sick."

Hazel put her tea on the small oak table between them. She squeezed Essie's arm affectionately. "You've been through so much. It's no wonder your mind is aloft."

Essie's face relaxed. She sipped her tea and savored the taste. "And if that's not enough, with Aquila gone indefinitely, I am running Cromwell's Passage. It is difficult to keep up with the needs of such a large estate, especially for a woman of my station."

"Your former station," Hazel gently corrected. "You have a new life here. You have climbed the social ladder, and you have risen to the occasion. Do not doubt yourself. You are a genuine wonder!"

Blushing, Essie waved her hand as if to say Hazel showered her with undeserved accolades. "I am still finding my way through this new life. I mean, can you imagine? The house I shared with my first husband in Wickhamshire would not have filled the stable at Cromwell's Passage."

Laughing, Hazel replied, "You mean to say the horses in Maryland live better than the people in quaint English villages?"

"I know ours do," answered Essie. Hazel was such a dear friend and always knew how to make Essie laugh when the moment called for it.

"What else is troubling you?"

"Laid up as I am, I sit here in the lobby and watch men stream through those doors. As long as the war continues, the flood of casualties will not stop. Many are beyond help due to the long distance they must travel over rough terrain. There must be a way to bring medical treatment closer to the battlefield."

"Isn't that what field medics are for?"

"Of course, but they have limited resources and can only do so much. Often, they must choose who to save and who to let go." Essie waved an exasperated arm in a circle to emphasize her point. "Can you imagine the plight of the field medic? One poor sod per battlefield, trying to treat dozens of wounded amid battle. It's preposterous."

Hazel blanched at the notion, her face crinkling as she responded. "How dreadful."

They sat in silence for a spell, and then Essie brightened.

"I know that look," Hazel proclaimed. "Your mind is conjuring some sort of scheme, isn't it?"

Essie grinned. She sipped the last of the tea and said, "I'm feeling much better. I think I shall write a letter."

"To whom?"

"My dear friend Benjamin Franklin."

CHAPTER 9

Lake Champlain, New York

"Unbelievable!" Aquila proclaimed as he peered through his spyglass. "The buggers are dismantling their fleet."

"To what end?" asked Captain Garrett Broadchurch.

Aquila, still focused on the scene, pulled his eye from the glass and looked over to the young officer in his charge. "My best bet is the British plan on moving the materials south of Lake Champlain and reassembling them to sail on the Hudson."

The distress on Broadchurch's face was instantaneous. "And we're here to build a naval fleet. Before we even attempt our mission, they could finish theirs." Broadchurch ran a troubled hand over his expansive forehead, knocking his hat backward. "If the British get their prime warships into the Hudson, the entire war will shift in their favor."

Aquila shook his head. "Not if we stop them first."

A flicker of understanding crossed Broadchurch's face. He nodded in agreement. Aquila kept low to the ground to avoid being seen. He waved to the young captain to follow. He held a finger to his mouth, indicating silence was required. They must not let their mission fail before they reported to General Arnold.

—ɷ—

Benedict Arnold slapped Aquila on the back in an ebullient display of gratitude.

Young Captain Broadchurch seemed dismayed. "General, sir, do you not find this news distressing?"

Arnold laughed. "Captain Broadchurch, I would have found the news far more distressing had I not learned about it when I did. We have time to sabotage the entire operation. It will prove easier than sinking these warships at sea. Don't you agree, Colonel?"

Aquila stood erect and nodded. "Yes, General. As soon as you give the order, I will take two regiments during the night to disarm the British operation."

Arnold reveled in the upper hand as he swaggered across the room. "We have time. Dismantling three warships is no straightforward task and will take weeks. We must plan carefully."

"I concur. Allow me to huddle with Captain Trumbull and Captain Broadchurch. We will devise a plan and present it to you no later than tomorrow morning."

Arnold seemed pleased. "That is acceptable. I must leave now to check on the progress of our shipbuilding operation. We can't fell timber and construct our fleet fast enough." And with that declaration, Benedict Arnold waved them away. "You are dismissed."

CHAPTER 10

Cromwell, Maryland

Essie sat on a chaise lounge with her legs tucked and her back against green down-filled pillows. Parchment and a quill rested beside her atop a maple tray. The scent of burning wood from the fireplace eased her frayed nerves, and the crackling fire sparked her creativity. She pondered the elements of the letter she was constructing and tapped the quill on the tray top. Ideas floated in and out, some good, some impractical. Essie weighed the proper words to bring a huge endeavor to fruition, brushing a lock of hair from her eye.

"Are you writing a letter?" asked her stepdaughter.

Essie looked up. She lost herself in thought. She seemed the only person on earth. When she failed to acknowledge Penny's question, the girl spoke again. "Essie, are you all right?"

Essie shook her mind's cloak and took the measure of her beautiful stepdaughter. Penny's dark hair shone amid the fire's glow. The alabaster skin of her youthful face had yet to display the aging that defined so many. Penny suffered significant grief during her youth, including her mother's death, a bear attack, capture by British soldiers, and the atrocities of war. But in Essie's opinion, Penny had weathered it well.

"Forgive me. My task consumed me. I am writing a letter to Benjamin Franklin."

"Isn't he in France with his grandson?"

"Yes, he is attempting to secure French military aid and recognition of the United States."

"Please extend my warmest thoughts to Dr. Franklin. Let him know that I still play the glass armonica he made for me."

Essie stood and embraced her stepdaughter while considering her good fortune. She married a remarkably kind and handsome man of means. She became a mother to Penny, to whom she had forged an indelible bond, and she was here in America, where anything seemed possible.

"I will apprise Benjamin of your regards and update him on all the news from Cromwell." Essie gazed into the fireplace. Her smile from moments ago faded, and an empty expression appeared.

"You are not writing Dr. Franklin just to be sociable, are you?"

Amazed by the intuition of a budding fourteen-year-old, she replied, "No. You are wise beyond your years. I am trying to formulate the best way to articulate an idea to aid our army in treating wounded soldiers on the battlefield."

With an arched eyebrow, Penny exclaimed. "That's astonishing! How will someone accomplish such a feat?"

"Well, I'm still trying to figure that out. Right now, too many soldiers are dying because the battles take place so far away from the few hospitals we have in America."

"And we can't move the battles closer to the hospitals," stated Penny eagerly.

"Nor would we want to. However, we can get better medical treatment closer to the battlefield without trying to open numerous hospitals in short order in the throes of war."

"So you've achieved the *why* of the idea, just not the *how*."

"Precisely. Hence the letter to Benjamin. He cofounded the Philadelphia hospital with the Bond brothers and helped us start the Cromwell hospital. And with his rich history as an inventor, well, I couldn't imagine a better person to help put meat on the bones of my skeletal idea."

"Tell me what you have so far."

Essie reveled in Penny's enthusiasm for ingenuity. "The basic thought is to get two or more doctors, a half dozen nurses, two surgical theaters, medicines, and medical supplies close to the battlefield with the capability to relocate quickly as our troops move to the next battle. A team of the fastest horses could carry the severely injured to the nearest hospital."

Penny's face revealed the deliberations of a young mind processing the complexity of an impossible idea. "It sounds like a grand notion, but . . . oh my gosh, I see why you are stuck on the *how*." Penny ran a hand through her dark brown hair and said, "Doctors are in short supply. That prospect alone seems daunting."

"You are so right, Penny. I think about my first husband. He attended a trade school for doctors in England. His training took years. Could we not have an experienced surgeon and an apprentice or two to assist in the field? There are so many other issues to address. It requires a wealth of resources and a strong leader. I'm unsure how these ominous hurdles will be overcome."

"I understand your angst. My hope is that Dr. Franklin can assist."

Essie placed an arm around Penny's shoulders. "That is my hope as well."

CHAPTER 11

Lake Champlain, New York

On the cusp of winter and facing a mammoth task, General John Burgoyne pondered whether he had erred in pausing his troops on the march from Canada. Certainly, the need to wait for supplies was paramount, but as he often reminded himself, delay kills. In Burgoyne's experience, taking things apart was far easier than reassembling them. This was true as a boy when, out of pure curiosity, he disassembled his treehouse. Burgoyne's stomach burned when he read the decoded dispatch from the commander in chief. Take apart three ships, carry the parts through miles of forest, and then reassemble them on the banks of the Hudson. It was madness. Alas, Burgoyne knew better than to engage in debate with the powerful General Willard. He was not a man who welcomed suggestions from the troops, regardless of the rank.

Scores of men worked at a furious pace, yet the task was insurmountable. Burgoyne shook his head and left his makeshift quarters to join the other generals by the campfire. An icy wind blew off the frigid waters of Lake Champlain. Burgoyne straightened his back and wished he were home in Sutton with Charlotte and his three children. Burgoyne pulled his red coat up to his chin and greeted his colleagues. Gathering Clinton, Howe, Cornwallis, and Carleton in one spot was perilous, Burgoyne thought. One rebel surprise attack could wipe out the better part of His Majesty's field generals. This was the wisdom handed down by Willard and those in charge in London. Who was he to protest?

"Are you weary of battle?" Burgoyne asked his colleagues.

Carleton, the next oldest, was quick to reply. "I much prefer the governor's house in Montreal, especially on these brutal fall nights with orders I deem near impossible."

"I rather enjoy the chase of the impossible. And the weather isn't that bad. I survived far worse as a youth hunting with my brothers outside Mayfair," Cornwallis chirped.

Burgoyne laughed at the much younger man. "Yes, talk to us when you've reached your fortieth birthday."

"Or better yet, when you are nearing sixty," quipped Carleton.

Howe, the former commander in chief, spat into the fire. In Burgoyne's estimation, he seemed bitter at being replaced by the less congenial Preston G. Willard. Who could blame him? Now, he sat idly by awaiting direction from leaders none of them liked or respected. Willard was inflexible, and Germain was an egotistical fool, a blowhard, nothing more. What Lord North saw in the lout was beyond Burgoyne's comprehension.

Burgoyne shuffled the fallen leaves with his left foot. It was a lifelong response when he was lost for words. Finally, he stammered, "General Howe, do you see our mission as achievable?" Despite the promotion of Willard, they all held Howe in the highest regard.

"Time is not on our side. With winter coming, moving the men and materials through miles of densely wooded terrain and reassembling three naval ships during harsh weather is a fool's errand."

"What choice do we have?" asked Carleton.

"I, for one, intend to resign my commission before winter's end," replied Howe.

Burgoyne didn't know how to respond. He was loyal to a fault. He would see the mission through or die trying. If it's what His Majesty required of him, that's what he shall do.

"I find the entire affair ironic," stated Cornwallis.

"In what way?" asked Clinton, his mentor.

"General Howe despised an order from Germain, who is hated because he did the same at the Battle of Minden."

Howe was furious. "How dare you compare me to that unscrupulous pig!" Howe removed a white glove from his right hand and threw it at the feet of Cornwallis.

"Are you challenging me to a duel?" inquired Cornwallis.

In a huff, the senior officer replied, "You have insulted my honor."

General Clinton stepped in to rescue his young charge. "William, I know Charles well. He is opinionated, as most young men are, but means nothing by the remark."

Clinton picked up Howe's glove and returned it to its owner. "Charles, is there anything you'd like to say to General Howe?"

Burgoyne wasn't sure if the chilly night air or embarrassment caused the redness in Cornwallis's cheeks.

"General Howe, I have the utmost respect for your military career and as a man to be reckoned with. I beg your forgiveness for my thoughtless quip." And with that, Cornwallis extended his hand, and Howe took it begrudgingly. While that concluded the incident, Burgoyne thought it just the beginning of a disjointed effort to defeat the Americans. London had little faith in the esteemed group of generals gathered around the fire on a frosty night by Lake Champlain. The generals had no respect for the commander in chief or the secretary for the American colonies. Worst of all, Burgoyne surmised, the generals' appetite for a lengthy war was fading. The esteemed group of British military leaders retired for the evening, one by one. Burgoyne lingered by the fire alone, wondering how the absence of a leader amongst leaders could produce victory.

CHAPTER 12

Lake Champlain, New York

Five days later, under the direction of Benedict Arnold, Aquila led two regiments guided by Captain Garrett Broadchurch and his family's longtime trusted mill foreman, Captain Isaiah Trumbull. Aquila possessed an adequate quantity of troops and, more important, the element of surprise. Captain Broadchurch was to lead an attack on the camp while Trumbull's men would scour the woods for British troops attempting to drag parts of the Royal Navy through the forest. The plan was conceived immediately upon acquisition of the intelligence. Aquila drilled his men hard for four straight days. They were ready.

Before midnight, Aquila and his two captains stood on the ridge of Lake Champlain. Drawing strength from the memory of Essie and Penny and the warm surroundings of Cromwell's Passage, Aquila inhaled and took in the cold white moon and all its brilliance. The grand celestial body would provide Aquila and his men all the light they required for a successful mission. He bade his officers luck and gave the order to attack.

Aquila accompanied Broadchurch's regiment. It was the larger of the two. Four hundred and fifty men equipped with muskets, bayonets, rifles, pistols, and knives made their way on foot toward the British camp.

—∞—

Isaiah Trumbull was no stranger to a hunt through the woods. Growing up in Cromwell, he spent his youth seeking deer in the forest and any other game he might happen across. He loved the challenge of navigating uncharted woodlands. It was even more enjoyable when there was a prize to be had. Isaiah mounted his brown steed, heaving his thick right leg over the saddle. He was a large and strong man who welcomed a scrap with anyone who might partake. He waved his arm to release five dozen men to their task. Riding out in front of the foot soldiers, Isaiah navigated his way while following his senses. Even with the bright full moonlight, he would rely on his ears and his nose to achieve victory. With Aquila's guidance, they made the troops drill in silence. Men practiced moving through the woods making minimal noise. Though the sounds of shuffled leaves and breaking twigs were unavoidable, refraining from speech was achievable. The only one who could make a sound in the woods was him, and Isaiah would not abuse the power.

They progressed deeper into the forest until Isaiah heard the first sounds. Voices. Grunting. Dragging. The sound of a nearby stream reminded him of the Nathaniel River near Cromwell. The redcoats were just up ahead. He had found his target. They needn't destroy all the parts being transported, just large sections, making the reassembly of the warships impossible without significant delay.

A scout approached Isaiah's horse and held up three fingers, signaling that intelligence had been gathered and needed to be communicated. Isaiah dismounted and walked with the scout to a group of northern red oaks thirty paces away. They whispered.

"Captain, downstream are a series of large sleds carrying ship components and materials. The redcoats are dragging the sleds with heavy ropes."

"Good work. I will send a corps of riflemen to take out the redcoats guarding the sleds. Another group will follow with torches."

Through a spyglass, Aquila saw smoke rise from the forest. It signaled victory in the first phase of the attack. It also created a diversion to occupy the British leaders stationed at Lake Champlain. From atop his horse, he sat on the edge of a bluff and turned his sights toward the second phase of the operation. Aware of the fire in the woods, the redcoats scurried about their camp in a frenzy. Aquila nodded to Broadchurch, who waved his arm, and hundreds of soldiers descended upon the enemy and, one by one, shot them dead.

CHAPTER 13

Cromwell, Maryland

Essie informally dubbed the holiday *Ladies' Christmas*. For the second year in a row, she and Penny would celebrate without Aquila. Essie's treasured friend, Celia Greene, was without her husband, Charles, and Hazel had yet to find a suitor. The only men who would attend Christmas dinner at Cromwell's Passage were Pastor Vinson, Dr. Timothy Clarke, and Dr. Henrik Van Der Beek. The latter would bring his wife, Fleur. Essie wished she could pair Dr. Clarke with Hazel. This, she pondered, would be no simple task, as both seemed happily single, married only to their work at the hospital. Moreover, Timothy had proposed to Essie on more than one occasion and was even prepared to leave Cromwell in the face of her polite refusal. Hazel, like Essie, had been widowed in England before being hauled off to the London Debtor's Prison after a failed, vain attempt to retire her late husband's mountain of bills.

"Are you planning Christmas dinner?" Penny inquired.

Essie blanched. "I apologize. I was lost in thought. You startled me. Yes, Ladies' Christmas is almost upon us."

"I always seem to catch you off guard when you are busy."

Essie beamed. "It's quite all right. I always place you first."

Her stepdaughter, wise beyond her years, noted, "Still, you seem troubled."

Sighing, Essie closed her eyes and stated, "Truthfully, I was daydreaming about how I might start a fire."

"Can't a servant accomplish this?"

Essie wrapped an arm around her stepdaughter's shoulders. "No, silly. Not an actual fire. I wish to fan the flames of love between Timothy and Hazel."

"Oh, a matchmaker, are you now?" exclaimed Penny.

"It just may prove impossible. Neither will confess their loneliness, but I see it in both their eyes. They want what I have with your father. And I want it for them."

"How will you manage it?"

"Well, I have no earthly idea. They see each other every day at the hospital. Maybe that could be a starting point."

Penny mused, "It might prove uncertain to assume that two people could somehow fall in love in a place where blood and guts are ever present."

Essie sighed. "I cannot refute your point. It feels like a hopeless endeavor."

"What if you could somehow get them to engage in an activity together? Sometimes at the schoolhouse, our teacher pairs us with another student for no other reason than to make a new friend."

Brightening, Essie replied, "That's a wonderful idea. I shall ponder how to create such a scenario."

Essie wrote the menu, but her thoughts remained on uniting Timothy and Hazel. They desperately needed one another. They just couldn't see it. The sun was fading in the early winter sky. The day was ending, and the hospital, barring any unforeseen emergencies, would be in a quiet period. Discarding the draft menu on the writing table, Essie jumped to her feet and ran to collect her cloak. Summoning the Wrights' ancient coachman, Clement, Essie left with urgency, destined for the hospital that bore her name.

Arriving in town, Essie jumped from the carriage, not waiting for the old coachman to open the door and help her to the street. She told Clement to wait for her as she crossed the threshold of the lobby and found Hazel.

Barely greeting her best friend, she said, "Quickly, find Timothy and Henrik and return with them. The four of us must meet to discuss an important idea."

Hazel scurried out of the room, and Essie walked into her modest office, removing her cloak and sitting down at her desk. Giddy, Essie rubbed her arms to help the goosebumps subside. She hadn't been this excited in months. Moments later, Hazel returned with the two doctors in tow. Timothy, the chief medical officer of the hospital, wore a look of grave concern. "Is everything all right? The suddenness of this meeting is quite unusual."

Sweeping a lock of hair from her forehead, Essie chuckled. "Yes, everything is fine. I had an idea and wanted to begin work on it immediately."

"What, pray tell, could not have waited till tomorrow?" Henrik asked. "It is finally calm here, and Fleur is expecting me for an early supper."

"This won't take long," Essie replied.

Essie studied the friends before her. Henrik fidgeted, eager to depart. Timothy stood erect, his face stoically awaiting the presentation of her thinking, and Hazel, with her blond hair pulled back under a white lace bonnet, gazed curiously with those brilliant emerald eyes. Before she spoke, Essie imagined Hazel gazing into Timothy's crystal blue pools and him desiring to kiss Hazel the way he once had with her.

From her office, Essie heard the front doors of the hospital open. The sound of the freezing wind accompanied the swinging door, and a momentary chill swept down the hallway into the room where they gathered. It snapped her back to the reason for the meeting.

"As you all know, some time ago, I had written a letter to Benjamin Franklin requesting his counsel on the matter of medical treatment closer to the battlefield. I've yet to receive his reply, but it occurred to me we can begin planning nonetheless."

"What do you have in mind?" inquired Timothy.

"Just the shell of a concept. I believe we need to create a hospital unit that can move as battle dictates. This will eliminate the patients traversing long distances to the nearest hospitals and save others from dying on the battlefield. We need to construct a plan of how to staff and supply these efforts. Battles rage from Massachusetts down to Georgia. We can be the salve, the secret weapon, that helps keep the American soldiers on their feet and focused on securing the future of freedom."

Henrik scoffed. "A noble thought, but realistically, we have all we can handle running one hospital. What you propose is a monumental concept worthy of consideration by the Continental Congress and General Washington, not the likes of us."

Timothy silently carried a torch for Essie. She knew this from the way he acted around her. No matter how outlandish her ideas had been in the past, Timothy always came to her aid. He didn't disappoint her now.

"I believe it is an idea worthy of exploration if for no other reason than for intellectual purposes. Who knows? The exchange of ideas, at a minimum, just may contribute to improvements here at the hospital."

"I'll do whatever you need, love," Hazel added in her Cockney dialect.

Beaming, Essie seized the moment. "I propose that Timothy and Hazel work on a framework for how to accomplish our transitory hospital. When you are done, you may present your ideas to me, and Henrik can consult as he can spare the time."

Henrik appeared relieved that he could gracefully extricate himself from what he saw as folly and concentrate on treating patients.

Hazel looked at Timothy and said, "Why don't we start tomorrow evening? I will prepare a meal, and we can eat here while we work."

"Splendid. I shall look forward to it," replied Timothy. He looked back toward Essie, as if seeking her approval. His youthful puppy-dog expression revealed his closeted feelings for her. Placing Timothy and Hazel together on a project where they would work together into the evening would transfer his feelings from her to Hazel. In this, Essie was confident.

A knock befell the doorframe of her office. It was Pastor Vinson. The older man shook off the cold and brushed errant snowflakes from his shoulders. The blue ribbon securing his gray hair at the nape of his neck still held traces of a snow shower. Pastor Vinson pushed his glasses up from the tip of his nose.

"Pardon the interruption. I was dropping off a post at the general store and noticed a letter addressed to Essie lying on the counter. I told Mr. Brown, the storekeeper, that I might find you here, and he entrusted the delivery to me."

Pastor Vinson reached into his black topcoat and pulled the letter from within. It originated in France. Finally, a reply from Benjamin was in hand.

CHAPTER 14

McConkey's Ferry, Pennsylvania

Aquila gained much favor with General Arnold for his successful mission at Lake Champlain. The commendation from General Washington was unexpected but appreciated. General Washington then transferred Aquila, Broadchurch, and Trumbull to his direct command in McConkey's Ferry. When Aquila arrived at dawn's first light at the winter quarters of the Continental army, Washington's aide-de-camp, a bookish man with round spectacles, greeted him. Aquila thought he resembled the screech owls common to the woodlands at Cromwell's Passage.

"I am Major Louis Pembery. His Excellency awaits your arrival. I am to show you to his tent forthwith."

Aquila signaled to his two senior officers to follow. The aide-de-camp held up one hand. "General Washington wishes to speak to you alone. After I deliver you, I will show your men to their quarters."

George Washington was a man completely in control. He took pride in having a neat uniform, holding proper posture, and always remaining even-keeled. Aquila knew few men who represented themselves in such a regal manner.

"Merry Christmas, Your Excellency. It is good to see you again."

Washington approached with his hand extended. Aquila noticed the powdered hair favored by the commander in chief. Most men of his stature would don the wig. Washington declined. In keeping with his earlier perception, Aquila noticed that no errant powder resided on Washington's epaulets or shoulder cloth. Washington moved to the tent flap and secured it to prevent any disturbance.

"And a merry Christmas to you, Aquila. I trust Essie and Penny are well."

"From recent letters, I take that to be certain. Since we conquered the British in Cromwell, redcoats have been sparse."

"That may be. But as you know, Cromwell is strategically located. It sits firmly between Baltimore and the Brandywine Valley. The presence of the hospital alone makes the town a potential target. And do not dismiss the notion that the British have spies everywhere. They may not be wearing red coats. They hide in plain sight as loyalists."

At that moment, Aquila felt a knot form in the pit of his stomach. He, at the behest of Maryland's deceased British governor, had established Cromwell as the hospital's site. The colonies had not declared independence. The notion of a war of the magnitude and scale they were in was not a certainty. Cromwell, the town founded by his grandfather, made all the sense in the world. Now, taking in Washington's words, he worried he had placed his family and the town in peril.

Gathering himself, Aquila steadied his nerve, and replied, "Yes sir, we must remain vigilant in all aspects."

"Which is precisely why I've ordered you here. You have arrived just in time. Tomorrow night, we shall embark on a surprise attack on the Hessian camp in Trenton."

"On Christmas?"

"I can't imagine a better scenario."

Aquila smiled. If Washington ever lacked confidence in the face of a fight, he never showed it.

"Take your men. Have breakfast. Settle in. We will meet here with the war council in one hour to review final plans for tomorrow's attack."

A ten-foot rectangular table held a map of the Delaware River. Surrounding the table was George Washington's war council. Aquila steadied himself. His legs felt weak in the presence of such ominous military prowess. He respected these men; inclusion in their company was an honor. General John Glover and his Marblehead Militia, a well-known band of mariners from diverse backgrounds, navigated waterways. Abhorring slavery and prejudice, Aquila respected General Glover's willingness to lead men of color, Jews, and Spaniards. Aquila suspected that a few of the other prestigious men around the table did not share his respect for the composition of Glover's Marblehead Militia. General James Ewing, a formidable leader of Pennsylvania militiamen, was contemplating the map. Washington referred to Colonel James Cadwalader as a military genius. Two less seasoned men rounded out the war council: a young general named Henry Knox and Colonel Alexander Hamilton, who Aquila had heard was a confidant of Washington. In the tent's corner, the owlish Louis Pembery, Washinton's aide-de-camp, stared at the group from afar, never uttering a single word unless called upon.

"Mounting losses, expiring commissions, and deserters have depleted our army," Washington lamented. "Recent setbacks in New York and the surrender of Fort Lee have sunk morale. Gentlemen, we desperately need a victory." The commander in chief arched his back, approached the map, and with a pointer, shifted his attention to the drawings on the table. "There are spies in our midst. Even though I remain sure that someone conveyed our plan for tomorrow evening to the Hessians, either in whole or in part, I still believe we have the element of surprise."

"How can you make such a proclamation? Surely, they are on high alert," said Cadwalader.

"I agree," added General Ewing. "Our army is low on provisions, numbers, and spirit. Losing a battle to the Hessians in Trenton could place our backs against the wall. We could lose the entire war."

Washington glanced at the waterman, General Glover, asking for his counsel.

"Crossing the Delaware in the dead of winter is no simple task. But as I've told General Washington, with the aid of General Knox, we have successfully run lines from bank to bank. Our flotilla will hold to these lines to hasten the crossing and ensure steady craft."

Aquila realized with admiration that Washington already knew what Glover would report. The commander in chief surmised that Glover's news would inspire confidence in the mission. The young Alexander Hamilton elbowed Aquila in the arm and smiled. Apparently, he found kinship with Aquila in their mutual respect for Washington's leadership.

Glover then reported, "We have gathered and confiscated every floating craft we could find. Our men have secured boats accustomed to hauling heavy shipments of iron ore. We also have flat barges to transport cannon and horses."

Washington, having listened to the opinions and reports of his trusted war council, took control of the meeting.

"The British hired the Hessians as mercenaries. They are known to be heavy drinkers. It is likely they will have had their fill in the face of the holiday celebration. At the hour of our attack, I suspect a drunken stupor will have occurred, with little or no lucidity."

Returning to the map, Washington continued. "We will cross the Delaware in the last hour of Christmas night. General Ewing and his troops will cross the river near Trenton, Colonel Cadwalader will cross near Burlington, and General Glover and I will cross near McConkey's Ferry. General Knox, Colonel Wright, and Colonel Hamilton will accompany me. Cadwalader's men will distract the British and Hessian troops in the south, preventing their northbound movement to aid the planned area of attack. Ewing's men will take up position just north of Trenton. We want you to wait in case they retreat. The rest of us will march ten miles south to Trenton and attack just before dawn."

Grateful to be assigned to Washington's command, Aquila relaxed. It would be a long and cold night. They would attempt a monumental feat with thousands of men, horses, and armaments. Aquila left the tent and gazed up at the clear blue sky. At least they would have good weather for their mission.

The Christmas celebration had been the best he could offer his men under trying circumstances. Johann Rall, commander of the Hessian forces in Trenton, pushed his chaw to the side of his mouth and spat tobacco on the ground. Rall was an experienced man with over twenty-five years of military service. He had seen it all, having fought in the War of the Austrian Succession, the

Jacobite rising of 1745, the Seven Years' War, and the fourth Russo-Turkish War. Working with the British to suppress the ragtag Continental army seemed like child's play. Could one even call it an army? From what he had ascertained from his British benefactors, soldiers fought in cobbled masses, comprising local militias with little training and deficient supplies. Despite warnings from two American deserters and Washington's aide-de-camp about an impending attack on Trenton, Rall concluded that the winter weather, the Christmas holiday, and the formidable Delaware River would render such talk as nonsense. Rall could think only about his return home. He threw back his jug of moonshine whiskey and fell into a deep sleep.

Although his military experience was slight, Aquila had learned that the best-laid plans often go awry. Such was the case on Christmas night as he stood on the banks of the Delaware at McConkey's Ferry in the face of a nor'easter. The icy wind penetrated his coat with the force of a cannonball. The snow raged. Aquila shielded his face with an arm. It was a hopeless endeavor. Bits of ice pecked at his cheeks, stinging as if he had disrupted a beehive. Seeking assurance that the mission was even possible, Aquila glanced up at the Delaware. A large portion of it had frozen. The water that flowed held pieces of broken ice dancing about the current. Any sane man would have aborted the mission in the face of such torrid conditions. Washington seemed undismayed. He was wagering an enormous sum. With a depleted army, investing in a mission with a high percentage of active troops in harrowing conditions could prove disastrous to the prospects of freedom. Once Aquila saw Washington give the order to General Glover to have his men begin, he shivered, took a deep breath, and summoned his courage. Washington stood tall, placed one hand on his hat to keep it from blowing away, and shouted, "Victory or death."

Aquila worked with Hamilton, Trumbull, and Broadchurch to supervise the loading of men, munitions, and horses onto the varied array of watercraft. Aquila worried about the men but more so about the horses. Could the men on the flat barges keep hold of their own legs and still steady the animals? If the horses didn't make it across the river, the ten-mile march to the Hessian camp in ominous wind and snow would be difficult if not impossible. The storm's strength grew as the hours passed.

The commencement of the mission was taking far too long. At every turn, the weather impeded progress. Aquila and Hamilton were among the last to cross. The iron ore boat they occupied bounced up and down while swaying from side to side. Icy water poured into the craft, and Aquila's toes went numb. He peered across the river. Most of the men ahead of him were standing. He understood why. Being seated would be too unpleasant with cold water filling the lower part of the boats. When he looked back whence they had come, Aquila noted General Glover helping half a dozen others to row a large craft with the commander in chief aboard. The wind whipped about, and Aquila turned his head, again using his arm in the useless attempt to protect his face from the force of the angry storm. Aquila heard a scream. Hamilton called out, "Look over there!" and Aquila observed the wind blowing four men and two horses off their barge and into the river. A rescue was impossible. Aquila prayed God would spare them a prolonged death and that the rest could reach the other side of the river without harm.

—m—

By 2:00 a.m., Aquila, Hamilton, and Broadchurch had gathered on the Jersey shore some ten miles north of Trenton. Damp and frozen, Aquila summoned his resolve, knowing full well that bravery was required to lead men on a tough mission in the harshest of conditions.

"Assessments," he commanded of his subordinates.

Broadchurch reported, "Colonel, we lost a dozen men to the river, but we have accounted for our munitions and the regiment's horses."

Glancing at Hamilton, Aquila gestured for an update. "Sir, my troops are present, accounted for, and ready to march."

Trumbull spoke last. "Aquila—" Quickly correcting himself, he began again. "Colonel Wright, all troops are present and accounted for, although if I may say, the men are freezing. The storm has not subsided, and a ten-mile march to Trenton seems ill-advised."

Aquila noted the surprise on Hamilton's face at the frank assessment by his man, Trumbull. Broadchurch was also troubled. Aquila reasoned he'd better clear Trumbull or risk dissension amongst his officers.

"Thank you, Isaiah. I shall consider your recommendation and confer with General Washington." Then to Hamilton and Broadchurch, "Isaiah has been our family's mill foreman for many years. I rely on his frank opinion on all matters and encourage the both of you to act in kind."

Aquila lowered his head to shield his face as he advanced in the harrowing wind. Snow and sleet barreled on. It felt like a long time ago when a schoolyard bully had hurled a handful of gravel at him. Then, as now, resilience served him well as he made his way forward in search of George Washington. A few minutes later, Aquila turned his back, letting the wind hit him from behind. He backed up against a large oak tree for a momentary respite. Gathering his strength, he heard what sounded like a cough. Someone was nearby. Aquila waited five minutes. The wind subsided as if a prayer had been answered, and the snow and sleet slowed to a crawl. Again, he heard a man coughing and then the sound of a throat being cleared. Aquila walked toward the sound with his pistol drawn. The enemy could be anywhere. He saw a man sitting on a boulder, his back arched and coughing.

"Your Excellency, I was looking for you. Are you unwell?"

George Washington straightened up and dried his face with a muckender he produced from the inside fold of his damp blue coat. He blew his nose, almost it seemed to Aquila, for effect. The leader of the Continental army stood up and replied, "I am fine. I fear the river and the storm took its toll on our men and our mission. We have lost nearly three hours."

"Hopefully, the storm is subsiding, and we can be on our way. Do you know whether the other crossings were successful?"

Washington shook his head. "There is no way to be sure until we reach the Hessian camp."

"Thousands of men are waiting for your command to begin the march to Trenton. Say the word, and I will commence the operation."

Washington looked despondent. He lowered his head and stared at the muddy slush surrounding his boots.

Aquila, unsure of what to do, bided his time for his orders. When Washington failed to reply, he said, “Sir, are you ready to proceed?”

Washington met his eyes, and in them, for the first time, Aquila saw fear. The man who exhibited nothing less than full confidence was vacillating. Finally, he stated, “The time we have lost and the weather have placed this mission in a state of peril. I have risked a great deal to effect this victory. Six thousand of our men are now stuck in a vortex from which there is no clear path forward.”

Stunned, Aquila inquired, “Are you considering retreat, sir?”

“I must consider every option. Crossing the Delaware again would be perilous. Remaining here makes us sitting ducks. Moving forward leaves no margin for error or the unforeseen.”

“Sir, if I may . . .”

Washington stared at Aquila. Those sure-minded eyes were lost.

Aquila was uncertain whether the general would welcome his advice or dress him down as an insubordinate.

“Speak your mind, Colonel.”

Breathing a sigh of relief, Aquila said, “If we arrive in Trenton just after dawn, we can still capture the Hessian camp. I propose we send our fastest unit to go first, establishing a position on the hills just north of the target area. They can fire cannon while the rest of the troops move east and west of the camp, filling in for the ground offensive. If the troops from the southern river crossing made it, they will move north, and we will lock the Hessians inside our ring of soldiers.”

Washington nodded in agreement. “It is similar to our original plan. I like your adaptation.” Washington coughed again. “Give the order. We have no time to lose.”

—∞—

The first thing Johann Rall heard was a low whistling sound. The thunderous crash of a cannonball in the tent next to his followed. His men were crying in pain. Rall sprang from his cot, grabbed his musket, and ran from his tent. The noise was deafening. The cries of unsuspecting soldiers mixed with the sounds of cannonballs landing in his camp. Men who were sleeping off the merriment of the prior evening's ale awoke in terror. Rall screamed to his troops in his native tongue, "Get up. Grab your weapons. We are under attack."

Before Rall could give another command to his disheveled troops, he watched with horror as cannonballs obliterated his camp. Grapeshot rained down from the northern hills, and a horde of Continental army men streamed into the camp from both the east and the west. Rall calculated he could retreat to the south. They were not completely surrounded. The chances of a successful escape were small, but surrender was not in his creed. Rall made the only decision possible. He looked back at the cadre of armed men under his command and yelled, "Attack!"

Rall, leading the effort, immediately encountered a barrage of bullets to his chest. He stumbled backward onto the cold, hard winter ground of the New Jersey shoreline. Gazing up into the early morning sky, Rall lamented that the money the British were to pay him for his services had not been worth it.

Aquila strutted onto the Hessian campground. Tired and weary, he found a second wind from the exhilaration of victory. He called to the three men leading troops under his command.

"Garrett, Isaiah, Alexander—round up the prisoners. Forge a pen and hold them under armed guard until we have further orders."

Aquila eyed the bodies of dead Hessian soldiers, the smoldering fires, and dozens of wounded, both mobile and immobile. They would need the better part of two days to organize the victory's remainder. He spotted George Washington atop his mighty white steed and trotted his horse to the general's side.

"A rousing success, sir. My heartfelt congratulations," offered Aquila.

"Our men achieved this victory, and they had the fortitude to persevere under the harshest of conditions and impossible odds."

Aquila expected Washington to show humility. He harkened back to their conversation after crossing the Delaware. The despondent leader had to make the toughest decision of the war and likely of his entire life.

"Do not underestimate the importance of good leadership, Your Excellency."

Washington smiled, with a slight nod to the compliment. Aquila knew that was all the satisfaction the commander in chief would allow himself.

"We will have a thousand or more prisoners. You are to take Trumbull and Broadchurch and march them to Lancaster. Those who survive the trip will work as indentured servants for patriot farmers for the rest of their lives. But first, gather their horses, munitions, and rations. Knox will handle the inventory and transport to our storage depots."

"Where are Cadwalader and Ewing, sir?"

"I sent scouts to both crossing points. Ice floes prevented both from achieving success."

"And you prevailed nonetheless!"

"No, Aquila, *we* prevailed."

Aquila nodded, admiring the general's humility. "What are my orders after delivering the Hessians to Lancaster, sir?"

"Return to Cromwell. I will join you within a fortnight. It is there that we will discuss your promotion and your oversight of the war's most important battle."

CHAPTER 15

Philadelphia, Pennsylvania

Just as old Clement piloted Essie and Hazel past the outskirts of the capital city, Hazel blushed and, to Essie's delight, poured her heart out.

"Timothy and I spent ten nights working late on the mobile army hospital plan. On the last night, I would have sworn he was smitten with me." Hazel laughed gently, belying her normal cackle.

"And you let the moment pass?" inquired Essie.

"I couldn't bloody well rip his clothes off and begin a tryst, now, could I?"

Essie admired Hazel's sense of humor and quick wit. "No, a lady must maintain decorum." Wanting to know more but without desire to pry, Essie continued. "Might you two get together upon our return from Philadelphia? I'm sure the meeting with Mr. Hancock will bring about more work for us."

Hazel was at a loss for words—an unusual spectacle. She bit her bottom lip, trying to hold her tongue.

"What? You look like you are swallowing your thoughts."

"It's just . . . well, I believe . . ."

"Spit it out."

Relenting, Hazel spilled out the words, forming a dagger between them. "Timothy is still in love with you. He cannot fully give his heart to another."

Essie's spirits deflated. How could she relieve Timothy of this burden? Their onetime dalliance was long ago, and Essie was now happily married. Timothy was being unfair to himself and, unknowingly, to Hazel. They both deserved love, and Essie remained sure they would find it with one another.

"I shall speak to Timothy when we return to Maryland. I will make him see the light of day."

Hazel took Essie's hand, and they both leaned forward in a warm embrace as the carriage stopped at Independence Hall.

Clement helped them to the street, and Essie remembered her last visit here as she stepped onto the cobblestones. John Hancock had given her a commendation before Congress for the killing of Robert Templeton, the evil Maryland governor and a lackey for King George.

The sun shone brilliantly. The cold air was refreshing. Hazel, who had never been to Philadelphia, was in awe.

"London wasn't nearly as clean . . . or new," she remarked.

The city felt as if it had matured in the past year. Essie noted many new shops on Chestnut Street. There was a printer, a notary, and, lo and behold, a decorator.

They entered Independence Hall, the seat of American government, and Essie was pleased. Someone had listened to her. In the year since she last visited, proper curtains and furniture had replaced the thrown-together look of disparate decor. On the left side of the hall, the meeting space was more organized. They had set rectangular wooden tables in rows, angled toward the front of the room. Continental blue table linen covered all the tables, including the desk in the front from which Mr. Hancock presided. Someone thoughtfully placed silver candlestick holders and quills for each delegate. On Mr. Hancock's desk, a brass bell rested near an ink blotter, four leather-bound books, and a sheaf of paper. The sight of Mr. Hancock's seat took Essie aback. It was a high-back oak chair with a carved sunrise at the top. Essie was sure the sunrise represented the dawn of a new age, the birth of America, her country, her home. Then, an errant thought breezed across her mind. Was someone in Congress wise enough to hire the new decorator on Chestnut Street? It had to be! No man could have transformed this hall into its present state of elegance.

Essie marveled at Hazel's wonder. Her friend looked up and down the building, taking in its majesty. She glanced to the right side of the hall and said out loud, to no one in particular, "It looks like a courtroom. I didn't expect to see that."

A loud baritone replied from behind, "If you think about it, the building's layout is perfectly splendid. On one side, we make the laws, and on the other, we enforce them."

Essie greeted the congressional president with a smile.

He took her hand and kissed it tenderly. "Mrs. Wright! It is delightful to see you again."

Essie blushed. John Hancock showed more charm on this occasion than he had on her prior visit. But that was a different time, a darker period wherein America was preparing to declare its independence. Now, Mr. Hancock appeared at ease, even jovial.

"Mr. Hancock, please allow me to introduce my friend, Mrs. Hazel Giddings. She has assisted Dr. Clarke in the plan's development we wish to discuss today. She is a nurse and helps in the management of the Cromwell Hospital."

Before turning to Hazel, John Hancock grinned and said, "I trust you mean the Esther Wright Hospital." Then, he turned toward Hazel, kissed her hand as he had Essie's, and stated gallantly, "Mrs. Giddings, it is my pleasure to make your acquaintance. Any friend of Mrs. Wright's is a friend of mine. She is a true American hero."

"I am unworthy of such praise. I simply acted in a manner befitting the day," replied Essie.

Hancock dismissed the notion as absurd. He beckoned for the two ladies to follow, and they climbed a staircase to the second level. In a large second-floor meeting room, a man sat with his back to the door, reading a document. Upon their entrance, he rose and turned. His face was stoic, and he emitted no emotion. After encountering Dr. Bond on her first trip to Philadelphia with Aquila to tour the Philadelphia Hospital, Essie knew not to take offense. Dr. Bond cofounded the hospital with Benjamin Franklin in 1751. He greeted Mr. Hancock heartily and grudgingly acknowledged Essie and Hazel. They sat at a round table, and Dr. Bond spoke to Mr. Hancock, failing to make eye contact with either woman. Now, Essie felt put off. Men like Thomas Bond would never see a woman as anything other than a vassal for children and chores.

"Benjamin has written to me about the plan for a mobile hospital system. His idea is to plan three or four mobile units with two or more doctors, a cadre of nurses, and a resupply system. He postulates we can ease unnecessary death due to long travel to our few hospitals and our lack of resources for transporting the injured."

Essie blanched. She wanted to hurl a candlestick holder at Dr. Bond's head. Her own reply from Benjamin acknowledged the idea was hers and that he would act as a facilitator to implement it. Should she speak up and defend her honor or remain muted to serve the larger goal?

"Excuse me, Dr. Bond," interjected Hazel. "I believe you are mistaken. This entire business was Essie's idea. Dr. Franklin confirmed it himself in his reply to her letter."

Essie's skin ran cold. Hazel had always had a penchant for speaking her mind in the face of authority. It often got her into trouble. Fearful of how Dr. Bond might react, she attempted to calm the waters. "It doesn't matter much whose idea it was, just that it may be best for our army."

Mr. Hancock chuckled. "Very diplomatic of you, Mrs. Wright. But we all know that you conceived the idea. After all, that is why you are here."

In his typical fashion, Dr. Bond ignored the moment's drama and plowed forward.

"I have engaged John Morgan and William Shippen Jr. in conversation regarding the training of doctors in field medicine specifically for this purpose."

Essie was confused until John Hancock came to the rescue. "Drs. Morgan and Shippen are the founding members of the medical school at the College of Philadelphia. It was the first such school in America. They are both eminently qualified to train the personnel for our mobile medical units."

Hazel ginned up the courage to begin her presentation. "Based on Essie's initial idea, Dr. Clarke and I envision three traveling units, each comprising at least three doctors, preferring at least two of whom to be surgeons, and a team of six surgical nurses. Now, as for supplies—"

Dr. Bond shot Hazel a look to kill. "Why is this woman speaking? I presumed she was here as a secretary or to bring tea." He folded his arms across his chest and sat erect in his chair, appearing as indignant as he sounded. Essie thought she might see smoke race from his nostrils.

"Dr. Bond, your eminence and career are well-established and highly respected. However, we will grant these ladies the proper opportunity to present their ideas to aid our country." John Hancock was firm in his admonishment.

Dr. Bond sat and fumed, offering only a small grunt in response.

Hazel, never one to be shy, hesitated. Essie gave Hazel a nod, urging her to complete her remarks.

"Now, of course, each unit will require a group of the fastest horses and carriages to serve as suitable ambulances for transporting the ill and injured over rough terrain. Medical supplies can be procured from the existing stationary hospitals, and after dropping off patients, the ambulances can carry medical inventory to resupply the mobile units."

John Hancock beamed. "You really have thought of everything!" Looking across the table at the curmudgeon of a doctor, he said, "Haven't they, Dr. Bond?"

"Yes, I suppose so," mumbled the doctor, who rose to leave as quickly as he could.

Upon his exit, John Hancock placed his hand on Essie's shoulder. "Would you remain behind? There is another issue we need to discuss." Then to Hazel, "If you would excuse us for a brief spell, I'd be most appreciative."

Hazel departed, stating that she would enjoy a stroll down the city streets and the fresh air.

Moments later, an old friend entered through the rear and ascended the steps of Independence Hall while escaping the public's notice. When he entered the room, the commander in chief looked as regal as he had the first time Essie had met him following the Battle of Cromwell.

She curtsied and proclaimed, "Your Excellency, it's so nice to see you. I did not know you would be in Philadelphia today."

George Washington extended his hand and drew Essie in for a formal embrace. "I am wherever I need to be. Now, nothing is more important than our pending conversation."

Essie squirmed. Her foot tapped the wooden floor. Conscious of her nervous habit, she tried to quell the activity. A cold sweat broke out across her nose, another anxiety response. Essie straightened her back and attempted to appear composed, awaiting the news from two of the country's most powerful leaders.

Hancock took over. "Yesterday, Congress passed a motion to create the position of director general for the Medical Department of the Continental army. The person in charge will oversee all medical activities for our soldiers, and I have full authority to appoint the appropriate person."

Essie breathed a sigh of relief. She had feared the president of the Continental Congress and the commander in chief were gathering to tell her Aquila had died.

"I presume you will appoint Dr. Bond," replied Essie.

Hancock laughed. "Well, he is expecting the appointment and there are no doubts about his qualifications, but I hesitated, wanting to hear your ideas for the mobile hospitals. Now I am thankful I did."

"I don't understand," Essie said.

"I am appointing you to the position," stated Hancock. "Congratulations."

"Me? I am not a doctor, just a midwife."

"Ah yes, but your accomplishments speak for themselves. Like Dr. Bond, you founded a major colonial hospital, Congress has decorated you for bravery in the face of the enemy, and you come with—how shall I put it?—less stuffiness than Dr. Bond." Hancock looked at George Washington. The two men exchanged smiles. Hancock continued, "Your country is calling. Will you accept the position?"

Essie swept a lock of hair from her forehead and steadied her voice. "Yes, yes, sir. I'd be honored." Then, almost as an afterthought, she looked at George Washington and inquired, "Perhaps I should confer with Aquila before accepting?"

Washington took her hand and said, "Your husband is traveling back to Cromwell from Lancaster, where he escorted Hessian prisoners. Before he departed Trenton, I told him I would see you in Philadelphia. He sends his love. Knowing him as I do, I believe he would be elated for you."

Essie relaxed. Discovering her internal fortitude, she announced, "You are so kind, Your Excellency, to journey here during conflict to receive me into this new role."

"Your appointment as director general for the Medical Department of the Continental army was news to me. I learned of it just now when you did. Like Mr. Hancock, I received a letter from Benjamin Franklin regarding your idea for the Continental army. I have come to speak with you about this and another role on behalf of your country, one that is no less arduous with far greater risk."

Confusion reigned as Essie once again began fidgeting under the table. Her leg twitched, and her foot tapped. She placed a hand on her thigh and closed her eyes for a brief flicker, willing the anxiety to pass. Then, her eyes took on a determined look. She was ready to hear what George Washington required of her.

"The news of your medical role will serve you well in providing what is the greatest need of the Continental army."

Since emerging from prison and indentured servitude, Essie had learned to think two steps ahead. It had become her survival tactic. Life could manage you, or you could manage life. She found it fruitful to practice the latter.

"Am I to help with ammunition or prisoner swaps?" she postulated.

Hancock had become an admirer. He grinned and said, "Your prowess in cogent thought is one of the many reasons we entrust you with critical strategy. But I fear you are on the wrong trail."

"What then?" asked Essie.

"Intelligence," responded Washington.

"Intelligence?"

"Yes, information to be received and passed regarding the actions and intentions of the enemy."

Essie grew exasperated when she heard Washington's proclamation. Uncharacteristic of her newfound penchant to think ahead of the moment, she blurted out, "A spy? You want me to be a spy?"

Washington's demeanor had a calming effect. Essie supposed that was one reason he was such a successful leader. He remained unflappable. He smiled warmly, acknowledging her prior question. "Yes, that's exactly what I envision. Without proper information, the British, who outman us four to one, and have a superior naval force, and far more money, will grind our new nation into submission. Good intelligence is our key to victory."

Essie could not restrain her emotions. What the commander in chief was asking of her was fraught with untold danger. She couldn't risk being sent to prison—or worse. She was now a wife and mother with important responsibilities. Essie fought her fear and summoned the inner strength to remain composed. "I wish to help in any way my country requires, but having been in prison, I am wary of returning."

Hancock replied before Washington could speak. Brazenly, he stated, "Prison? You needn't fear prison. They hang captured spies. Sometimes they are shot."

Now, Essie's fear was evident. She could feel her cheeks turning crimson.

Washington, the omniscient father figure, spoke calmly. "Essie, I foresee your mobile hospitals as an ideal mechanism for covertly exchanging information while minimizing the chance of detection. I have done extensive research on the matter, and we will keep you safe at every turn."

Relaxing, Essie bit her lip. "What if a British soldier intercepts our printed intelligence? What then?"

Washington placed his hand atop Essie's. The warmth was reassuring. "The British pass intelligence on paper. They write it in codes that they invent, so only they can decipher the messages. Sometimes our officers can break the code, but other times they cannot. The presence of code, however, is clear, and its mere existence would place you in grave danger."

Washington paused and removed a document from inside his blue coat. "Here is an example of what our new intelligence corps will employ."

Essie took the paper and began reading. It was a handbill advertising a new show at a playhouse in New York. "I don't understand," she said.

Then, Washington took the paper and produced a small glass vial of clear liquid and a tiny brush. He wet the brush with the liquid and ran it over the blank lines between the handbill's advertisement. It was like witchcraft. Out of nowhere, words appeared with each stroke of Washington's secret elixir. Flabbergasted, Essie read the message.

MRS. WRIGHT—YOUR COUNTRY NEEDS YOU.

"I hardly believe my own eyes," she stated.

"Invisible ink. We write in invisible ink and use acid to produce the words. It is one way we shall keep you safe," said Washington.

"Tell me, Your Excellency, if you were unaware of my new appointment as director general for the Medical Department of the Continental army, how was it you saw me aiding the intelligence effort?"

Washington asserted without deliberation. "This effort will employ citizens who are not soldiers. Nonmilitary personnel will draw less suspicion. You can move about freely and create reasons for meeting and visiting information drops.

We will teach you all you need to know. The hospital structure was news to me, but as I mentioned, it is an opportunity, not a drawback. And I must still emphasize in the strongest possible terms that this is a very dangerous undertaking."

"How will I lead such an effort and fulfill my new role as director general for the Medical Department?"

"You will not lead the intelligence effort. A new general will have this responsibility. He has begun his training, and you will report to him."

"Is this general someone with whom I am acquainted?"

Washington stared Essie dead in the eyes and replied, "Yes. It's your husband."

CHAPTER 16

Cromwell, Maryland

The long-awaited reunion left Essie both full and anxious. George Washington had made her promise not to discuss her intelligence service with Aquila before they could all meet at Cromwell's Passage. Such a secret was an unbearable burden. She sat with Penny at sunrise on the elevated porch of the main house and tried to lose her thoughts with the sight of the landscape. The Maryland winter had been kind to them. The air was unseasonably warm, and snowstorms had been scant. Now at the tail end of the colder months, Essie noted the rolling brown hills beyond. The landscape's anticipation of spring and its renewal of life, green and lush, was much like the next phase of her life, equal in its hope for a brighter future and a way to serve her young country. Wrapped in her favorite violet cloak, Penny nestled close to Essie. They watched the magnificent orange sun rise boldly over the towering collection of maples and conifers.

Ingesting the chilly air, Essie luxuriated in the dewy scent of pine gracing the early morn. From her vantage point, she could see the buildings making up the mill, the cottage she once shared with Hazel, and in the distance, the lands of their close friends, Charles and Celia Greene. The long, winding path leading up the hill to the main house called to her, or perhaps she was calling to it, willing the path to deliver her beloved husband.

Penny sneezed, breaking the spell this land had cast upon Essie.

"Father should be along any time now," lamented Penny.

"I should think so, but many things could cause a delay." Essie noticed her stepdaughter's runny nose and offered, "Let's get you inside by the fire. There's no need to catch your death of cold while awaiting your father's return."

Essie gave Penny a white linen foulard and escorted her across the porch's long expanse toward the home's front door. Before they could enter, Essie heard the faint sound of hooves beating the cold dirt path.

"Look, it's Father and Isaiah," proclaimed Penny. And with that, she broke from Essie and raced down the dozen porch steps.

Essie followed, and they stood watching the distant figures become larger with each advance.

A servant brought them tea. Aquila, vibrant and healthy, told tales of the New York City fire, escaping the British at Fort Lee, foiling the enemy plan to move ships through the forest near Lake Champlain, and their victory at Trenton. Curiously, he omitted a promotion to general or his pending role as chief intelligence officer for the Continental army. Essie considered breaking her promise to George Washington. She wanted to blurt it out and rid herself of the burden. Instead, Essie detailed her new responsibilities as director general of the Medical Department and her trip to Philadelphia with Hazel.

"You never cease to amaze me," her husband proclaimed. Aquila's face revealed his pride in her.

Essie's mind, however, was ablaze with questions. Did Aquila know George Washington had enlisted her help for his new role as spymaster? Were they both hiding the truth from one another? Like a swarm of gnats about her nose, Essie couldn't shake the uneasiness from the joyous reunion with her husband.

"I must spend the day with Isaiah inspecting the mills. We plan to restore each building to its full capacity."

"But what happens when the two of you must return to the war?"

"Isaiah served his country with honor. He has resigned his commission and will remain here to lead the effort."

Essie saw an opening. If Aquila were to volunteer information about his promotion and begin discussing the spy network, she could learn the details and keep her promise to Washington. "And what of you, my love? When will you depart? Where will you go?"

Aquila just grinned. "That, my dear, is a conversation for another time." And with that simple, empty proclamation, he gathered his tricorn hat and rose from the settee.

Essie sat stunned, wringing her hands together until they turned white. Her stomach fluttered. She stood up to embrace her husband, but a servant interrupted her by announcing the arrival of three men: General George Washington, Major Benjamin Tallmadge, and a gentleman named Nathaniel Sackett.

Aquila revealed no surprise at the announcement of such prestigious company. He requested tea and crumpets from the servant, and they all sat by the crackling fire where Washington and his two men shook off the chill from their long journey to Maryland.

Washington rubbed his hands together and inhaled deeply. Once settled, he stated, "These men are from New York. Mr. Sackett resides in Fishkill, and Major Tallmadge is from Setauket on Long Island." He shifted in the overstuffed highback chair and crossed his legs. "A New York congressman introduced Sackett to me. We share a belief that an intelligence ring is of paramount importance if we are to vanquish our foes." Then, directing his attention to the other man, stated, "Young Major Tallmadge has been training under Mr. Sackett, who has mastered the ability to decipher British code and who commissioned the use of the invisible ink I demonstrated for both of you."

Essie studied Major Tallmadge. He was a boy in a soldier's uniform. Despite his serious outlook, he appeared to be a teen under apprenticeship and not old or wise enough to be a confidant of the commander in chief. Blindly, Essie heard herself asking Major Tallmadge how old he was. Aquila was aghast at her rudeness. Washington grinned, enjoying the confrontation.

Tallmadge's deep voice and self-assured response overshadowed his boyish face. "I am twenty-three, Mrs. Wright. I led the Second Regiment of Light Dragoons and am quite capable of pursuing any assignment my country requires of me."

George Washington chided, "But Major Tallmadge is far more than a capable military leader. He failed to state that he attended Yale at fifteen years of age and possesses a mind for strategy that few experienced men may claim."

Essie said to the young officer, "I beg your pardon, Major Tallmadge. I disrespected you, and for that, I am sorry."

Tallmadge smiled. "Think nothing of it, Mrs. Wright. I have become accustomed to people doubting me at first blush. I have overcome the injury of it and use it as a tool for success."

"You are most gracious. Perhaps we can start over. I wish to help your mission in any way I can. I hope we can be friends."

Tallmadge beamed. "Of course. It would be my great pleasure."

Washington resumed control of the conversation. "Aquila received a promotion to general and will oversee the country's spy ring formation. Major Tallmadge shall concentrate his efforts in New York, and Aquila, working from Cromwell, will establish a southern network. Mr. Sackett has begun training both and will continue that effort here with Essie until I deem the operations ready to commence."

"I wanted so badly to tell you all of this," Aquila said to Essie. "But, as you now know, I had to keep it secret."

Essie returned her husband's regret and took his hand. "I already knew."

"Let's review the framework. Mr. Sackett will explain the overarching plan to be adjusted as we learn more," stated Washington.

"Thank you, Your Excellency," said Sackett. "This operation will aid the military but will involve mostly civilians. Nonmilitary people, both men and women, will arouse far less suspicion, and we can recruit them in greater numbers. Major Tallmadge will report to General Wright. Upon the conclusion of his training, he shall endeavor to develop the people and processes to convey intelligence from British strongholds in New York City and Long Island." Sackett stopped to sip the tea in his hand. He continued after setting the fine ceramic on the table next to him. "General Wright will engage in similar actions in Pennsylvania, Maryland, and points south, first finding an equivalent to Major Tallmadge to lead the effort." After another sip of the tea, he finished his thought. "You, Mrs. Wright, will be the binding, the one whose efforts galvanize the entire operation."

"Through the hospital network," Essie said.

"Yes, the extensive nature of the mobile medical units, coupled with the hospitals in Cromwell, Philadelphia, New York, and Boston, will provide a unique opportunity to pass intelligence to General Washington in a baton race of sorts."

"There is so much to do," exclaimed Essie. "I can hardly wait to get started."

"Mind you. This is a dangerous road," proclaimed Washington. "Everyone must work together but also in isolation. It will be an underground alliance. Each member will take a vow of secrecy that will hold for all eternity."

"We must forsake our individual liberties in the quest for our country's freedom," Aquila proclaimed.

"If a tree falls in the forest and no one is near, does it still make a sound?" Washington asked. "The lonely cry for freedom will resonate loudly for generations to come."

CHAPTER 17

Brooklyn, New York

General Willard stood before his new subordinates, chastising their leadership and current situation. Pacing back and forth before Burgoyne, Howe, Cornwallis, and Carleton, the heavyset man puffed out his enormous chest and pounded it with his right hand.

"You have no heart! This effort is not worthy of the world's greatest military. These rebels should have been squashed at the outset. Our ships have fallen into disrepair, our troops are too scattered, and there is no cohesive strategy for victory. At least not that I can discern."

The generals who had led the British to a state of disarray sat in silence. Finally, Howe found the courage to speak. "General Willard, with all due respect, we have supply line issues across the Atlantic and conflicting instructions coming all the time from London. What would you have us do?"

Willard's temper flared, and he pounded his meaty fist on the table before them. "Think, General Howe. Think! Military leaders of the highest order are commissioned to do that."

Exasperated, Howe shook his head. "That devil Germain is incompetent in strategic planning."

"He, like I, expects you to adjust as conditions dictate. We are not order takers at a pub. It is we who must bring King George the glory of victory. There are no excuses, just performance!"

Willard filled his pipe, tamped it down, and lit it. After inhaling deeply, he continued. "General Howe, since I am assuming your command, I shall have your report forthwith."

General Howe straightened his back and rose from the table. "We have command of New York City and Long Island and the northern section of New Jersey. While we maintain an active presence in Massachusetts, Connecticut, Rhode Island, Pennsylvania, and points south, the rebels are holding steady. We lost three warships in the Lake Champlain operation." He paused, cleared his throat, and then added, "And General Arnold is working at a furious pace to build the rebels a navy."

"We must not underestimate their efforts. Underestimating the enemy has been the ruin of many armies. We shall create three primary forces with the idea of surrounding the Continental army, converging on a central chokehold point."

Howe grimaced. "How exactly do you see that taking shape? It feels like a return to an earlier strategy."

Willard boomed, "The strategy did not fail." Glaring into Howe's tired gaze, he declared, "It was the leader."

Howe appeared defeated. In Willard's estimation, the worn-out general couldn't wait to board the first ship back to England.

Willard didn't wait for his field generals to offer an opinion. He just gave them their orders. "The three primary forces will be led by Cornwallis in the south, Clinton in the mid-Atlantic, and Carleton, aided by Burgoyne, in the northeast. We shall plan to defeat the rebels in all three regions, pushing the fight to the central point of victory . . . Philadelphia."

CHAPTER 18

Baltimore, Maryland

As they waited under the shade of the enormous oak on Charles Street, Aquila, in a muted voice, reassured Isaiah. "Don't be ridiculous. Your job as the foreman of the mill is the perfect cover. The job requires you to move around the region. The British will never suspect you."

Despite the cool breeze from the early spring day, Isaiah blotted the sweat from his brow with a dark blue fogle. He squirmed, leaning against the trunk of the massive tulip poplar tree for strength. "I am uneasy but will do what you ask in service to America."

"I assure you that taking care will prevent any harm from coming to you."

"It is not I for whom I am fraught. What of you, Essie, and even Penny? You cannot forget the British imprisoned your daughter and sentenced your wife to be hanged following the Battle of Cromwell."

Aquila had always viewed Isaiah as a friend. His normally placid manner melted away in the face of their mission and the need to defend his own honor. "How dare you question my loyalty to my family? Essie acts of her own free will. And I would lay down my life without hesitation to save her and Penny. Never doubt it."

Taken aback, Isaiah retorted, "My apologies, Aquila. I meant no malice. My words were merely an expression of concern for you and the girls, the people on this earth I love the most."

With that, Aquila relaxed his manner and collected his thoughts, preparing for the meeting to come. Pointing north, he said, "Here comes Charles. After his horse is secure, we shall proceed to the meeting place."

Charles dismounted and embraced Aquila and Isaiah. "Do you not find it amusing that we live next to one another but have traveled hours upon deviant routes to meet clandestinely in the city?"

Aquila replied, ignoring his friend's attempt at humor. "Our contacts from the Sons of Liberty are domiciled here. They will be instrumental in drawing up plans." Then, he turned south and stated, "Gentlemen, shall we proceed to the tavern for a beverage?"

The three men strolled down the street and entered the Walters Tavern just prior to midday. The establishment was devoid of patrons. Aquila noted a woman in an apron, waxing the top of the bar. Her bonnet dipped across her forehead. Aquila judged her to be in her late thirties, perhaps forty. It was difficult to tell. Her youthful face gave way to the beginning of gray locks invading the sheen of her light brown hair.

In his jovial manner, Charles cried out, "Is it too early for a man to get a drink around here?"

Heather Walters came from behind the bar and gave Charles a hearty embrace.

Charles made introductions and asked her, "Did you round up the old gang?"

Heather dropped the polishing cloth on the bar and turned her back to the door, seeming afraid of being overheard. Aquila surmised that this woman was experienced in the business of clandestine communication. Her husband had been a founder of the Baltimore chapter of the Sons of Liberty. After he died in an early militia raid, his wife had assumed the tavern's management while playing the unassuming role of grieving widow. But as Charles had explained it, Heather Walters was an active force in aiding the revolution.

"They are waiting for you," Heather stated. "You know the way."

"Will you be joining us?" asked Aquila.

Heather stared him in the eye. She had a self-assuredness about her. Oddly, Aquila couldn't shake the feeling that Heather Walters was assessing him, as a man and a leader.

Charles looked over his shoulder toward the front door and the tavern's street window. He wanted to make sure no one was watching. "Follow me, boys," he said to Aquila and Isaiah.

Charles led them to the back room. He lifted a beaten shag rug, pulled the secret hatch from the floor, and descended the stairs into the storage cellar.

Once they were in the subterranean space, Aquila inhaled the stale odor from the cold, dank room with no air. Old dusty crates sat stacked against the wall, and a rectangular wooden table that looked like a relic from the seventeenth century rested in the middle of the floor. Three men murmured over a bottle of whiskey. Aquila wondered if they were sober and how leading a military mission with civilians would be successful.

William Lux and Robert Adair had founded Baltimore's Sons of Liberty chapter in '66 in response to the Stamp Act imposed by the British the prior year. Samuel Chase joined them soon thereafter. In the eleven years since its founding, the group had dissolved, but the threads of acrimony inherent in these men still pierced their pleasant demeanor.

When Isaiah asked how they stayed safe from the British noose, Lux stated proudly, "The secret is acting. We go about our day, pretend to mind our own business, and even feign allegiance to the crown. Meanwhile, we turn our shopkeeping profits into funds for the revolution and pass information up and down the coastline by word of mouth."

Aquila relaxed. Lux's response assured him that these men were serious and would aid the cause. "Your roles in the Sons of Liberty and your willingness to further serve your country in association with the women of the Daughters of Liberty and many other well-meaning citizens shall comprise an offspring effort. The Agents of Liberty will be the name of our collective body. I am establishing operations throughout the colonies to collect actionable intelligence to aid the Continental army in defeating the British."

"Do you have a mind to tar and feather British soldiers we find lurking about?" asked Adair.

"No," Aquila stated emphatically. "While those tactics might have been useful following the Stamp Act, the Agents of Liberty will not deal in violence."

Chase chided, "It seemed to work just fine back in the day."

"You could make an argument in favor of those types of actions in the time before the Continental army. Not anymore," Aquila emphasized. "Let me be clear. Our mission is solely one of gathering and passing intelligence. We are to find out British troop locations, fleet movements, and knowledge of strategy. We will employ a combination of word-of-mouth and circuitous routing of both coded messaging and those written in invisible ink."

Samuel Chase looked despondent. "I would be less than honest if I said I didn't prefer the old methods, but we will do whatever you need, General."

"Very well," responded Aquila. "Colonel Greene will be your commanding officer. He will have domain over the Agents of Liberty from Pennsylvania south. Major Tallmadge will assume command from New Jersey north."

"Who will recruit citizens to aid the cause?" asked Adair.

"That's my job," answered Charles. "As the leader of the southern regiment of the Agents of Liberty, I will work with each of you and the men of our former chapters in the other colonies to recruit and train citizens in sufficient numbers to aid our cause."

"What type of people are we looking for?" asked Chase.

Charles Greene smiled confidently. "People just like you."

"One more thing," added Aquila. "My wife will establish mobile army field hospitals. Along with existing stationary hospitals, we will endeavor to transmit messages via ambulance drivers and whatever other means make sense."

Lux stroked the long, scraggly beard flowing from his chin. "A field hospital? Your wife must be an astonishing woman."

Aquila nodded. "That she is."

CHAPTER 19

Cromwell, Maryland

The morning sun gleamed. Essie lingered under the expansive branches of the two-hundred-year-old tulip poplar on the old Main Street, renamed Mordecai Way for the town's founder, Aquila's grandfather. The grand old shade tree hovered along the developing thoroughfare, offering its strength and resilience to all who gathered around it. Like their brethren in northern states, they dubbed the enormous poplar a Liberty Tree, a place for gathering to discuss the rebellion while enjoying the outdoors and remaining out of earshot. Essie inhaled the tree's placid aroma, aided by the whispery breezes of late spring. The air was heavy, as was her mood. There were no shortage of tasks to accomplish. She had scarcely seen the inside of her home since her visit with John Hancock, George Washington, and Dr. Bond. Simply put, she was exhausted. *A good tired,* as her mother would say after a day of hard work and accomplishment.

In the months since her appointment, Essie established field medicine training in Philadelphia, ambulance routes, and resupply strategies. Now, she aimed to begin the equally arduous job of finding and training people to become Agents of Liberty within the confines of the hospital composition. She was expecting Pastor Vinson and Hazel. The portly clergyman frolicked across Mordecai Way with a smile on his face. Farther down the street, nearer to the hospital, Hazel made her way toward the enormous Liberty Tree. Essie welcomed them. If any redcoats or loyalists were around, she wanted it to appear that this was a chance meeting between the pastor and two members of his church. As instructed, Hazel carried an empty basket as if she were on a shopping expedition. It only bolstered the illusion.

"Thank you both for meeting me here so early," Essie said. "There hardly seems enough time in a day to eat or use the loo."

"Take a deep breath," urged Pastor Vinson. "God will provide you with all the strength you need to achieve His purpose."

Essie relaxed and presented them each a jar of apple preserves. "I bought these in the Brandywine Valley on my last trip home from Philadelphia. Old Clement paused the journey to give the horses a rest and some water, and I found the loveliest little store outside Wilmington."

"It looks delectable. I can already taste it on a biscuit," said Hazel. "Thank you, love. You are so very kind."

"We must be quick about our conversation," Essie declared. "Pastor Vinson, you will play an instrumental role in the intelligence operation. Anyone who naturally moves around town and the region is invaluable. You will deliver messages inconspicuously."

"With pleasure, my dear," responded Pastor Vinson.

"Hazel, your mission is far more complex—and dangerous," Essie stated.

"What, pray tell, could be so difficult?"

"The British need nurses. Since we have blocked their access to our hospitals, and they have a dearth of field medics, trusted and experienced nurses are in demand."

"And you want me to apply for the position of a British field nurse?"

Essie noted the shock on her best friend's face. The sharp tip of irony's dagger ran through Essie's mind like a hot knife through a slab of beef. Here were three people born in England, standing under a Liberty Tree in the New World, plotting to overthrow the tyrannical rule of the country that abandoned them. And here she was, asking Hazel to return to the enemy.

Essie summoned the courage to guide Hazel according to the plan. "Yes, that's exactly what I am asking. You will extract the most valuable intelligence from the British front lines. We will teach you to pass messages securely."

"What about my role here as the Cromwell Hospital administrator?" Hazel paused and then said out loud what Essie feared most. "And what of my budding relationship with Timothy?"

"Timothy and Henrik have already signed on to the idea. They have agreed to absorb some of your administrative duties while training one of the senior nurses to do the rest." Essie hesitated, searching her mind for the right words to ease her friend's troubled mind. "As for Timothy, he will wait for you, as Aquila did for me."

To relieve the tension, Pastor Vinson asked, "When shall we begin?"

"Training starts tomorrow. Hazel, you should be prepared to leave in a week."

"A week it is," she said dejectedly. "Where shall I go to fulfill my mission?"

"The British have a new commander in chief. It makes the most sense to attach yourself to his regiment. Intelligence indicates that he will soon be in Maryland."

"Does this varmint have a name?" Hazel inquired.

"General Preston G. Willard. I am told by General Washington that Willard is a seasoned military leader, a no-nonsense type." Then, remembering Hazel's penchant for speaking her mind, added, "It is imperative that you play your part well, and for God's sake, hold your tongue."

CHAPTER 20

Head of Elk, Maryland

Unlike many field generals of his day, General Willard never minded the choppy waters of the open sea. He found it exhilarating. Once on dry land, Willard felt the power bestowed on him, along with the solidity of the earth beneath his feet; he was invulnerable, surmising that if he could withstand the sometimes-brutal ocean transport, he could conquer anything that the land might present. Once anchored, Willard was the first to disembark from the gallant warship and, as was his custom, crushed the first bit of earth he encountered with his boot, moving the toe left and then right to pulverize the dirt.

General Clinton and scores of redcoats followed him. "We shall make camp here in the northern part of Maryland, a day's march to Philadelphia," he said to Clinton, who merely nodded and said, "Yes, sir."

Willard proceeded forward, located a tree with a modicum of privacy, and relieved himself. After the respite from his pressing bladder, Willard noted an odd etching on the tree. From his vantage point, he saw a cutout segment of the trunk. Someone had created a storage compartment in the tree. It was a drop! A place for enemy spies to leave messages. This tactic was as old as time. He'd seen it used many times over his illustrious military career.

With a knife he pulled from his scabbard, he examined its innards; it held nothing. For a moment, Willard considered stationing a man to watch for the next drop. Alas, he knew that may prove fruitless. The rebels might have abandoned this tree, or they might not use it again for weeks or months. He did not wish to spare the manpower. But it made him wonder. As the new commander in chief, wasn't it his responsibility to engage in intelligence gathering? Heretofore, the British effort in this area was circumspect at best. Willard walked forward, taking in the aroma of the many pine trees. He vowed to outsmart the American intelligence effort at every turn. Then, deep in thought, General Howe interrupted Willard, appearing distressed.

"General Willard, we have come across a small village nearby. The colonists there are suffering from smallpox. I suggest we move our camp farther north to the Brandywine Valley."

"Agreed," replied Willard. "Before the men get settled here, let's pack up and move out."

"Yes, sir. Right away, sir," replied Howe.

Willard resigned himself to a camp selection farther north. While his men were less likely to contract smallpox because of inoculations administered in England, he did not want to take any unnecessary chances. Then, as if struck by lightning, he had a brilliant idea.

"General Howe, wait up. We have something further to discuss."

CHAPTER 21

Brandywine, Delaware

Aquila's encounter with General Washington was well-timed. Half the year was gone, and the British were attempting to outflank them at every turn. Washington's need for intelligence was greater than ever if they were to prevent Philadelphia from capture and the fall of their fledgling nation. When Aquila reported to the tent of the commander in chief, William "Billy" Lee, the general's valet greeted him. Next came Alexander Hamilton, who beamed and embraced Aquila like a sibling. Hamilton escorted him into the tent and heard an unfamiliar voice, one with a French accent. A tall young soldier was conferring with Washington.

"Aquila, meet the Marquis de Lafayette, recently arrived from France." Washington was filial in his introduction. "The marquis has volunteered to fight for the Continental army."

Aquila embraced the young Frenchman, but his youth surprised him. The man couldn't be over eighteen or nineteen. Aquila surmised that for Lafayette to curry immediate favor with Washington, he must be from a well-to-do family. Washington was likely betting on the young man's influence for further aid more so than his military prowess. His age alone limited the amount of field experience he might possess.

Aquila stood back. "It is a pleasure to make your acquaintance, Marquis. I look forward to serving with you."

"Oui, General Wright. We shall fight arm in arm until the British are driven from your land."

Turning his attention to George Washington, Aquila suggested a private conversation regarding the reason for his arrival. Lafayette, Hamilton, and Billy Lee filed out of the tent.

"Plans are proceeding accordingly, General. Colonel Green is establishing the southern tier of intelligence while Major Tallmadge prepares in the north. Tallmadge is young and has much to learn. Despite his vast academic achievements and ability to think strategically, he is at least six months from starting the northern operation. Colonel Greene's efforts in the south will proceed in a few weeks' time."

"Excellent," the commander in chief replied. "And what of Essie?"

Grinning, Aquila responded, "My dear wife, although frantic at the enormous responsibilities given her, is making progress on both fronts. She has appointed key people in both areas and is working to establish the required crossover between the two operations." Aquila hesitated, unsure of how much detail to reveal. "And she even has a nurse penetrating General Willard's camp."

"A mole? Won't the redcoats suspect an American nurse wandering into their camp?"

"Well, yes, sir. I would agree, but Essie chose a young lady from London who journeyed to America as an indentured servant on the same voyage she did. Essie believes she can pull it off."

Washington seemed pleased. "Very well. Keep me posted on any issues. I will look for the first intelligence dispatches within the coming month."

"Yes, sir," Aquila replied. He exited the command center tent to find the form of Louis Pembery lurking about.

CHAPTER 22

Brandywine, Delaware

Safety was theirs to claim. The peaceful green pastures of the Brandywine Valley provided General Willard with the opportunity to give his soldiers a rest before proceeding to Philadelphia. There, he would do what his predecessors had failed to accomplish—capture the city representing the heart of the rebellion. The American capital was a heartbeat away. Capturing the city was the beginning of the end of the revolution. Willard would restore order and proceed northward, bringing New York and Boston to heel.

Willard left his command tent and stretched his arms outward, trying to shake off the stiffness of sleeping on a cot. It was the one thing he would not miss after this conflict, his last for sure. Once he had put the Americans in their place, under King George's control, he would return to England and retire from his military service. Perhaps a cushy job in Parliament. Or maybe he would just enjoy the land of his family's vast estate outside Bristol and watch over the sheep in the endless rolling hills. All Willard knew was that he was tiring. He wanted the war to conclude and would act to advance matters swiftly.

"Good morning, General Willard," exclaimed an exuberant General Howe.

"Your demeanor is rather spritely. Heading back to England tomorrow?"

"Yes, sir. I admit I was initially deflated when I heard you would take over my command, but now I look forward to spending the rest of my days with family and friends back in England."

Willard made a *humph* sound acknowledging the comment. Inside, he conceded to himself he envied Howe.

"General Clinton is a good man, as are Cornwallis, Burgoyne, and the rest. They will serve you well," stated Howe.

"I have no doubt," replied Willard. "We are meeting in a few minutes. Join us."

"Of course. I would be honored."

The two men walked to a clearing where breakfast was being served. Willard wasn't hungry. A cup of tea would do just fine. Maybe a bite of fish and a strip of bacon, for sustenance.

Clinton opened the meeting. "Good morning, General Willard. One of our scouts has provided more information about the American naval effort near Lake Champlain. General Arnold has completed one ship and has embarked on the creation of a second. Both of which are to be sailed down the Hudson to engage our forces in New York."

"Those ships must never reach New York City. I want a plan forthwith to reduce them both to ash," Willard grumbled.

"Yes, sir, we will get right on that," replied Clinton. "General Burgoyne is quite familiar with the New York geography. The two of us will caucus and deliver a plan by nightfall."

"I expect nothing less," Willard growled. His command was based on respect. Fear generated respect. Good fellowship played no part in Willard's thinking. All he knew was to rule with an iron fist.

Regarding Generals Clinton, Howe, and Burgoyne, Willard clenched his jaw and spat out his proclamation. "With the fledgling Continental navy destroyed, the capital city captured, and the northern cities soon under hand, I expect the Americans to surrender by fall. We shall all be home for Christmas."

The other generals applauded the notion. Willard saw nothing that stood in the way of total victory. He deliberately kept the final assignment of General Howe quiet from the group. Howe discovered the village infected with smallpox. He had a large contingent of soldiers enter the village; men who had either been inoculated in England or who had survived the disease. Their mission was twofold: Order the villagers to disperse amongst the other colonies and to retrieve as much infected clothing and blankets as they could. The first order would spread the disease amongst the colonies and ravage the Continental army and its resources; the second would further the spread of the disease through charitable redistribution. Washington had hesitated to inoculate his troops. A foolish miscalculation, thought Willard.

Once in Philadelphia, Willard would engage in his masterstroke. The young, handsome, and resourceful Major John André would spearhead the quest for intelligence.

CHAPTER 23

Cromwell, Maryland

Isaiah Trumbull ambled into town. He whistled a cheerful tune and greeted Pastor Vinson, who smiled warmly and handed Isaiah a copy of the upcoming Sunday service.

"There is a new hymn for you to learn before church. You are one of our strongest voices. The hymn is abstract, so you may need to read between the lines," proclaimed the pastor.

"Understood," Isaiah replied. "I shall study the words carefully and receive their full meaning."

For safety, Isaiah walked into the church, removed his boot, and placed the folded paper into his sock. Replacing the boot, he bid the pastor good day and proceeded to the apothecary. There, he picked up an elixir, an ordinary activity that would be questioned by no one.

—ထ—

Essie received Isaiah in the drawing room at Cromwell's Passage. To Essie, his normally grizzled and determined face held a modicum of doubt. This spying business was new to all of them, and they were all uneasy.

"Here is the elixir from the apothecary and this week's hymn from Pastor Vinson," he said flatly. "If there is nothing else, I have business at the mill."

Essie relieved Isaiah of his discomfort, thanking him for his service while politely ushering him out. She returned to the drawing room and sat down at her writing desk. Unsheathing the elixir from the burlap bag, she removed the cork and, with a tiny brush, coated the blank lines between the hymn. Her eyes flew open wide as the strength of the young Agents of Liberty movement shone through.

An ambulance from Trenton, New Jersey, transported a Patriot soldier with a gunshot wound to the chest to the Philadelphia hospital. The man was an impostor, a British spy. Interrogation revealed British plans to attack Lake Champlain. The goal is to destroy the new US Navy.

Essie placed her hands to her mouth in disbelief. This information was of paramount importance. She must create a new dispatch with the invisible ink General Washington had provided her. She withdrew a fresh sheet of paper and wrote a mundane letter to General Washington informing him of the new ambulance routes and the early success of the mobile hospital. Then, between the lines, Essie constructed a concise communication using the invisible ink regarding the intelligence she had deciphered. After blowing on the ink, she folded the paper with care and would place it into the hidden compartment of the giant tulip poplar on Mordecai Way. From there, Aquila would have a courier, unknown to Essie, pick up the letter and transport it to the next drop. As Aquila had explained, the letter would see three or four drops on a circuitous route before it reached the commander in chief. Essie prayed it would not be too late.

CHAPTER 24

Brandywine, Delaware

Willard was in a foul mood. He had slept poorly, and his stomach was in an uproar. Cursing, he kicked a wooden bucket towards the privy. He saw a young major, who looked smitten with a woman who followed him dutifully. She was young, perhaps thirty, and was petite with blond hair. Willard reminded himself to inquire as to her identity. Thirty minutes passed, and he had his opportunity. The same young officer brought the woman to Willard's tent for an introduction.

"Who is this little crumpet?" Willard asked condescendingly.

"General Willard, please allow me to introduce our new head nurse, Mrs. Hazel Giddings."

Hazel curtsied and stated, "Pleased to make your acquaintance, General."

Willard growled to himself. His stomach was still in an uproar. "What part of London are you from?"

"East side, sir. Strictly working class."

"And where did you learn to nurse?" Willard inquired.

"My mum was a nurse in London. I apprenticed under her."

Willard detected hesitancy in the reply. A telltale sign of a liar. "How did you come to the colonies?"

"After my husband died, I was remanded to the London Debtor's Prison and then sold into indentured servitude in Maryland."

"And how is it you are free?" Willard asked suspiciously.

"I worked off my debt, and they set me free. I have been wandering ever since. A loyalist I stayed with told me the Royal Army needed medics in the field. I just wanted to help."

Willard didn't reply. He looked her up and then down. "Tell me, Mrs. Giddings, can you make the fire in my belly cease?"

"What exactly are you experiencing?" she asked.

"It feels as if someone took my insides and twisted them into knots."

The nurse didn't flinch. "Any fever, rashes, or headaches?"

"No, just the confound cramping."

"Leadership's strain often causes stomach upset. The burdens endured by prominent men take their toll on the body, particularly in the stomach. I recommend you start with ginger paregoric. That should settle you. If not, we will look for a deeper cause."

Although it seemed reasonable to Willard, he recognized when someone was kissing his ass. He vowed to keep a close eye on the new nurse. "Fine, fine," he grumbled. "Prepare it at once."

CHAPTER 25

Cromwell, Maryland

Determining that the drop system they had concocted would take too long, Essie approached her husband.

"I know my instructions were to destroy the communication," Essie exclaimed, "but as the leader of the intelligence effort, I thought it paramount that you see the original."

Aquila patted his wife on the shoulder. This, he knew, was the danger in engaging civilians in clandestine military operations. He valued Essie's judgment. How could he inform her that her actions, although noble, imperiled everyone? Aquila took the hymn and read the message scrawled between the lines. When done, he nodded but said nothing. Then, he went to the candle on the drawing-room table and lit the corner of the paper. Dropping it into a ceramic ashtray, he watched it burn and pondered how to neutralize the British plan. He was due to depart Maryland for New York, where he would work with young Major Tallmadge to begin the northern intelligence operation. Tallmadge had a friend, a young man who had impressed General Washington. His name was Nathan Hale. Hale would become the first active spy in the Northern Department of the Continental army. On his way to New York, Aquila could rendezvous with General Washington in Pennsylvania and forge a plan to foil the British effort to destroy the young naval fleet. He pledged to deliver Washington's orders to Lake Champlain and collaborate with Benedict Arnold to defeat the British attack, regardless of any delays to Tallmadge's mission.

"Thank you, my love. This hymn is of great value." He held her and said in a loving but firm tone, "In the future, however, for your own safety, our family's safety, and America's safety, burn the notes as soon as you read them."

A tear ran down Essie's cheek. Aquila wondered whether he had been too harsh.

"I understand," she replied.

Needing to change the tenor of the conversation, he inquired, "Where are you off to next?"

"My plan is to stay here with Penny. I can direct the medical efforts adequately and use ambulances coming into our hospital for dispatching instructions to the field."

"Very well. If you are called to leave town, I trust Penny will stay with Celia?"

"Yes, Celia has been most gracious. She enjoys Penny's company, and Penny regards her like an aunt."

"This war has caused her to grow up too fast," Aquila lamented. "I am sorry that she lost the chance to enjoy the innocence of youth."

Essie embraced her husband's arm, placing her cheek against it, and said, "Penny has her girlish moments. Before we know it, she'll fall in love with some young man and want to start a life of her own."

Aquila kissed the top of Essie's head. "Don't rush things. Let a father hold on to the image of his little kitten for as long as he can." Then, he turned and faced Essie full on, kissing her fervently and stating, "I have an hour before I must depart. Would you join me in our chamber?"

CHAPTER 26

Cromwell, Maryland

Even though war had made it so, Essie thought she might never become accustomed to being without her beloved. Aquila left for New York two weeks ago. It felt like two years. After dressing, Essie made her way to the dining room where the staff had laid out a small spread of hard-boiled eggs, sausage, fruit, and freshly baked cherry pastries. Penny was just finishing her breakfast and was ready to depart for school.

"I need to go to the hospital. I shall accompany you to school," she said to her stepdaughter.

Penny brightened, shaking off the morning doldrums Essie recalled from her own teenage years. Somewhere, she remembered, a young woman gets stuck between holding on to the carefree nature of childhood and the growing responsibilities of being an adult. In a few short months, Penny would be sixeen, old enough to be courted, although in Essie's opinion, Penny did not yet know anything of love. The only man in her life was still Aquila, and Essie could tell that Penny missed her father dearly. Since their trip to Europe to repair facial wounds inflicted by a bear, Penny and Aquila had grown closer than ever before. They were all learning hard lessons from America's quest for independence. The road to freedom was long and lonely.

The early winds of fall swirled the colorful leaves around their feet. Essie clutched her cloak around her petite body, seeking warmth from the unexpected chill.

"Do you think Father will be gone long?" Penny asked.

"I wish I could say for sure. He doesn't know when he'll be home." Essie thought of the additional journey to Lake Champlain and considered explaining this to Penny as a reason that Aquila might be gone longer than expected. But she dismissed the idea. Ignorance is bliss, and disclosing the details could endanger Penny.

"Do you see an end to the war? Will the British ever give up and go home?" she asked innocently.

The breeze caused Essie to shiver. "No, I don't think they will ever give up. They are too powerful and too proud."

They continued in silence for a hundred or so paces, and Essie finally asked, "Are there any young men at school you are interested in?"

Penny's cheeks turned red.

Essie wasn't sure whether it was from the cold or she was blushing. She decided on the latter. "There is, isn't there?" She beamed.

Penny brushed a lock of her lustrous brown hair from her eyes and responded, "Yes, there's this one boy. His name is Marcus. Marcus Stapleton."

"What's he like? Have you spoken to him?"

"Spoken to him? Oh my gosh, no! I think I'd wither and die before I had the courage to do so."

"Is he popular with the girls?"

"All of my friends talk about Marcus's good looks. And he's smart and funny. My friend Bess is sure Marcus will be somebody important one day."

Essie loved the high spirits accompanying a girl's first crush. "What is Marcus most interested in?"

"I'm not sure. I hear he has a penchant for debate."

"Perhaps he is a budding politician," Essie remarked. "Today, if the opportunity presents itself, go up to Marcus and ask him if he could help you with your latest philosophy assignment. Didn't you say you had an essay to write about Socrates?"

"Why, yes, but I need no help. I have the assignment well in hand." Then a flash hit Penny. "Oh, oh, I see where you are going. Just let him think I need help."

Essie smiled at her young charge. "You are learning."

After seeing Penny off to school, Essie entered the hospital and went right to the office. She longed for a slow day with a cup of warm tea. Out of curiosity, Essie shuffled through papers. She saw purchase requisitions, receipts, and a few bills of sale. Henrik and Timothy had begun the practice of keeping a treatment record of each patient seen. Although the intention was well-meaning, Essie surmised they were both far behind in this duty and feared they might never catch up. She organized the messy array and was deep in concentration when she heard Timothy's voice from down the corridor.

"Get this man in quarantine, *now*!"

Essie hurried to the examination room. There, she witnessed Timothy and the nurses rushing to cover the lower half of their faces with handkerchiefs. When Timothy saw Essie in the doorway, he yelled, "Essie, don't come in. We have a smallpox patient. This man is highly contagious."

After watching her first husband die an agonizing death in England from this horrid disease, Essie knew full well what the real danger was. Epidemic. The spread would be devastating. She retreated to the safety of the office. Henrik followed her in.

"Someone brought the patient in late last night. At first, he had only a headache and a fever. This morning, the telltale rash broke out. Unmistakably smallpox. Worse yet, when questioned, the man said he was from a small town near Head of Elk. The British took their blankets and clothes. Then, for some inexplicable reason, they ordered the townsfolk to disperse."

"Disperse? There is only one reason they might do that," Essie exclaimed.

Henrik, with bags under his eyes and his usual look of exhaustion, replied, "Do you think they are intentionally trying to spread smallpox? As a weapon?"

"Think about it. Henrik. England required all its soldiers to be inoculated before coming here. Many others of us have survived the disease or built up an immunity. America has no such advantages."

Henrik exhaled. "You make a good point. The primary question now is what we can do about it. General Washington has waffled on the question of vaccines. Many congressmen, as I understand it, have opposed inoculations. The idea of being injected with the very disease that could kill them is a frightening prospect to the uninformed."

Essie's plans for a quiet day had gone to hell in a handbasket quicker than one could blink. She would prepare a coded message for General Washington. The ill effects of the British plan could prove deadly.

CHAPTER 27

Lake Champlain, New York

Aquila thought Benedict Arnold might be the most self-assured man he had ever met. The general had a drive to prove his worth, and it was relentless. Upon learning of the British plan to foil his shipbuilding operation, he shouted to no one in particular, "Over my dead body!"

With the blessing of George Washington, Aquila brought reinforcements from Philadelphia and New York City. Arnold now had hundreds of additional men at his command and relished the opportunity to lead. With Aquila and the other generals in his tent, Arnold laid out the plan for a surprise attack. "The British will come up through Fort Edward, the site where we plan to launch our completed ships. I will send a reconnaissance team to the site to see if they have arrived. Presuming they are still in transit, we will lie in wait with cannon and sink them before they get off the Hudson."

"What if they are already here?" inquired Aquila.

Arnold frowned. "Then, my good man, we shall defend this camp with everything we've got while a contingent of our men takes out their ship on the north end of the Hudson."

Arnold seemed so sure of his plan. Aquila had doubts, yet he knew he could say only so much. Benedict Arnold was the ranking officer and had dominion to direct the men as he saw fit.

—℘—

Fort Edward was a two-hour-long ride on horseback from where the Continental army staged its shipbuilding operation. The reconnaissance team departed, and Aquila, with a regiment of five hundred men, occupied the position midway between the two points. Aquila was ready with cannons. His men were prepared to join the attack on the British ship or to defend the camp's perimeter. Should they join the attack, Arnold would send five hundred men to Fort Edward as reinforcements. Aquila was more at ease now that he understood the details behind Arnold's strategy. He reckoned he would have drawn up a similar plan.

Aquila instructed his troops on what was to come, attack or defend. They would not have to wait long to find out. With his men prepared for either contingency, Aquila mounted his horse and looked out through the forest. It reminded him of the hundreds of acres he owned at Cromwell's Passage. How his father had built the gristmill and left his own father's farming operation behind. Aquila had helped his father reforest that portion of the land. He supposed he was a naturalist. Unity with the land signified freedom. To Aquila, it was the essence of freedom, and he would fight with everything he had to defend its cause. The recon team's appearance in the distance interrupted his rumination.

Aquila could see the lead man's face and knew instantly something was amiss.

"General Wright, there is no sign of the redcoats at Fort Edward."

Now Aquila wondered whether they had the wrong landing spot. Arnold, who knew the terrain far better than he, was sure that Fort Edward was the only reasonable place for the British to land. It was the only true access point to Lake Champlain from the Hudson River. Then Aquila smiled. He recognized that his intelligence operation was succeeding. They hadn't misjudged. They outmaneuvered the British, who would arrive at any time. Rather than send word back to General Arnold, Aquila moved his men and cannon to a concealed spot on the banks of Fort Edward. He would send the recon team back to camp to inform the general. This way, they would lie in wait for the British to arrive.

"Move out!" he shouted across the sea of men behind him.

Though Fort Edward had no leader, a few troops patrolled the station. Aquila sent two men to advise the small fort. The men there needed to be aware of the current operation and join if necessary. Two hours later, they positioned themselves on the banks of Fort Edward. The British would peer through spyglasses from the choppy waters of the Hudson to make sure the coast was clear. Anticipating this, Aquila camouflaged his men well. They positioned themselves back from the edge of the coastline, taking cover behind trees and beyond the reach of the redcoats' view. They hid their cannon under loose branches and stationed them much closer to shore. A scout with his own spyglass was on the muddy embankment waiting for any sign.

Unsure of when or whether they would see the British, Aquila urged his men to remain alert. The Continental army had not come this far only to fall prey to weariness. With his own spyglass, Aquila saw the Royal Navy ship in the distance. The warship, built for smaller waterways, would bombard shorelines like the one Aquila now occupied. He second-guessed himself. Had he underestimated the British? Should he have gone back and collected revised orders from General Arnold? Aquila gazed out over the Hudson and estimated the ship to be more than a hundred and twenty feet. It would hold close to two hundred men and contain armament of more than a dozen twenty-four-pounder guns. The Continental army outnumbered the ship's troops by a margin of two to one. They had cannons at the ready. Aquila dismissed his doubts and reassured himself that General Arnold would approve of his revised strategy once he learned they had destroyed the Royal Navy ship.

"A ship is on the horizon," cried the scout, affirming what Aquila had already seen.

"On the ready! Move into position and prepare to fire," Aquila shouted across his troops.

The Continental army advanced to the shoreline, no longer worried about being seen. Aquila had cannons aimed at the bow, stern, and mid-hull. One clean hit would end the threat.

"Fire!" yelled Aquila as the warship approached. Two cannonballs burst into the air, heading toward the target. The cannon aimed at the bow fell just short. The second cannon directed toward the stern grazed the ship but failed to inflict significant damage. Aquila ordered the cannon to be reloaded, wondering why the third cannon designated for the hull had yet to fire its first shot. He looked over; the soldier was having difficulty. Aquila sized up the soldier's inexperience and ordered a replacement. The next soldier assumed the responsibility of firing the cannon and let go of its shot. While the cannonball was airborne, the redcoats returned fire. Aquila watched in horror as the redcoats took out one of his cannon operators, and men fell. Looking back at the warship, Aquila witnessed the answer to his prayer. A direct hit to the mid-hull! The warship cracked in two, and Aquila and his cheering men watched the burning sections of the wounded ship descend into the Hudson.

Just as the cheers abated, Benedict Arnold rode in on his black steed and stared at Aquila. Then, looking at the men, he stated, "Excellent work, men. I knew my revised plan would succeed."

CHAPTER 28

London, England

George Germain sat in the palatial office of the prime minister. Lord North was berating him in a manner that made his skin crawl. General Howe had arrived back home and submitted his detailed report. Germain knew the scolding from Lord North was forthcoming, and frankly, he was wondering why it had taken so long.

"I was skeptical when you sent Old Warhorse Willard to the colonies as commander in chief. His methods are archaic." Lord North paused in his rant and paced anxiously back and forth in front of the seated Germain. "Your poor decision has likely set our efforts back years. The king wants an end to this conflict and demands we bring the colonies to submission."

Germain sat there brooding.

"Don't you have anything to say for yourself?" Lord North demanded.

Germain considered his position. He might get fired for speaking his mind. If he remained quiet, Lord North would judge him weak. He saw himself in a lose-lose situation. So he opted to speak his mind.

"As I'm sure you ascertained from General Howe, he was weary of war and ready to return home. A leader cannot be effective without being fully committed to the mission. A change had to be made."

"But Willard? He should have been put out to pasture years ago."

"I doubt the strategic capabilities of Clinton, Burgoyne, and Cornwallis. Willard is bold and decisive."

"Not necessarily in the proper way," grumbled Lord North.

"What shall you have me do?" inquired Germain, perhaps too eagerly.

Lord North continued to pace. "I don't know. A change of command takes too long to implement. We may have to ride it out with Willard and hope he prevails."

Without thinking, Germain tried to score points by adding, "The idea to eliminate the fledgling continental shipbuilding effort was a good idea."

Lord North made a muffled sound of disapproval. "Yes, we know how that worked out. We lost a warship and two hundred men in the bloody Hudson River." Lord North became more agitated. Germain reasoned he must escape the meeting lest he be terminated. Before he could react to Lord North's last tirade, the prime minister spoke again. "And what of the weaponization of smallpox? Has Willard gone totally mad?"

Germain tried to speak calmly, hoping it would reflect positively on his command. "As General Howe explained it, Willard saw an opportunity and took it."

"We haven't employed those sorts of tactics since the French and Indian War. When the king hears of this, he will call for both your heads. Now, get out of my sight!"

Germain left the prime minister's office with his job intact. Everything would turn out fine as long as Willard followed the plan to capture Philadelphia.

CHAPTER 29

Philadelphia, Pennsylvania

Although she had made the trip to Philadelphia many times, Essie deemed this journey slower than the rest. As the director general for the Medical Department of the Continental army, Essie wanted to race to her command post to confer with doctors under her charge and with the leaders of Congress. She implored her coachman, old Clement, to drive the horses as fast as they might go. There would be no stopping for any reason other than the well-being of the horses.

When she finally arrived in the city's center, Clement stopped the carriage near Independence Hall and Essie sprinted inside, speaking to the first person she could find and telling him to convene a meeting with President Hancock and all available doctors from the army's central command post. Essie's nerves caused her to sweat. She had a mild headache, likely from the chaos of recent events. Then it occurred to her. She had early symptoms of smallpox. Could she be coming down with the disease? Perhaps her belief that she had built an immunity in her stricken hometown of Wickhamshire was no longer accurate. Essie spied a serving trolley in the hallway separating the courtroom from the meeting space and poured herself a glass of water. She sipped, gathering her resolve when the president of the Continental Congress appeared. His dark blue coat with gold buttons and gold trim covered the white shirt that was wrinkled from wear. Hancock wore a warm smile, although Essie assumed he was working too hard in the face of America's struggle for cohesive independence.

"Essie, you look exhausted. Are you unwell?" Hancock inquired.

"I felt fine along the journey from Maryland, but I admit I am feeling queasy."

He approached to greet her politely when she warned him it might be better to keep his distance. She was not yet sure if she was contagious. Then Essie thought, when she told Hancock the real reason for her visit, he would order her to be quarantined.

"I see you have some water. The other doctors are not immediately available. Our sentry was able to round up Dr. Bond, who will join us upstairs. Please take a few minutes to collect yourself. I shall see you shortly."

Thirty minutes passed, and Essie felt better. She realized she had not yet eaten and was famished. On the serving trolley, she found a plate of apple crumpets and partook. Wiping a crumb from the corner of her mouth, she said hello to the surly Dr. Bond and ascended the grand staircase by his side. They arrived in the same room the three had met in when she was appointed director general for the Medical Department of the Continental army. Dr. Bond, expecting the appointment, had left in a huff.

John Hancock entered and closed the door behind him. "Now, Essie, what is the crisis you came to discuss?" asked Hancock.

Essie rushed to relay the information she'd learned at the Cromwell Hospital regarding the British plot to weaponize smallpox, beginning with the small town near Head of Elk.

Hancock immediately connected the dots. "The symptoms you displayed when you arrived. Are they not early indicators of smallpox?" he asked.

"What symptoms?" inquired Dr. Bond.

"A mild headache and a sweat," Essie replied. "But I must tell you I had just finished a long journey from Maryland and had taken no food or drink in too long a period."

"Were you exposed to smallpox in Cromwell?" Dr. Bond pressed.

"Only from a distance. I am fine, really, I am. We should be more concerned about General Washington and the troops."

"I am concerned about you and them," Hancock replied gently.

Dr. Bond proclaimed, "Mrs. Wright needs to be quarantined here in Philadelphia for two weeks. We cannot risk an outbreak in the capital city."

Hancock regarded Essie and stated, "I'm afraid Dr. Bond is correct in his assessment. He shall accompany you directly to the hospital quarantine rooms."

"What of the two of you? Could I not have infected you?"

Dr. Bond quietly said, "We have both received the inoculation." Rising, he reached for her arm and said, "Now, if you will come with me. We shall cover your face and get you to the hospital."

"But what of my duties?" she pleaded. "To the army and . . ." She froze, not knowing if Dr. Bond was aware of her role in the Agents of Liberty.

"Not to worry," Hancock replied. "Dr. Bond will temporarily assume your medical duties with the army." He paused and then added, "And I will send for General Washington to discuss other matters. He has just established winter camp at nearby Valley Forge."

Essie left Independence Hall on the arm of Dr. Bond. In her own mind, she knew she did not have smallpox. Some water and a crumpet, with a short break, made her feel better. Yet she couldn't argue the need for quarantine. Clement would ride home and inform Celia to look after Penny until she could return. And she would ask President Hancock to conceal this news from Aquila. With all he had on his plate, she did not want him to worry about her.

CHAPTER 30

Philadelphia, Pennsylvania

Almost two weeks had passed since their victory at Fort Edward. Aquila felt no remorse in his actions even if Benedict Arnold rode in at the last minute and took credit for the operation. It mattered not to Aquila. The Continental army's success stemmed from the intelligence effort he had established. The Agents of Liberty were making an integral difference in the war, and to Aquila, that was satisfaction enough. His long journey from Lake Champlain through to New York City had concluded. Although the Fort Edward battle delayed the initial reason for his New York trip, Aquila spent a brief spell with Major Tallmadge discussing plans for intelligence in the northern states. Aquila sat tall on his gallant steed. He was tired but proud. He had made Philadelphia by nightfall.

The city was eerily quiet. Aquila wanted to stop at Independence Hall before retiring to the inn for the evening. Inside, a single candle flickered, about to die. Aquila called out, hoping John Hancock was still about. He found only one aide preparing to lock up the hall.

"I am General Wright," he proclaimed. "Where is President Hancock?"

The timid aide was anxious to leave. Aquila thought he must fear his own shadow. He did not reply. He put his head down and raced toward the door.

"Did you not hear me?" Aquila demanded. "Stop at once."

"I am sorry, sir. I must leave immediately. The city is under an evacuation order. Congress left for Lancaster a week ago and may yet retreat farther to York."

The news distressed Aquila. He furrowed his brow and said, "Have we abandoned the capital city?"

"For all intents and purposes, yes. General Washington suffered a defeat in the Battle of Brandywine. As I understand it, thousands of redcoats will swarm the city anytime. Oh dread! I should have left days ago." The nervous aide wiped his forehead with a white mouchoir. "I'm sorry, General. What did you say your name was?"

"Wright, Aquila Wright."

"Wait here," the aide said. "I have a letter for you from President Hancock. He thought you might pass through and wonder what is happening."

The aide retrieved the sealed letter and ran out the door. Aquila stood alone in the great hall and broke the seal of John Hancock. Unfolding the paper, he read the brief but deliberate warning:

Dear Aquila,

If you are reading this letter, I, along with the rest of the Congress, have fled to safety in Lancaster. I fear you may not be aware that Essie is under quarantine at the hospital here in Philadelphia. She came to let us know about the British plan to spread smallpox among the Continental army and exhibited early warning signs. Dr. Bond insisted Essie remain at the hospital. I do not know her current condition, but her quarantine period should soon be at its end. I pray she is okay. Assuming this is the case, bring her to us in Lancaster. I shall ensure her safe passage back to Cromwell.

Godspeed,

John Hancock

Aquila dropped the letter on the floor and raced out the door. Mounting his horse, he raced to the nearby hospital. Once there, he dismounted, tied his horse to a post, and ran through the hospital's main entrance. The hospital was in a state of bedlam. He reasoned that once Washington conceded in the Battle of Brandywine, the facility would be overwhelmed. Essie's field medic units would not have been able to offer much help in such a grand battle. Throughout the hallways of the hospital occupying a full city block, men and women were running back and forth. Some were screaming at the loss or injury of a loved one. Others were begging to be seen by a doctor. Overwrought doctors in bloodstained garments rushed by.

Aquila had to find the quarantine unit. He located a nurse, pleaded for directions, and jogged to the area on the other side of the hospital. Sweating heavily and out of breath, Aquila saw the double doors with a large sign:

QUARANTINE!
NO ADMITTANCE
MEDICAL PERSONNEL ONLY

Ignoring the sign, Aquila burst through the double doors and began pulling back curtains until he saw her. She lay still as a board in the dark space, looking pale and weak. Aquila reached for his wife, wrapping his arms around her upper torso and pulling her to his chest.

Essie opened her sleep-laden eyes. "My love. You shouldn't be here. You could take ill."

"There's no time to talk," he said. "We must leave the city."

"When? Why?"

"The British have already overtaken Washington in Brandywine Valley. Congress has abandoned the city. We must leave tonight. Now!"

"But I am not through with my quarantine. I could place you in danger," she warned.

"How long have you been here?" Aquila asked his wife.

"Twelve days. Two to go."

"Have you developed a rash?"

"No, in fact, I have felt fine almost since the day they quarantined me."

"That's all I needed to know. Let's get you dressed. We must make haste."

CHAPTER 31

York, Pennsylvania

Essie thought the York County Courthouse was a mundane version of Independence Hall, although smaller and incapable of staging the Continental Congress. Aquila had been surprised to learn that John Hancock had left Congress to tend to matters at home and Henry Laurens had been elected to take his place. Upon first sighting, Essie found herself taken aback by the surprising difference between Laurens and Hancock. While Mr. Hancock was at ease and charming, Mr. Laurens was much too serious. His long face, prominent forehead, and enormous eyes showed his worry.

Aquila approached him and inquired about the state of Congress.

"After the British took Philadelphia, we retreated to Lancaster, but the redcoats maintained a heavy presence there. It felt safer to travel further west to York," Laurens explained.

"What exactly happened to John Hancock?" Essie inquired.

Laurens patronized her, as if intelligent conversation with a woman was beneath him. In a stuffy tone, he said, "Mr. Hancock stated only that he had business in Massachusetts. Without a certain date of return, I was elected to replace him."

"Funny, he mentioned nothing of leaving his post in the letter he left for me at Independence Hall. On the contrary, it seemed he would most definitely be traveling west with Congress."

Laurens snorted a reply. "I suppose something came up after he penned the letter. Nevertheless, it is what it is, and we are likely here for several months."

"Months?" Essie asked, surprised. "Is there no countermeasure planned to regain control of the capital city?"

Again, Laurens appeared put out. He looked at Aquila to answer the question posed by his wife. "That, of course, is up to our commander in chief, George Washington. I should hope that he will retake Philadelphia in good time."

Aquila thanked Laurens for his time and escorted her away. Essie was sure her husband knew her tolerance for misogynistic behavior was low.

"What a dreadful man," Essie proclaimed when they were out of earshot.

Aquila replied, attempting to keep Essie's attention on the larger picture, "He is well-respected by Congress and in his home state of South Carolina. His wealth is abundant." Essie huffed, still reeling from the encounter. "How did he become so wealthy?"

"He is a rice farmer and the largest slave trader in the colonies."

"Slave trader? Now I know I detest him," Essie decried.

"'Tis of no consequence whether we like him. Mr. Laurens is a capable successor to John Hancock. I trust he will make the right decisions."

"I trust you," Essie stated. "Mr. Laurens? Not so much."

"Come, we shall pitch a tent and remain here for the night. In the morning, I shall take you home to Cromwell. It is a daylong journey, and we shall leave at sunrise."

An hour into their journey southeast toward Harford County, Essie had yet to utter a single word.

"Tired, my love?" Aquila inquired.

"A little," she replied.

"You are uncharacteristically quiet, almost sullen."

The *clip-clop* of the horses impeded her thoughts. Her forehead throbbed. After a too-long silence, she said, "It is you who haven't uttered a single word." Essie found her tone surprisingly sharp. She couldn't recall a time when she had felt anger toward Aquila. At least not like this. This was different.

"I'm not sure what you mean," he said somewhat defensively. "I've been trying to engage you in conversation since we left York."

With fire in her eyes, Essie almost shouted, "I'm not referring to your banal effort to engage in small talk. I'm talking about our child. We've journeyed from Philadelphia to Lancaster and York, and you haven't said a thing. You haven't inquired about how I feel."

As the tears flowed, Essie saw the realization on her husband's face. Their child died while he was at war. Aquila had written expressing his sorrow, but they had yet to discuss it. For Essie, it was the first time she had been with child—and to lose it. The heartbreak knew no bounds. While her mood sometimes subsided, the knot in the pit of her stomach remained.

Grasping the depths of her despair, Aquila took Essie's hand. "It broke my heart to receive the news. I cried in front of George Washington. He offered me leave. I refused. Now, I regret I chose poorly."

Essie couldn't speak through the sobs. Aquila pulled a handkerchief from his inner coat pocket. The chill winter air almost froze the tears on her cheeks. Essie blotted her tears and composed herself. But then, just as suddenly as they first began, the tears returned.

"When will this bloody war finally end? When can we be a family?"

Aquila patted her hand. "I wish I knew. But it will end one day. We will be together. You, Penny, and I, and we can try again to have a baby."

"War is a lonely affair, tearing apart families and communities and ravaging the land," Essie lamented. "Why can't men work out their differences in a more civil manner?" Through the next round of sniffles, she added, "If women were in charge, things never would have gotten this bad."

Aquila looked lost. Perhaps in her state of melancholy, she had said too much. At that moment, Essie cared little for how her husband felt or, for that matter, the foolish men on both sides of the conflict who perpetuated death and its accompanying grief. She was still mourning the loss of her child. Men grieved and moved on. For a woman, it just wasn't that easy. The life inside her, once extinguished, left a gaping hole in her spirit, perhaps never to be repaired. All she wanted was a normal existence in the peaceful pastures of Cromwell's Passage and the will to keep moving forward.

CHAPTER 32

Philadelphia, Pennsylvania

Willard felt like a king. Once he took total charge of Philadelphia, he was lodged in the magnificent home of the city's richest man, a patriot merchant named John Arbogast. Willard's men cast out Arbogast and his family, caring little for where they wound up. They did, however, keep the staff, who would work for the British for no more compensation than the privilege of serving and, of course, room and board.

Willard was tired. He arched his back, trying to loosen the tense muscles from too many years in the field. As commander in chief in charge of the enemy's capital city, Willard was now entitled to remove himself from the drudgery of field operations and enjoy the luxuries associated with his position. With Howe back in England, Willard would send Clinton north and Cornwallis south. He would remain in Philadelphia to guide the effort.

Willard stepped into the dining room. It vastly exceeded the one on his English estate. The silver service sparkled. Arbogast had good taste, almost as if he were a Briton. He took his seat at the head of the table, and a servant poured the day's first cup of tea. A plate of eggs, sunny-side up, and bacon accompanied the beverage. The servant laid the meal in front of Willard while offering a warm, freshly baked muffin. Willard gruffly accepted, offering no thanks or courtesy to the staff to whom he granted favor.

Sipping tea, he read the morning paper, a patriot rag from town. He forced himself to keep up with the opinions and happenings of the rebel force, no matter how distasteful the reading. He took off his glasses when a young officer entered.

"Good morning, General. I am Major John André at your service."

Willard gazed upon the much younger man. He was tall and devilishly handsome. Although Willard knew from background reports that André came not from wealth, he held himself as if he did.

"Sit, sit," Willard commanded. "Dine with me."

André sat and poured tea for himself. Adding a twist of lemon, and extending his elbow like a gentleman, André smiled at the general and inquired, "How may I help?"

"It seems as if the rebels have developed some sort of, I assume, ragtag intelligence unit. Upon landing in Maryland, I discovered a tree being used as a drop. Where there is one, there are others." Willard shoveled bacon into his mouth and chewed. After sipping the tea, he continued. "This is war, Major. Make no mistake about it. The enemy has spies everywhere. Your job is to form a British intelligence effort and ferret out the Americans taking part in treasonous activity."

"Yes, sir, of course. May I ask why me?"

"You come recommended, and I am told that your intellect and ability to think for yourself are beyond reproach. I require this of all my leaders."

"Understood, General. Thank you for the opportunity. I shall not let you down."

"I should hope not. You will have free rein to conduct your duties as you see fit and shall report directly to me. The fewer people that know about your activities, the better."

"I agree. Since arriving in Philadelphia, I have been able to ingratiate myself with the city's society through the arts and other social gatherings. The American aristocrats have been most welcoming."

Willard huffed. "No doubt because people know you for your charm. But I caution you, Major. That attitude will surely change now that we have control over the city. Be wary of this."

"Yes, of course. With your permission, sir, I shall take my leave and begin at once."

André hesitated, and then added, "General, you should know there has been a severe smallpox outbreak in the city and its surrounding areas. It's a rapidly forming epidemic. This may hinder our early intelligence efforts."

Willard stared him down with a stone-cold expression. "Fancy that. Smallpox, you say?"

CHAPTER 33

Cromwell, Maryland

Aquila treasured the time with Essie, Penny, and his beloved estate at Cromwell's Passage. The idea of running the Continental army's intelligence operation from his own home held great appeal. These were the thoughts that paraded through his mind on a beautiful winter's morn as he walked to the gristmill's main building to converse with Isaiah. The brilliant morning sun warmed him. He inhaled, savoring everything he encountered, from the dewy scent of the nearby woods to the latent smell of manure as he meandered past the stable.

The mill was preparing to reestablish operations gone dormant while Isaiah and most of the men were off to war. Aquila entered to find Isaiah giving instructions to a group of older hands on how he wished the grinders to be cleaned and tested. The mill came to life with its accompanying screech and then a steady chugging sound. Isaiah spotted Aquila and waved, motioning for them to walk outside where they might converse without the noise.

"I figured you'd be sleeping in after such a long journey," remarked the mill foreman.

Aquila, with a wave of his hand, dismissed the notion. There was always so much to do. His mind was not one that condoned sleeping beyond the minimum time required. With the pleasantries out of the way, Isaiah motioned again for Aquila to accompany him. The two men walked forty or fifty paces to a massive, ancient oak tree Aquila had climbed as a child. Legend had it, his grandfather,

Mordecai Cromwell, had planted the tree as a sapling. They moved behind the trunk and into the shade of the old tree's strong branches.

"I was preparing one of the invisible ink messages for you, unsure of when you would return," Isaiah began. "But, as you know, I'd much prefer to speak in person."

"Of course," Aquila replied. "Coded messages are a necessary evil, given the times and the mission at hand. What have you learned?"

"I received a post from Mr. Lucas in Philadelphia. He desires a substantial order of the grain we are storing for him. I'm not sure this qualifies as intelligence, but it seems, according to Mr. Lucas, the redcoats have taken complete control of the capital city. General Willard forced John Arbogast, one of the city's wealthiest men, out of his home to use it for quarters. Mr. Lucas also mentioned there is a severe outbreak of smallpox in Philadelphia."

Aquila didn't disclose that he knew most of this already. He appreciated the loyalty shown by Isaiah, the reluctant intelligence draftee.

"Well done, my friend," Aquila stated just before raising his right hand to his head. A wave of nausea overtook him. It rushed in like the wind from an unforeseen storm.

"Are you unwell?" asked Isaiah.

"I felt fine a moment ago. Suddenly, I find my head is pounding and my stomach is queasy."

"Let me accompany you to the house. You can lie down while we summon a doctor."

"Thank you, but I'm quite sure—" and before Aquila could complete his protestation, his knees buckled, and he fell to the ground. He heard Isaiah call out for three men from the mill. Aquila could feel himself being loaded onto a wagon used for hauling sacks of grain. He was barely conscious. The short, bumpy ride on the hard wooden floor of the wagon did nothing to aid the sickness in his stomach. He thought he might vomit before the ride had concluded.

As they approached the house, Isaiah hopped off his seat, giving instructions to the men to bring Aquila into the house while he set out to find Essie.

She appeared disheveled from sleep at the top of the grand staircase. "Isaiah, what is wrong?"

Aquila could hear his friend describing to his wife the sudden illness that befell him. His eyes were shut as the men brought him into the house.

Essie cried out, "Oh my God. Lay him on the chaise lounge by the fireplace. Make haste—go to the hospital. Fetch Timothy or Henrik. Hurry!"

CHAPTER 34

Cromwell, Maryland

Three-quarters of an hour passed as slowly as molasses traveling downhill. Essie was frantic. She expected Timothy or Henrik to arrive promptly, perhaps even both of them. Aquila was the hospital's benefactor. She paced back and forth from her husband's side to the big windows overlooking the path leading to the main house. Back at Aquila's side, she applied a cold cloth to his forehead. He had lost consciousness and appeared chalky white. Essie assured herself the illness was something a simple elixir might cure. Left to her own devices, she might try a simple salve, but with a doctor on the way, she decided to wait.

Essie heard Penny exclaim, "Someone's coming up the path."

"Thank the heavens," stated Essie. "Is it Timothy or Henrik?"

"I can't quite make out the rider." Then, a moment later, "Wait, it is that young doctor, Dr. Robinson."

Dr. Robinson? Essie lamented inwardly. The hospital must be busy. Still, she was grateful for the help and walked to the foyer to greet him.

Dr. Robinson dismounted, tied his horse to a hitching post, and raced up the stairs to the main house. Handing his cloak to a servant, he wasted no time, stating, "Take me to General Wright."

Essie led the way. Unable to resist, she inquired, "Were Timothy and Henrik unavailable?"

"Yes, Mrs. Wright. A smallpox outbreak overran the hospital. Thank goodness

Dr. Van der Beek insisted we all get vaccinated."

Essie scrutinized young Dr. Robinson as he began his examination. As upset as she was, Essie couldn't help but notice Penny stealing a look at the handsome young doctor.

"Tell me what happened," said Dr. Robinson.

"Aquila was down by the mill with Isaiah when he fainted. Isaiah said Aquila complained of nausea and a headache beforehand."

Dr. Robinson loosened Aquila's neckerchief and unbuttoned his top shirt buttons.

And there it was. The crop of small red pustules with which Essie was all too familiar. *Smallpox.* The illness that took her first husband's life and ravaged their quaint hamlet on the outskirts of London. Was there no end to the devastation brought on by this horrid disease?

"You see what I see," stated Dr. Robinson stoically. Essie was sure he measured his words and manner to keep her calm. "There is no need to take General Wright to the hospital. He is better off recovering here."

"Yes, I most certainly agree," Essie replied. "Penny and I can nurse him back to health." A knot in her stomach twisted. She swallowed hard, praying they could.

"One more thing," said Dr. Robinson as he rose to leave. "The two of you, Mr. Trumbull, and anyone else exposed to General Wright must quarantine here for two weeks. I am required to post a sign to this effect at the base of the road leading up to your house. I will be back tomorrow to check on General Wright."

CHAPTER 35

Cromwell, Maryland

It had been a long night. Sleep proved elusive, although Essie admitted to herself that she didn't try. Aquila remained unconscious. She was up and down the staircase with cool compresses. Listening to his breathing had proven a nightlong labor of love. Essie was prepared to have Clement transport the doctors to Cromwell's Passage at once if his breath became shallow. She glanced out the window from the splendor of the large chamber. The sun was beginning its ascent over the long line of hundred-foot pines. This was a sight Essie had loved ever since she had arrived. It calmed her. She inhaled and drew strength from the yellow sphere, appearing like an inverted first-quarter moon.

Leaving the window, Essie checked on her beloved. The rash engulfed his face, rising all the way to his hairline. With her hand against his brow, Essie decided the fever had gone down. The pustules on Aquila's neck and chest had dried and were turning dark. This differed from the smallpox she experienced with Thomas in Wickhamshire. With Aquila, the illness progressed swiftly. Essie didn't know what to make of this observation. Maybe he was healing much faster and would soon be on his feet or—she swallowed hard—it might mean his death was imminent.

Penny wandered in, her hair tousled and her nightgown askew. "How is Father this morning?"

Essie jumped out of her skin. She had expected no one else to be up this early. Collecting her wits, she hugged Penny and attempted to spin a pleasant yarn. "Look here," she said, pointing to Aquila's neck and chest. "The lesions are healing."

Penny brightened. "That's encouraging."

Essie embraced her stepdaughter. "Let him rest. The staff will have breakfast ready soon. Let's you and me have a bite and maybe a short walk through the grounds. The fresh air will do us good."

"That sounds lovely, but can someone stay with Father?"

"I have arranged for one of the staff to perch at his bedside. Besides, we shan't be gone long."

An hour later, Essie and Penny entered the gardens and strolled along its wide path. Essie breathed deeply. The air was pleasant but not like in spring and summer when everything was in bloom. Today, the air was cool as winter got underway. Goosebumps enshrouded Essie's flesh as she shook away the cold.

"I took your advice," Penny vibrantly stated.

"With the boy at school?"

"Yes," she blushed. "The Honorable Marcus Stapleton and his dreamy brown eyes."

"So you feigned ignorance on your philosophy assignment and asked for help. Then what happened?" Essie's mind momentarily left the tedium of her husband's illness.

Penny giggled. "Well, he stuttered out some words indicating his disbelief, and then he just walked away."

Essie put a loving arm around Penny's shoulders. "He's obviously a fool. An immature fool at that." They took a few steps toward the dormant rose bushes, and Essie said, "Here is a secret. Boys are stupid. They don't know a good thing when it stands before them."

Penny squeezed Essie's hand. "How old are they when they finally figure it out?"

Essie half laughed and half snorted. "Some never do."

As they made their way back to the main house, Essie saw a carriage pull up in front of the porch steps. It was Henrik! He was here to check on Aquila. While she appreciated the efforts of young Dr. Robinson, the sight of her friend, an experienced physician, warmed her heart.

"Come inside," Essie implored. And then, quietly so Penny would not overhear, she said, "I am worried. Aquila's smallpox is not behaving in a manner similar to my first husband. I can't be a widow again. Please, Henrik, do all you can."

Henrik nodded and tried to smile. The man's face bore the exhausted look of a doctor whose life never settled down. "The hospital is overflowing with smallpox patients. Most of the sick are from major outbreaks in other parts of Maryland, Delaware, and Pennsylvania. I don't know how we can keep up." Henrik adjusted his black top hat. "The hospital in Philadelphia is full. Their quarantine hall is closed, and I fear that smallpox is moving rapidly north, bound for New York and New England."

Remembering her stay at the Philadelphia quarantine ward, Essie had an idea. "Henrik, we will establish a pesthouse on the outskirts of town." Essie was delighted with her sudden inspiration.

"We can use the old Bartholomew place. His lands have been vacant since the British abandoned Cromwell. Bartholomew was a tanner. There is a large barn we can use as the pesthouse. Medical personnel can stay in the house and . . ." she gathered her final thought on the matter, "we can use the adjacent land for a cemetery."

"That is a magnificent idea." Henrik replied. "Then, we can wash down the hospital and resume normal operations." Reaching the foyer of the grand home, he said, "And I have just the person to run the pesthouse."

"Who?" inquired young Penny. Essie had forgotten Penny was lingering.

"Why, young Dr. Robinson," answered Henrik.

Essie glanced at her lovestruck stepdaughter as Penny asked, "Won't that place him in grave danger?"

"He received the vaccine. No need to worry, young lady."

They ascended the staircase, and Essie escorted Henrik into the bedchamber with Penny in tow. Upon their entrance, the chambermaid took her leave. Essie brightened as a groggy Aquila finally came to.

"How long have I been out?"

Essie took his hand. "A few days. Henrik is here to check on you."

Penny moved to the other side of the bed and took Aquila's hand. "Father, it is so good to see you awake. You have been quite ill."

Aquila tried to smile. Essie thought the pustules on his face tightened his skin and kept his mouth from fully expanding.

Henrik reached into his leather medical bag and removed a glass cylinder with a small cork. "I want you to drink this. It's been effective in combating smallpox."

Aquila bristled at the sight of the brackish solution. What appeared to be water sat atop a thick black substance flaking at the top.

Noting his patient's disdain for the sight of the medicinal solution, Henrik offered an explanation. "It is water settled over tar." He chuckled at the ingenuity of the elixir and stated, "A physician friend in Holland said they have had tremendous success treating smallpox symptoms with it."

Fascinated, Essie inquired, "And you just pour the water over tar?"

"No," responded Henrik. "It must cure for several days before administering it to a patient. I have a barrel behind the hospital."

"Is it really necessary?" asked Aquila in a scraggly voice.

Henrik tried to smile in appeasement. "It will taste as bad as it looks, but it certainly can't hurt."

His daughter chided, "Don't be a baby. Down with it."

Aquila looked up at Henrik. "General Washington changed course on vaccinations for the Continental army. I received the inoculation before returning to Cromwell."

Essie was astonished. "We traveled all the way from Philadelphia together, and you didn't think it was important to tell me?"

Henrik interceded. "It is of no consequence now. People who have received the vaccine can contract a mild form of smallpox before realizing the serum's benefit."

"So Father will make a full recovery?" asked Penny.

Henrik placed a gentle hand on her arm before replying. "Yes, his lesions are healing rapidly." Then to Aquila, "I expect you to be up on your feet within the week. Now drink the water and tar."

Essie watched as her brave husband, a general in the Continental army, drank from the glass vial and made the face of a boy tasting something undesirable.

CHAPTER 36

Philadelphia, Pennsylvania

Willard sat at the handsome wooden desk belonging to John Arbogast. All four corners of the top surface held hand-carved eagles. Caressing the top of an eagle's head, Willard's finger skimmed a rough patch of wood, irritating his fingertips. Dipping the quill into a jar of ink, he began the report to Lord Germain. He considered encoding the report or using the invisible ink André had procured, but, being set in his ways, he simply chose to write. Once completed, his report would travel with two armed troops in a cylindrical sheath straight to the next ship bound for London. The captain of the ship would guard the letter in his quarters and deliver it to the final armed couriers only upon disembarkation at His Majesty's port.

Willard wrote for the better part of an hour. He signed the communique and stretched while the ink dried. From the stiff leather-bound chair, Willard contemplated his plan to debilitate the Continental army and the people of the colonies using smallpox. The plan flourished. Smallpox was spreading from Virginia to New York. Soon, the disease would overwhelm all the English colonies, and his remobilization of men, ships, and munitions under Generals Clinton and Cornwallis would end this colonial insolence, and deservedly so. What if thousands died in the process? A new generation of proper Britons would repopulate these lands, people loyal to the crown.

Willard blew on the letter, folded it in thirds, and applied his wax seal. All in time to greet his next appointment.

"Good morning, Major André. Come. Sit. I am eager for your report."

André sat in a chair covered in crushed blue velvet facing Willard's grand desk. His back was straight, and his legs crossed, befitting the gentleman he was. "Sir, General Washington has finally succumbed to pressure from Congress to inoculate his troops. I believe the scourge of smallpox has caused him to get off the fence of indecision."

"Imagine that," replied Willard. "Seems it's an action that will prove too little too late."

"That is likely an accurate assessment, General."

"What else have you learned?" grumbled Willard.

"For starters, the man leading the American intelligence effort is General Aquila Wright. His base of operations is at his estate in Cromwell, a small town in northeastern Maryland. But like many others, smallpox has struck General Wright."

Willard was pleased. The rebels' fledgling effort was already severely hampered. "Who is second in command?"

"General Wright's main confidants are Colonel Charles Greene, also of Cromwell, and a young major named Benjamin Tallmadge. The former is heading up southern operations; the latter is based in New York City."

"Are these men to be taken seriously?"

André winced at the question. Willard saw the younger man's comprehension that he was being tested. "I believe all men rebelling against the crown are to be taken seriously, sir."

Willard was pleased. André was proving to be a good choice. "I have a full calendar today. Is there anything else, Major?"

André hesitated. His mouth gaped, but he strained to hold back the words.

"Out with it, Major. I haven't got all day."

"Well, sir. It's likely nothing. It's General Wright's spouse, Essie."

"What about her?"

"They appointed her director general for the Medical Department of the Continental army."

"So what?" Willard bellowed. "Does their foolishness in appointing a woman to an important position bother you?"

"Not exactly, sir. I hesitated to report this as the intelligence is not solid. One loyalist in Cromwell overheard a muted conversation between Mrs. Wright and the town pastor and another woman beneath a poplar tree outside the church. The man reporting couldn't be sure, but he left with the impression that Mrs. Wright was using her new position to aid her husband's intelligence effort."

CHAPTER 37

The Diary of Hazel Giddings
Philadelphia, Pennsylvania

I fear I have accepted a challenge for which I am not worthy. While I have entrenched myself as the in-house medic in the palatial home taken over by General Willard, I have no faith in my prolonged ability to be a matron of the theater. I am inclined to speak my mind and have little resourcefulness in telling lies. Yet that's what is required. I miss Cromwell. Essie, Penny, and my hospital job are all missed. I especially miss Timothy. I pray he will wait for me to return—that is, if I am able to return. At present, I see no end to my current plight.

Writing in this diary is my one temporary solace. In doing so, I have defied my orders from Essie and General Wright. But I fear I will go mad if I can't get my feelings out. This is my only device.

The only time I feel safe is in the sanctuary of my chamber. I wait until the wee hours of the night to pen my "letters back home." My observations are buried between the lines of ink in those letters. The letters will be left in a hollowed-out tree trunk at the southern end of Chestnut Street. The letter I must now write is the most dangerous of all. I ask God to give me strength.

CHAPTER 38

Cromwell, Maryland

Despite Essie's hope that Aquila's new role would keep him home more often, he set off to join the Continental army's winter encampment at Valley Forge. General Washington was dealing with an epidemic of smallpox, he had said, and he would expect Aquila to be close at hand. Recovered, Aquila was strong-willed in his effort to assist the Continental army in combating the disease. He had departed Cromwell's Passage two days earlier, carrying a letter from Henrik containing instructions on how to create the tar and water solution that possessed some inexplicable healing power.

Putting her personal feelings away, Essie couldn't argue. They all put the needs of their new country above all else. Still, she found herself alone more often than she cared for. A pervasive sense of isolation had overcome her. Not as melancholic as when she lost her baby, but a deeply embedded pain enshrouded her being. With Hazel off on her mission and Celia minding the needs of her own estate while Charles pursued the southern intelligence operation, Essie was alone. While she normally contained a strong inner constitution, on this blustery winter morn, Essie wanted nothing but a good cry.

Summoning her inner strength, Essie wandered to her writing desk to begin the day's first task. She sat down, removing the quill from the glass jar of black ink and began the letter to George Washington. With no end in sight to the smallpox scourge, Essie was more convinced than ever that pesthouses were a growing necessity. She had drawn up a plan to create pesthouses in all afflicted towns. In collaboration with Henrik, she included instructions on physician and nurse care, cleaning of the facility, burning of disease-infested clothing and linen, Henrik's tar and water solution, and guidance for disposing of the bodies of those that didn't survive. She wrote at a furious pace. There was so much to say, and the pent-up feelings catalyzed the desire to help bring this miserable war to an end in any way she could. Essie paused with the tip of the quill over the paper as she contemplated weighing in on the controversy of inoculation. But as quickly as she considered it, she placed the notion aside. After all, General Washington had already ordered mass inoculations for the troops. He never consulted her. She found out weeks after the fact from her husband after he fell victim to the shot's side effects. Even though she was in charge of all medical matters for the Continental army, a man she revered disrespected her gender and station once again. Essie reasoned she could only do what she could do. Bruised feelings bore no fruit. Her opinion on the matter was now moot. Essie signed the letter, sealed it, and handed it to Clement with instructions for its journey to Valley Forge.

CHAPTER 39

Philadelphia, Pennsylvania

The Philadelphia hospital was the largest in the colonies. Its size and capabilities rivaled the treasured institutions of healing in London. Major André found it impressive. Today, he was hellbent on uncovering the truth, if any, that the Continental army was using medical facilities to aid the transfer of intelligence. Now that the British had captured Philadelphia, this grand hospital was under their control. André would find Dr. Bond and see what he knew.

Standing in the doctor's doorway, André removed his hat and stood erect without revealing the slightest crease in his spotless red uniform. He folded his right arm, hat in hand, across his abdomen and introduced himself.

Dr. Bond appeared frazzled. He was a man who had too much to do and not enough time. Some men wore their hardships on their faces. Dr. Bond was one of them.

"I am interested in learning if you have borne witness to any activities in this hospital aiding the transfer of intelligence against His Majesty's government," André stated.

Dr. Bond sipped water from a glass on his desk and cleared his throat. The bags under his eyes were profound, with their dark hue making it seem he had just lost a prizefight. "I don't know what you mean," he replied.

André, never taken as the fool, sat down in the hardwood chair facing the hospital's lead doctor and said, "Let's not play games, Doctor. I have eyes all over this city. I am keenly aware of your friendship with Benjamin Franklin and other patriot hooligans. This will go much easier for you if you cooperate."

Dr. Bond stared grimly, looking André directly in the eye. "I make no apologies for my friendship with respected members of Philadelphia society. My primary job is to cure the sick, and I take that seriously."

André nodded. "Very well, Doctor. Then I shall expect your complete cooperation and that of your staff if you see any nefarious activity against the crown."

Dr. Bond stood and did not offer his hand. "Good day to you, Major."

"I shall take my leave, but before I go, a look around the building is in order."

With that, André turned and walked out into the cavernous hallway and inhaled the stale odor of illness. Not more than ten paces forward, he encountered a beautiful blond nurse on a furious pace to the first-floor patient ward. She slammed into him as her shoulder brushed his side. The impact caused the young nurse to fall, leading André to extend his hand, helping her to her feet.

"Where are you off to in such a hurry?" he inquired.

The nurse straightened her shawl as she regained her composure. "Forgive my clumsiness. I was merely running late for duties and was trying to make up for lost time."

André held her hand perhaps longer than he should have. His charm and smile had a certain effect on women. He knew how to use it to his advantage. "You are British? Judging from that accent, I'd say London's east side. My name is Major John André, at your service."

The young nurse blushed, taken with his disarming outreach. "I am Hazel Giddings and yes, you are correct, I am from east London."

Her hand rested in his. Her skin was smooth. "You are unwed?" he asked sheepishly.

"I am widowed. My husband died back in London. I am here working as a medic for General Willard. He sends me here to help out during the day."

André arched his right eyebrow. "General Willard? I was with him this morning. I also report directly to him." Then, he let go of her hand, and she turned to walk away.

"It was nice bumping into you," Hazel said with a soft giggle. "Perhaps we shall see each other again."

As she walked down the corridor, André blurted out, "Wait!"

Hazel stopped and turned around. Her eyes revealed her interest. Saying nothing, she seemed to look up at him like a lost puppy desiring a pat on the head.

"I hope you don't think me too forward. I have a social engagement this evening, a party of sorts, at the home of Judge Shippen. Would you accompany me?"

As she hesitated, André speculated whether a man already existed in her life. Even if true, it wouldn't deter him. She was so strikingly beautiful.

Finally, she stammered out, "If it's okay with General Willard, I'd love to."

CHAPTER 40

Valley Forge, Pennsylvania

Aquila's first glance at the Continental army's winter encampment was beyond belief. Men stricken with smallpox lay everywhere. Many appeared near death. An overworked doctor from one of Essie's mobile army hospitals ran from patient to patient in a hollow attempt to provide comfort. Equipment, clothing, and uneaten rations lay askew in the camp. General Washington was a man who demanded order. Aquila could only imagine how the commander in chief dealt with the crisis. Aquila made his way to Washington's tent where he found Billy Lee, Washington's valet, arguing with Alexander Hamilton, the recently appointed aide-de-camp. They were embroiled in a dispute of some sort.

"You can't block access to General Washington. We are at war!" Hamilton decried.

"I ain't gonna risk the general contracting smallpox. I'll take the messages to him," Lee responded.

"And what of your own health?" inquired Hamilton.

"I accept the risk without hesitation," Lee stated emphatically.

"But don't you see? You carry the risk into the tent every time you enter," Hamilton implored.

"Easy, gentlemen," Aquila said. "I overheard your conversation, and I am afraid I must side with Colonel Hamilton. General Washington had smallpox way back in '51 while visiting his brother in Barbados. He is immune. Did he not tell you?"

Hamilton looked as if someone had robbed him blind. Lee was flabbergasted.

"Now, stand aside. I must speak to His Excellency alone."

Aquila entered the cavernous tent and found Washington sitting up on the side of his bunk. "Are you unwell, sir?" he asked.

Washington smiled. His unsightly teeth made a cameo appearance. "I'm fine. Just sitting here bemused at the frivolous debate occurring outside my tent. Had you not come by, I was ready to put an end to the nonsense." Washington stood and extended his right hand. "It's good to see you. Feeling better, I trust?"

"Yes, Your Excellency. Thank you. I carry with me a letter from Dr. Henrik Van der Beek. A physician friend in Europe shared with him a solution speeding the recovery of smallpox."

"Is it accessible to us?"

"Yes, surprisingly. It's nothing more than tar and water cured in a specific manner over two days' time. I can have your doctor make some immediately."

"Excellent!" proclaimed Washington. "We need to get as many of these men back on their feet as soon as possible. Winter is nearing an end, and the British are moving troops, ships, and armaments to end the war quickly." Washington straightened his white ruffled cravat and added as an afterthought, "And this camp is a deplorable sty. The mere sight of it makes my stomach sour."

"Let's get the men back on their feet, and then we shall all work together to straighten up in time to break camp."

Then, Washington moved over to his oak-top writing desk and motioned for Aquila to join him. "Tell me about the Agents of Liberty," he said.

"The pre-revolution Sons and Daughters of Liberty have been engaged in Atlanta, Richmond, Baltimore, Philadelphia, New York, and Boston. We coordinated with doctors at every field hospital. They trained to receive and pass messages. Intelligence should begin arriving regularly any time now." Aquila chuckled and added, "That is, if the messages make their way past Hamilton and Lee."

Washington didn't accept Aquila's attempt at humor, only replying stoically, "They have my best interests at heart."

Conceding the potential for a lighthearted moment, Aquila proceeded with his report. "And through Essie's efforts, we have successfully embedded a young nurse of British origin at the home of General Willard. Her name is Hazel

Giddings, and she has overcome initial suspicions and earned the position as Willard's personal medic."

Washington, pleased with the news, replied, "Excellent. We are off to a fine start."

"Yes, sir. And given her proximity to the Philadelphia hospital, she can spend considerable time there, where she is aiding our efforts even more."

"You and Essie have done well. Our intelligence effort is off to a remarkable start."

"Colonel Greene has things well in hand in the south."

"What of the north?" inquired Washington.

"I have heard from young Major Tallmadge. He is establishing routes for message drops and enlisting the services of friends from his hometown of Setauket. I shall journey to Long Island soon to aid its launch."

CHAPTER 41

Cromwell, Maryland

Essie eagerly unfurled the rolled-up parchment. The coded letter was from Hazel. How she longed for her best friend's company and news of her well-being. The letter was a handbill for a small theater on Second Street in Philadelphia. Seated at her writing desk, Essie removed the jar of acid and a small brush to reveal the message between the lines. Anxiously, Essie read as the brush revealed the words scribed in invisible ink. There were no pleasant exchanges between friends. The letter began on a disturbing note. The acid did not reveal the words fast enough to quell Essie's heightening alarm.

Willard engaged in a plan to extinguish . . .

Essie brushed the solution across the page at a furious pace, eager to learn what appeared to be a dire warning.

. . . the entirety of the Continental army and what Willard calls the disloyal citizens of America . . .

The fear swept Essie away like a gust of wind carrying the leaves from the forest floor. She continued to brush between the lines on the theater handbill until she reached the end.

. . . through the intentional spread of smallpox. Philadelphia is drowning in smallpox cases, and Willard received intelligence that the disease is spreading through the colonies.

Aghast, Essie sat up straight, tapping her right index finger on the desk, wondering what to do with this information. She was already aware of the smallpox outbreak and its rapid advancement throughout the colonies, but this fresh development—that the British were using the smallpox as warfare — well, that was almost unbelievable. Essie contemplated her recent letter to George Washington and the recommendation of creating pesthouses and the use of tar and water to combat smallpox. Knowing what she now knew, it seemed inadequate. Essie fidgeted with a lock of hair, contemplating how best to relay this urgent news. As instructed by Nathaniel Sackett, Essie rose and proceeded to the fireplace in the great room and tossed the handbill inside. She stared into the smoke and rising bits of ash, and an idea formed in her mind.

CHAPTER 42

Philadelphia, Pennsylvania

John André stood in the foyer of Edward Shippen's home. Nowhere else in America had André seen a more grandly appointed home than the magnificent Victorian. Glancing to his right, he glimpsed the awe on the face of his evening companion.

In a hushed tone, he said to Hazel, "Mr. Shippen is a judge. The family has been in Philadelphia for generations. In fact, Mr. Shippen's great-grandfather was the first mayor of the city."

Hazel said nothing. But André watched as her eyes moved around the entryway. Servants bustled about to take cloaks from visitors and offer drinks and hors d'oeuvres. Judge Shippen approached with his daughter by his side, extended his hand, and welcomed them. André stood tall in his starched white pants and red military coat bearing epaulettes and a single gold star, the symbols of his rank. He introduced Hazel, and as he spoke, he couldn't help but think that this young English beauty was not accustomed to attending such events. The dress she wore was more appropriate for a Sunday church service. André surmised it was likely the best she had. Returning his attention to the host, André listened as Judge Shippen spoke.

"I believe you already know my daughter, Peggy."

André smiled, almost forgetting about Hazel. He took Peggy Shippen's hand, kissed it, and replied, "Yes, we seem to travel in the same social circle." He felt a small pang of guilt as Peggy Shippen blushed and his date did a slow burn.

Hazel pursed her lips, and André assumed she was holding in the angry words swimming through her head.

"Peggy has recently become engaged to General Benedict Arnold," Judge Shippen stated matter-of-factly, as if he noticed the flirtation with André and wished to quell it.

"I had heard that news." André looked down at the toes of his spit-shined black boots and replied, "Congratulations, Miss Shippen."

Unexpectedly, Peggy Shippen removed a small, rolled piece of paper and delicately attempted to place it inside André's coat. Failing in the attempt, the paper fluttered to the parquet floor where André scooped it up and pocketed it.

It was Judge Shippen who spoke first. "Are we passing notes like schoolchildren?"

"No, Father. This is a note from General Arnold to Major André. Despite being on opposite sides of the conflict, they had become acquainted some time ago here in the city and struck up a rapport."

"Hmph," grumbled Shippen.

Peggy Shippen clasped her father's arm tenderly. "Father is a stout loyalist, although our family has always been divided on the matter. Some controversy accompanies my engagement."

"The real controversy remains with General Arnold's precarious financial status and legal troubles," said Judge Shippen.

Peggy elbowed him. "Father, this is not the time for such talk."

André bowed gracefully to his host and his daughter. "Thank you for inviting us."

And with that, André took Hazel's arm and presented her to society's finest as they strolled through the house. After two glasses of wine, the petite figure of Hazel Giddings was showing signs of inebriation. André took the glass from her hand, set it on an elevated disposal table, and accompanied Hazel to a magnificent spread of food. The meal presented lamb with mint jelly, roasted chicken, and cod, accompanied by white, rye, and pumpernickel breads. Roasted turnips, carrots, and squash dotted the outer rim of the serving table. At the far end, many fruit pies and pastries drizzled with molasses sat near a tray of gingerbread cookies.

"It's enough food to feed an army," Hazel said.

"I imagine food was scarce, growing up in east London," replied André.

"Terribly so. We were a poor, working-class family. I am not accustomed to such lavish displays. I'd wager a good bit of this food goes to waste. But you are a man of means. This is all quite familiar, I am sure."

André was unapologetic. "I grew up on the other side of London. My father was a successful merchant, and we lived comfortably."

They ate, drank, and socialized until the clock struck twelve. André judged his date at her tipping point and didn't wish her to be ill the following day. He had guaranteed Hazel's return to the Arbogast house by midnight, and he was already late. As they boarded the carriage, he pulled her close, wrapping her in his cloak outside the Shippen home. Once seated, Hazel nestled up to him and tilted her head back while gazing into his eyes. Her full lips parted, and he was sure she would like to be kissed. And so he obliged. André's passion rose, and she returned it without restraint. She placed her arms around his neck and pulled him closer. Breaking free from their passionate exchange, André commanded of the coachman, "Change of plans. Take us to my quarters on Second Street."

CHAPTER 43

Cromwell, Maryland

Before she had endured the agony of prison, indentured servitude, and pompous men standing in the way of her every dream, Essie would never have imagined writing a letter to England's prime minister. Today, she summoned her newfound courage and resolved that she, a humble villager from the outskirts of London, might just hold the key to ending the yearslong war between the country of her birth and the young nation she had grown to love. Essie, at her writing desk, ran her hand over its surface, hoping beyond hope that her plan would make relations between the two countries as smooth as the oak-top desk. Essie reached for the fine stationery emblazoned with the Wright family crest and her favorite quill, a stark white swan's feather. Dipping the nib into the blue and white porcelain inkwell, she concentrated, wanting to exhibit her very best penmanship, and wrote.

To Lord Frederick North, 2nd Earl of Guilford, Prime Minister of Great Britain,

I write to convey the most disturbing developments emanating from America. General Willard is engaged in the deliberate spread of smallpox. His aim may be to extinguish the Continental army, but the perhaps unintended consequence is killing many tens of thousands of innocent citizens. As someone who was born and raised in Great Britain, I have witnessed many an armed conflict and have never known the country of my birth to engage in such a ruthless and willful process to murder innocent people. While we remain on opposite sides of this conflict, I appeal to your senses as a leader and a gentleman and ask that you cease this horrid warfare and admonish those responsible.

It is my fondest hope that you see what I do. This war has stretched over many years and appears almost unwinnable for either country. Would not a peaceful resolution where both nations live in harmony be preferred?

Respectfully,
Mrs. Esther Wright
Director General for the Medical Department of the Continental Army

Essie gently blew on the ink, hoping with each exhaled breath that the carefully chosen words would have the desired effect. She folded the paper and applied the wax seal bearing the Wright family crest.

CHAPTER 44

Setauket, Long Island, New York

Aquila had survived impalement and a blast from a cannonball, but the recovery from the smallpox episode proved challenging in its own right. He tired easily and found himself short of breath. A heaviness lived in his chest, and the faded lesions always seemed to itch. Perhaps most troubling was the effect on his eyesight. Once proud of his eagle-eye vision, Aquila struggled to see far in the distance. The problem was pervasive in poor lighting. As he entered the town limits of Setauket, Aquila stopped his horse, removed his wide-brimmed brown felt hat, and rubbed his tired eyes. Then, replacing the hat, he trotted toward the town's main street. Hitching his horse to a post in front of a local tavern, Aquila sought a whiskey to ease his frayed nerves. He worried about his health and thought about how his acceptance of chief intelligence officer for the Continental army had come with the promised benefit of working from Cromwell's Passage. But the needs of war dragged him up and down the coastline in a state of perpetual motion. He missed Essie and Penny and the serenity of his family's homestead.

Aquila saw a collection of redcoats hoisting ale and singing in a drunken stupor when he entered the tavern. New York was still under the control of the British, and Aquila knew he must tread with care. He commended himself for choosing to dress out of uniform. His best bet for a successful mission hinged on his ability to navigate enemy territory. Aquila took a seat at the bar and waited. After an hour, he wondered if he had arrived at the right place. The promised contact had not yet arrived. Then, a young auburn-haired woman, dressed as a barmaid, emerged from behind with a small plate holding a baked muffin.

"Enjoy this treat. It holds greetings from Benjamin Tallmadge," she said politely. Before he could respond, the young woman vanished. Breaking the muffin apart with a fork, Aquila found a tiny rolled-up piece of paper, which he removed and stored in his inner breast pocket, wary of reading it inside the British watering hole. He walked out, mounted his horse, and trotted slowly to the edge of the nearby wood line. There he reached for the rolled-up note and found not words, nor a coded message, but a small map showing a red barn on the east bank.

—ꟿ—

The wind murmured from the Long Island Sound, easing Aquila's fatigue from the day's long journey. Tallmadge was overjoyed to see him. The two men embraced and entered the cavernous old barn that had resided on the site since Tallmadge's ancestors came to Long Island 150 years earlier. The barn held a few horses, some farm equipment, and bales of hay. In Aquila's estimation, it was a neglected relic, largely ignored by Tallmadge's father, a clergyman whose sons were engaged in the revolution.

Tallmadge led him to the back of the barn, removed several large bales of hay, and revealed a trapdoor leading to a cellar. This cellar resembled the one in Aquila's barn, where he had instructed Penny to take refuge if the British menaced Cromwell's Passage. Tallmadge lifted the hatch, and the two men descended the stairs. Lighting a Betty lamp, Tallmadge directed Aquila to a desk with a worn top and a long drawer underneath. Aquila took in the musty smell of the cellar and stood at the desk alongside Tallmadge, who unfurled an expansive parchment revealing a map of New York City and Long Island. With his finger to guide Aquila's attention, Tallmadge began his report.

"I am pleased to say that the northern intelligence operation is almost ready to commence." Pointing to Setauket, he continued, "We are here. I have enlisted the services of civilian volunteers who will work through various clandestine means to convey messages and move them along the water and the roads with multiple handoffs. Information will flow both ways and reach General Washington as expeditiously as the process permits."

Aquila affirmed with a nod. "You organize things well. How many civilian volunteers have you cultivated?"

"Four so far. One of these men is recruiting a man inside New York City. His enlistment in our cause is central to its success." Tallmadge eagerly opened the desk's long drawer and removed a skin-bound notebook. He set it on the desktop and turned over the scratched, soft, floppy cover to point to the first page. A list of numbers appeared.

"Is this some sort of code book?" Aquila asked.

Tallmadge smiled. "Yes, in a manner of speaking. This list contains the key players in our effort. I am listed by my code name, John Bolton, with a corresponding number; others are merely defined by a number. They include everyone pertinent from Washington to a local farmer here in Setauket."

Turning the page, Aquila viewed columns of numbers and letters that appeared unintelligible. "What is this?"

Tallmadge beamed. "This system is a cypher. I have created a unique method of conveying information through seven hundred and sixty-three numbers, each representing a place, a name, a phrase, or a single word. We will replicate the book for the people in our ring, and if the enemy finds it, it will prove fruitless."

"Ingenious," Aquila remarked. Pointing back to the map, he said, "Explain the detailed routes for conveyance of intelligence."

"Certainly," Tallmadge replied. "My friend, the aforementioned farmer, will make frequent trips from Setauket to New York City to visit his sister and her husband. Another friend, a local tavern owner, will travel along a different route to procure supplies for his tavern. While in the city, the farmer will pass him the information, and he will carry it back to Setauket, conveying it to a third friend, who will then row across the Long Island Sound to Fairfield, Connecticut. The information will pass back to me, and I will place it in the hands of General Washington."

"It's cautious, as it should be, but I worry that the circuitous nature of your route will needlessly delay vital intelligence," Aquila stated.

"Understood, General Wright. However, what I have described is just one of many plans to convey information. We cannot be reliant on only one method for fear of discovery."

Aquila nodded. "I agree with your assessment. In my judgment, your northern operation is not yet ready to join the Agents of Liberty. I will give you six months to continue recruiting assets, establishing dead drops, and refining movements."

Tallmadge looked wounded. Aquila hated breaking the spirit of the young major, but as the one in charge of intelligence for the Continental army, Aquila was resolute in his drive to succeed. Putting a theory into practice ahead of schedule was dangerous.

CHAPTER 45

London, England

"I received the most interesting letter," stated Lord North. His voice was deliberate. His tone was stern.

Germain sat upright, awaiting the lecture that was sure to follow. His relationship with Lord North was anything but congenial. It was inconceivable that Germain was being called to the primary office in Whitehall for anything other than a rip.

"It came on a recent ship from the colonies. A woman of some standing has written to me about our war tactics."

Germain felt his face go flush. He had no idea what woman had written to his prime minister or why Lord North exhibited such hostility. He sat still and revealed none of his anxiety.

"Heaven knows why the colonists placed a woman in charge of medical affairs for their army, but apparently, they have. It seems this Mrs. Wright, the wife of a prominent general, is appalled that we decided to intentionally spread smallpox, which would wipe out the Continental army and our colonists. I knew this was going to bite us in the posterior."

Germain was sick. He admired the old warhorse for his ability to think on his feet. But this? It was unbelievable. Germain sat and listened. Try as he might, Germain knew his face revealed the regret coursing through his brain.

"The letter states the spread of smallpox has invaded nearly all the northern colonies. Did you authorize this insanity?" Lord North's voice was now raised in a manner that Germain had never experienced. The worn and weathered lines on the prime minister's face crinkled in disgust. His eyes held the fire of a thousand suns. "You controlled the power of the world's finest military. You held my trust to end the colonial revolt employing a dignified war strategy befitting Great Britain. You have failed me. You have failed your country!"

Finding his voice, Germain stammered, "But milord, I assure you I authorized nothing of the kind. Smallpox as a method of combat was never a topic of conversation. I knew nothing of this horrid and shameful strategy."

Calming down, Lord North replied, "It matters not. You chose General Willard. He completely understood his actions, and you must be responsible for the entire sordid mess." Before Germain could reply, Lord North continued. "I have sent an urgent dispatch to the colonies placing General Clinton in charge of our affairs. Because of his many victories in past wars, we will relieve General Willard of his rank and send him to the English countryside to retire in a much nicer manner than he deserves."

"And what of me?" Germain asked timidly.

"I have half a mind to send you to the gallows. Instead, I strip you of all titles and property and banish you to the Forton Prison in Gosport."

Lord North clapped his hands. Two guards appeared. "Take him away. I never wish to see this bugger again."

CHAPTER 46

two months later
Philadelphia, Pennsylvania

The early morning sun shone brightly through the second-story window of the Arbogast house, where Hazel resided in service to General Willard. She lay in her bed, luxuriating in the soft confines of the feather mattress. Staring at the white linen canopy, Hazel knew it was time to rise. Still lost in thoughts about her torrid affair with John André and the dangerous game in which she found herself involved, she tossed and she turned, hoping for another brief spell of sleep. Other than John, the only man she had ever laid with was her late husband. Remembering, Hazel smiled at the gentle lovemaking from her first years of marriage. Lying with John was a different experience altogether. He was virile but tender. The touch of his body against her lit a flame. He made love the way he painted, like a genuine artist.

Tossing around in the down-filled quilt, Hazel decided to start her day. If General Willard did not require her attention, she would report to the hospital. As she sat up and stretched, a crash startled her. Hazel ran to the window and looked down to see six redcoats and a battering ram tearing the front doors from their hinges. The soldiers screamed for General Willard as a mature, grizzled general followed them into the house. Hurriedly, Hazel dressed in her nurse's uniform and made her bed. She decided it was best to wait in her room. She hurried to the door of the chamber and cracked it open to provide a sight line. The soldiers confronted a startled but still groggy General Willard just rising from bed in his long, striped nightshirt.

"What's the meaning of this?" General Willard responded angrily. "I'll have you all court-martialed!" Recognizing the older man leading the revolt, Willard screamed, "Clinton! Is this how you repay my trust? With a mutiny! I'll see you hanged!"

Hazel watched, aghast, as the soldiers apprehended the disheveled general and held him steady.

With an even temperament, General Clinton addressed Willard. "I'm afraid they recalled you, old chap," he said. "My orders originate from the prime minister. It appears your benefactor, Germain, has been sacked. I am the new commander in chief. These men will escort you to the port where you will await the next ship back to London where, as I understand it, you may retire at your country estate."

Willard's bald head with its wisps of white hair combined with his fiery dark eyes to create what Hazel thought was a crazed appearance. "And what, pray tell, am I being charged with? Winning a war that my predecessors did not know how to fight?"

Clinton smirked. "Lord North did not take kindly to your germ warfare. Your intentional spread of smallpox mortified him. We can and should win wars by preserving dignity."

"And I am to be put out to pasture—like an old cow?"

"Take him away!" commanded General Clinton. "Search the house."

Hazel stood frozen. She steadied herself on the door trim, overcome with emotion. At least in some small way, she hoped that what she had just witnessed was a manifestation of the intelligence she had passed to Essie. On the other hand, she had won the trust of General Willard and was now vulnerable to this new man, General Clinton. It was as if she were starting over with the hardest part of the mission right before her once more. Hazel trembled at the thought. She was unsure she had the strength. Maybe this was a blessing! Just maybe, General Willard's downfall was her opportunity to escape and return to Cromwell . . . and Timothy. But what of John? How could she leave him?

Confusion reigned as a light sweat appeared on her forehead. It gave way to unadulterated fear when the redcoats barged into her chambers and ransacked the room. Soldiers tossed her bedding, spied under the bedframe, yanked everything from the closet, and then, to Hazel's chagrin, opened the drawer of the writing desk. And there it was, in the hands of a British soldier, the little book containing her innermost thoughts and secrets, not spoken aloud nor otherwise conveyed to another living soul. The soldier skimmed through the pages. His eyes bulged at the revelations. Hazel was nauseous. When the soldier declared, "It appears we have a spy," Hazel turned and vomited.

CHAPTER 47

Cromwell, Maryland

On the cushioned platform beneath the window in Penny's chamber, Essie brushed her stepdaughter's lustrous brown hair. They prepared for Sunday morning services at the Cromwell church. Today was to be Penny's first day as the church harpist. Essie had spent what time she could spare teaching her teenage pupil the subtleties of playing, and Penny had mastered her craft. Essie's heart held pangs of regret that Aquila was not present to escort them to church and share the outpouring of pride she would no doubt experience on her own at seeing Penny excel before the townsfolk. With each brushstroke through Penny's hair, Essie's mind raced between Aquila, the letter she wrote to Lord North, how Hazel was faring, and how to embed her husband's Agents of Liberty into her collection of fledgling mobile army hospitals. She was lost. Lost in the melee of conflict between her duties as wife, mother, medical leader for the army, and now supplemental spymaster. Essie felt her head might explode. She summoned her innate courage, inhaled deeply, and slowly expelled the air from her lungs, hoping beyond hope she had concealed her angst from Penny.

"You seem troubled," Penny remarked.

Essie knew right then she had failed at masking her inner thoughts. She had always been guilty of wearing her emotions on her sleeve. Her stepdaughter was far too perceptive. This wasn't the first time Penny had inquired about her thoughts when she was adrift in her mind's overgrown brush.

"No, sweet girl. I am burdened with many thoughts, but your church performance is the priority. I will beam with pride." Essie hoped her enthusiasm veiled her anxiety.

Once seated in the front row of the church—reserved for the Wrights, the town's founding family—Essie sat straight up against the polished wooden pew and watched as Penny strummed the harp's strings. They agreed on a gentle excerpt from Handel's "Messiah" for the parishioners' entry. Penny played as if it were as natural as breathing. She was beautiful. Now at sixteen, Penny had developed a woman's body. The royal blue dress with the white lace neckline nestled beneath the sheen of her rich brown hair. Her cheeks held a bit of natural blush, and her eyelashes fluttered in a manner Essie suspected one day would drive young men crazy.

Pastor Vinson assumed the pulpit and began his sermon. He spoke of these times. "War. Death. Destruction. While we endure these travails, is it not crucial that we continue to embrace the Lord's message of love and compassion?"

Essie tried to hold these tenets in her heart. After all, she was born a Briton. It was impossible not to feel some compassion for the men in red coats, even though they were the enemy. But her thoughts quickly veered in the other direction. These were scoundrels who would use the spread of smallpox to disable and kill their enemy—and innocent men, women, and children. Before conceding it to the enemy, they'd burn down a city. The British evicted people from their homes to house their own officers. And they were cold and diabolical. Weighing the circumstances, Essie saw no possible way in which Pastor Vinson's well-meaning sermon would overcome her hatred of men so wicked.

Essie felt a hand on her right shoulder. She turned to see Isaiah sitting directly behind her.

"I need to speak with you after church," he whispered.

Essie smiled and nodded. Then she turned back around to face the pulpit, where Pastor Vinson was completing the day's sermon. As people filed out, Essie remained and listened as Penny played an uplifting piece from Mozart. When the church emptied, Essie embraced Penny, kissing her on the cheek.

"I wish your father had been here to see you play. It was magnificent!" Essie said. "Please, wait in the carriage with Clement. I will be along in a moment. I must speak with Isaiah."

Pastor Vinson remained at the doorway, wishing his parishioners well.

When they were finally alone, Isaiah spoke quickly. "Aquila told me they are using hollowed out quills to transfer messages for the Agents of Liberty. That got me thinking. As you know, I've been making stretchers for the war effort in my spare time."

"Yes, the army and my medical corps appreciate your service."

"Of course, milady. What I wanted to tell you is that Aquila's quills gave me an idea. What if I hollowed out one of the stretcher handles and placed a cap on the end that would barely reveal a seam? Then, through the hospital efforts, you can aid the Agents of Liberty in communicating intelligence from the front lines?"

Essie beamed and hugged her family's longtime foreman. "It is a brilliant idea. Please begin immediately. I will send a coded message to the agents we have at the mobile hospitals informing them of the new method."

Essie's spirits lifted. She always hoped that Pastor Vinson's beloved messages of optimism would ease her troubled mind. Today, that wasn't the case, but the act of going to church and the whispered message from Isaiah brought optimism of accelerating the conclusion to this never-ending war. Shouting at the church's entrance broke her thoughts.

"Mrs. Esther Wright! Where is she?" demanded one of the two Continental army officers.

A startled Pastor Vinson, having said goodbye to the last of the Sunday parishioners, stood in their way. "What is the meaning of this? You cannot barge into the church on the Lord's Day and behave so garishly."

Ignoring the pastor, the men pressed forward toward the front of the church. Isaiah stood to protect Essie. "Out of the way," the lead soldier demanded. "Our orders are to take Mrs. Wright into custody and transport her to Philadelphia for trial."

Essie came from behind Isaiah. "Trial? On what charge? I have done nothing wrong," she challenged.

The soldier in charge was a tall man. His look of disdain showered down upon her. "Treason against the United States of America," he stated coldly.

"There must be some mistake," Essie declared. "On whose orders is this arrest being carried out?"

The tall soldier reached into a pocket beneath his blue coat and unfurled the order. Essie read the words in disbelief. Henry Laurens, the president of the Continental Congress, had signed it. Before she could respond, the soldiers gripped each of her arms and began dragging her down the aisle. Penny, who had reentered the church, cried, "No, you can't take her."

Essie's stomach soured. It transported her back years when men she once respected dragged her from her beloved cottage in Wickhamshire and hauled her off to debtor's prison for a crime she did not commit. She glanced over her shoulder and yelled to Isaiah, "Take Penny home. Inform Celia. And get word to Aquila."

CHAPTER 48

Philadelphia, Pennsylvania

Aquila's doubt about the Marquis de Lafayette was all but vanquished as he fought side by side with the young Frenchman. Lafayette commanded a battalion against the British, repelling a complacent opponent content with masquerading as an elite military force while enjoying the spoils of the city. As Aquila rode into the city's center, near Independence Hall, he glanced at Lafayette and smiled in appreciation of his exuberant, hard-fought effort.

"It seems the British forces became, how do you say it, fat and lazy while occupying the city," Lafayette remarked. Then he laughed and said, "I am not surprised. It is typical of British arrogance, but one cannot assume a victory or rest on his laurels."

Aquila nodded in agreement. "General Clinton, the newly appointed commander in chief of the British forces, made public his orders to vacate Philadelphia. I expect the redcoats to be gone by sunset tomorrow."

"And your Congress will return to Philadelphia from its temporary location in York?"

"A dispatch I received shows they are already on their way."

"Magnifique!" replied Lafayette in his native tongue. "Where will the next battle take us?"

"That will be up to General Washington, but if I had to hazard a guess, I'd say up north. Retaking New York is of paramount importance."

"Very well, General Wright. I shall await further orders. In the meantime, I shall honor my men with a good meal and a few hours in one of the city's finest taverns." Then, he laughed again in his boyish manner and said, "But not to worry. It is a brief respite. We shall not become fat and lazy like the British."

CHAPTER 49

Philadelphia, Pennsylvania

Standing in abject fear, Hazel's thoughts traveled back to her young life. After enduring the London Debtor's Prison and a brutal life as an indentured field hand, she would welcome a return to those past hardships if she were to be spared the wrath of General Clinton. She stood before him in the office that General Willard once occupied. Two soldiers stood on either side of her as she tried not to tremble. General Clinton held her diary. He set it down on the desk and flipped the dog-eared pages.

"Mrs. Giddings, this is terribly interesting reading. You admit to being a spy for the Continental army, and you are currently engaged in a romance with a trusted British officer. Do you have anything to say for yourself?" Clinton glared at Hazel. A wave of nausea swept through her stomach again. Never one who was at a loss for words, Hazel cleared her throat and tried, with little ammunition, to defend her honor. Whispering, she replied, "No, milord."

"Very well," General Clinton replied as he gently tapped his pipe against the desktop, filling it with fresh tobacco and pushing it down. "There is only one punishment befitting a spy. Mrs. Hazel Giddings, I sentence you to be hanged today before sundown." Then, using the candle on the desk, Clinton lit his pipe. Puffing in rapid succession to start the pipe, he blew smoke toward Hazel's face. The smell of Orinoco tobacco swept over her as the two soldiers gripped her arms and led her away. She was almost to the doorway when she heard Clinton bark one more order. "When you have secured the prisoner, find Major André and have him report at once."

—∾—

With the setting sun came a chill. Hazel had no cloak and felt goosebumps forming on her arms. The redcoats threw a black hood over her head as they escorted her from the prison to the gallows. Hazel gasped for breath. Why, she wondered, did they cover her face? She knew exactly where she was, and her destination was clear. It was for theater alone. They wanted to make a spectacle of her. Hazel had seen public hangings. Sometimes the prisoner died beneath the darkness of the black hood. Other times, they removed the hood so the prisoner could witness public ire. Resigned to her fate, she trudged. The weight of the shackles prevented anything more. She could hear a crowd forming as they led her up the steps. Loyalists were cheering. Outrage gripped the patriots. Hazel heard alternating cries of "Kill the spy" and "Cut her loose."

Finally, Hazel stopped moving. She felt the soldiers' hold on her arms loosen as one of them ripped the black hood from her head. The light stung her eyes, and the wind blew her tousled hair across her face. Hazel listened as the hangman attempted to speak. The raucous mob was too loud. The next thing Hazel knew, a gunshot rang out to quiet the crowd. A soldier had fired a pistol into the air. The mollified crowd gazed up at the platform. The hangman spoke.

"This woman, Mrs. Hazel Giddings, is a confessed spy. By the order of the commander in chief, General Henry Clinton, she is to be hanged by the neck until breath shall forever leave her body. Does the condemned have any last words?"

Gathering her spirit and innermost strength, Hazel reverted to the sharp-tongued, independent-minded woman she was. Defiantly, she spoke as forcefully as she could manage. "I was born a Briton. My country tossed me aside like rubbish. I love America. Britain is evil . . ."

"Enough of your treasonous talk," growled the hangman. Showing no compassion, he placed the noose around her neck and pulled it taut. The hangman fumed and released the sandbags. Hazel felt her body run up toward the overhead beam as the noose tightened around her neck. She heard a mix of horrified gasps and cheers from the crowd. Dangling in the wind, Hazel could still smell the acrid odor of Clinton's Orinoco tobacco on her clothes. Within minutes, her sense of what was occurring in the town square vanished. Hazel felt as if she were floating. It was like being in a dream state. She had left her body and was watching from above, contemplating her life and the friends she was leaving behind.

CHAPTER 50

Philadelphia, Pennsylvania

"We are leaving tonight," stated General Clinton to his newly inherited spymaster, John André. "Willard has been put out to pasture where he so dearly belongs, and our troops are moving north. It is critical that we fortify New York."

André nodded in reply. He took the measure of General Clinton and was determined to escape unscathed from his indiscretions.

"As for you, I have half a mind to send you back on the next ship to London with your coconspirator."

André stood erect, holding his tongue but wanting to defend his honor. He said with deference, "General Clinton, I had no involvement in the smallpox matter."

Clinton lowered his head in disgust. "Perhaps not, Major, but your torrid affair with a patriot spy leaves your judgment in question." Rubbing his left hand over his forehead, Clinton then said, "What were you thinking? Reportedly, your intellect placed you in such a prominent position of responsibility. Now, I wonder whether you are fit to serve by cleaning the privies in His Majesty's army."

André bowed his head. The scathing rebuke by his commander in chief made him realize Clinton was likely to carry out his threats of sending him back to London. André had thought his worst-case scenario was a reprimand and a demotion. In his estimation, he needed to play a card he had wanted to hold for a while longer. The ace up his sleeve that would ease the general's ire and place him back in a position of prominence. André cleared his throat, hoping it would cause Clinton to halt his tirade.

"You have something to say?" bellowed the general.

"Yes, sir. I have been working covertly to turn an American general."

Clinton froze behind his desk, as if he couldn't fathom the crux of what he had just heard. "You've got my attention," he replied calmly.

CHAPTER 51

Philadelphia, Pennsylvania

The patriot soldiers whisked Essie away without a cloak, a meal, or a pleasant night's rest. The carriage traveled swiftly without delay; the cold, bumpy ride ended on the streets of Philadelphia, brimming with activity on this overcast Monday afternoon. Weary to the bone, a soldier yanked Essie from the carriage and led her into the hallowed hall that once again housed the Second Continental Congress. Essie had entered Independence Hall mostly in good times: to receive her commendation for valor in the Battle of Cromwell, and to accept her commission as the director general for the Medical Department of the Continental army. Today, the anxiety of ignorance about the reason behind her arrest left her queasy.

The officers led Essie up the flight of stairs to the same meeting room in which she had last met with John Hancock and Dr. Bond to warn them of England's weaponization of smallpox. Now, Essie stood before President Laurens and General Washington, her hair askew and her clothes disheveled, wanting just to sit and have a warm cup of tea and a proper conversation regarding what this misunderstanding must be about. These men wore scowls. Neither rose to greet her. They did not invite her to sit, nor did they offer her a beverage. Before she could utter a single word, Laurens began his tongue-lashing.

"I understand you have been busy writing letters to the enemy," he said in a tone she had never experienced from his predecessor.

With the realization of the reason for their ire, a prickly sensation raced down Essie's spine. *The letter*. The one she wrote to Lord North, the British prime minister. Her intention was honorable. Why were these men so displeased?

Laurens continued, "I don't recall any proclamation appointing you as a diplomat on behalf of the United States of America." Then, with Washington watching, Laurens slammed an angry fist on the oak table and barked, "What have you got to say for yourself?"

Essie trembled. She fought the urge to cry, seeking the right words from deep within. Finally, she stammered, "My letter to Prime Minister North merely informed him of General Willard's intentional use of smallpox and asked for his aid in ending this dreadful form of warfare and a peaceful resolution to the war."

Her words rang hollow. Laurens was more infuriated than before she had spoken. "Does that not sound like diplomacy to you?" he asked mockingly.

Gathering her resolve, Essie stood tall, looked at George Washington, and declared, "Is this not what you asked me to do the last time we met in this very room? To gather intelligence for the betterment of America?"

Washington rose from the table and addressed Essie's plea.

"You are correct, Essie. Your chartered role prescribed the gathering of intelligence for the betterment of our nation. Where you failed was in acting on your own. The consequences are profound. Britain has replaced the aging and vulnerable General Willard and installed General Clinton, seen as a steadier hand and a more formidable foe. Your good intentions have likely prolonged the war's duration."

Exasperated, Essie shot back without forethought. "But Your Excellency, the intentional spread of smallpox has ceased with General Willard's departure."

"True," replied Washington. "But the prolonged war under General Clinton will cause immeasurable patriot soldiers to die. A heavy price to pay for ending the smallpox warfare, where the bulk of the damage had already been incurred."

Essie stood there shaking. Her anxiety overwhelmed her ability to form cogent thought. Despite her best efforts, a tear rolled down her cheek as Laurens carried on.

"You are being stripped of your position as director general for the Medical Department of the Continental army. Dr. Bond will assume the role in your stead.

You are accused of treason against the United States of America for unauthorized diplomacy with the enemy."

Processing the vastness of her situation, Essie questioned in a weakened voice, "Who will defend me at trial?"

"Trial?" Laurens huffed. "There will be no trial. You have confessed your crime. Treason is punishable by death. By the authority of the Second Continental Congress, you are to be hanged in the town square within a fortnight."

CHAPTER 52

Philadelphia, Pennsylvania

Let me through!" Aquila roared.

A small, squat guard, his rifle resting upon his shoulder, replied in a voice revealing not an ounce of flexibility. "I am sorry, General. By order of His Excellency, George Washington, the prisoner is to receive no visitors."

"We shall see about that," Aquila replied, and he turned on his heel and barreled his way down the street and around the corner to Independence Hall. As he got to the entryway, Aquila leaned his right arm against the enormous door, breathed out, and checked his anger. Berating the commander in chief and facing charges of insubordination, or worse, would not help Essie. He passed through the vast archway and encountered an aide. In a voice most would deem too aggressive, Aquila asked, "Where is General Washington?"

Saying nothing, the aide gestured toward the stairwell.

Aquila's boots hit the stairs. The noise announced to anyone listening that someone with urgent business was on the way. Reaching the top, Aquila proceeded to the private meeting room favored by the congressional leader. He rapped on the door in a manner he hoped did not convey his ire.

"Come," Laurens's muffled voice stated through the thick wooden door.

Pushing his way through, Aquila saw Laurens and Washington standing over the table reviewing a map.

"We've been expecting you," Laurens stated matter-of-factly.

Then, Washington motioned toward a chair. "Please sit, Aquila."

Laurens began. "Before we discuss the crime committed by your wife, we are duty-bound to ask if you had any knowledge whatsoever of her intentions to write to Prime Minister North."

Aquila knew he must proceed with caution. Words must be measured and emotions held in abeyance.

"I most assuredly did not."

Washington was the first to respond. "You are a decorated general and a valued soldier. Your word is enough for me."

Aquila was pleased but somewhat perplexed at how trusting the commander in chief was. Were he in Washington's shoes, Aquila was unsure he would offer the benefit of the doubt. Seeing Laurens's face, Aquila surmised he felt the same.

Aquila gathered his strength and began. "The very qualities of Essie's nature that you have celebrated on more than one occasion are what led us to this point. While I could not speak to my wife, I could easily assess her intentions. Essie is the type of person who gets an idea and simply presses forward. She spends little time in calculation. She is a woman of action. Her results speak for themselves." He was no lawyer, but Aquila worked his brain to its full extent to defend his wife's honor.

Laurens made a guttural sound and replied, "In my estimation, she should have spent a bit more time in calculation before engaging the enemy without authority."

"I am sure, as I live and breathe, that her intentions were pure," Aquila implored.

"Perhaps," answered Washington, "but, as you know, the purest of intentions aligned with poor judgment often lead to catastrophic results."

"Is it so?" Aquila asked, his voice rising ever so slightly. "Essie wished to stop germ warfare. She succeeded. General Willard was recalled and replaced with General Clinton. Is he not a known entity and certainly not the formidable foe we assume him to be?"

Aquila could see that Laurens was losing patience with the conversation. He was being heard only in deference to his service to the Continental army. Laurens's obligatory reception to his concerns was exhausted. His reply galvanized Aquila's assumption.

"She committed a crime—high treason against the United States of America. For this, there are no excuses, nor exceptions!" As a gesture of finality, Laurens pounded his fist on the oak table in a fit of anger. "I delayed her sentence out of respect for you, which is not the standard procedure in these cases."

Aquila resigned himself to the meeting's inevitable conclusion. Reasoning with Laurens and Washington yielded no progress. His mind raced in contemplation. Unlike Essie, Aquila normally pondered important matters for long periods to eliminate any inkling of doubt. But now, at this moment, Aquila's fierce love for Essie blinded him, and he would place her above all else. He rose from the table and stated as elegantly as he could, "You leave me no choice. I resign my commission immediately. I cannot be part of an institution that so callously passes judgment on someone who has worked tirelessly to aid the country she loves."

With his proclamation, Aquila half expected Laurens to do an about-face and offer some shred of mercy. Laurens's troubled expression and Washington's last words extinguished the hope. "So be it."

CHAPTER 53

Philadelphia, Pennsylvania

Benedict Arnold is a well-respected and decorated general in the Continental army," proclaimed John André. "I swear by all that's good in this world, he is ready to turn."

Clinton seemed skeptical. "To what do you owe such a bold assessment?"

André smiled, displaying his well-known cockiness. "Let's just say it's because of my friendship with his betrothed, Miss Peggy Shippen. She introduced me to General Arnold, who claims he is owed a substantial sum of money from the cash-strapped Continental army. What's more, he feels disrespected and desires not only to convey American secrets but to lead men under the British flag."

Clinton did not seem convinced. "What tangible reward would we reap from such an alliance?"

"General Arnold is presently in command at West Point. He will open the gates and surrender the fort to us. Imagine the pathway to victory with West Point flying under a British flag," proclaimed André. "If we control the Hudson, we eliminate access to New England and effectively divide the colonies."

"And what exactly does he wish in return?"

"He requires twenty thousand pounds and a command post in the British army," André replied. "Shall I proceed, General?"

"Not so fast, Major. Given the many missteps of my predecessor, I am inclined to seek a show of good faith from General Arnold."

"What do you have in mind?" inquired André.

Clinton clasped his fingers together in a steepled manner. "I shall leave that to your determination. Once we have something tangible, we can decide if we wish to proceed."

André didn't immediately reply. He stood, brushed the toe of his boot across the polished wood floor of the Arbogast home, and meekly uttered, "We need to take this opportunity seriously. It's a once in a lifetime chance to end the war."

Clinton puffed furiously on his pipe.

André thought the smoke leaving Clinton's nostrils resembled the mythical fire-breathing dragons from the stories of his youth.

"How can you be certain General Arnold is not feigning his interest in joining us as a trap?" Clinton bellowed.

With no guarantee of success, André was chastised into submission. "I cannot immediately allay your concern," he said rather obligingly.

"You should know better than to question my judgment in all matters," Clinton barked. "Now go get on with it. We leave Philadelphia for New York City tonight. Bring me some tangible show of good faith or drop this foolishness."

Turning on one heel, André left the Arbogast home and hit the street, wondering, *What show of good faith would satisfy Henry Clinton?*

John André returned to his quarters and completed the quick work of packing his belongings for the trip north. He was sorry to leave Philadelphia, where he had made so many acquaintances and contacts. Mostly, he was sorry to be leaving the beautiful Peggy Shippen behind. In his private thoughts, André dreamed of Peggy, sailing to England and sharing his life with her. Her beauty captivated him. Peggy's sass inspired him to be at his best. His best artist. His best poet. And his best intelligence officer. It was a double-edged sword. The woman he desired was engaged to the man on whom André's career success depended. He applied a spritz of cologne to his neck and straightened his uniform. Breezing out the door, he confidently sought the woman of his dreams.

Arriving at the palatial Shippen home on the west side of Philadelphia, a servant greeted André and invited him into the marble foyer adorned with large oils depicting hunts in the Pennsylvania countryside. *Hounds leading men to their prey. Wasn't that why he was there? Was he using Peggy as the means to Arnold?*

"Major André," said Peggy Shippen. "What a pleasant surprise."

André bowed before her in a manner of gallantry, taking her hand and gently kissing it. The servant departed, and the two agreed to stroll through the gardens. André knew from experience that they could speak privately in the winding gardens with their six-foot hedges.

"We are pulling out tonight," André began.

"Did you speak to General Clinton regarding my fiancé's proposal?" she inquired.

He exhaled. "Yes." Hesitating, André searched for the right words.

"Well, did he accept?" she asked.

"Not exactly. He wants a show of good faith. The manner of such demonstration has been left to me. I confess I am unsure what would please General Clinton."

"He questions Benedict's veracity?"

"Of course," André replied. "The concern is that he is merely pretending to turn to lure our side into a trap of some sort."

Peggy rolled her eyes in disbelief. Then, she indignantly proclaimed, "I can assure you that he is quite serious. I shall send a coded message with word of your need. Once I have a reply, I will send a courier to New York to let you know."

With no further recourse, André escorted her back to the house and took his leave. Her fragrant scent still permeated his every thought.

CHAPTER 54

Philadelphia, Pennsylvania

Walking briskly down Chestnut Street, Aquila heard the *clip-clop* of boots gaining on him from behind. Then, he heard the voice call out, "Aquila, wait."

Aquila turned on one heel and, to his surprise, saw the commander in chief, out of breath, struggling to catch up.

"Your Excellency, is everything all right?"

"Yes, yes," Washington replied while catching his breath. "I needed to have you out of earshot of Independence Hall. You see, I serve as commander in chief at the pleasure of Congress. Therefore, I must publicly support the decree from Henry Laurens."

Sensing the meaning between Washington's words, Aquila replied, "And you wish to help?"

"Most certainly," stated Washington, now standing tall with his breathing settled. "Do not mistake me. I don't believe what Essie did was right, but I admire her tenacious approach to achieving a most difficult objective."

Aquila, without forethought, embraced Washington, and said, "Thank you, sir."

"I have a plan, but I cannot let people see me as a participant. No one can know of my involvement. Not even Essie."

"I understand," replied Aquila.

"And I have one nonnegotiable condition."

"Anything. Just name it."

Washington stared into Aquila's eyes in a manner that only he could and said, "You will rescind your resignation and continue to serve as my chief of intelligence."

Aquila, feeling grateful for Washington's lifeline to Essie, replied, "Done."

CHAPTER 55

Philadelphia, Pennsylvania

Essie's mind resembled a tornado's funnel cloud. Errant thoughts swirled as melancholy took hold. She had been in dire circumstances before, the London Debtor's Prison, and being sentenced to death by the evil Governor Templeton but, even in those situations, she had not lost all hope. Now, on the day she was to be hanged, Essie could see only her lack of a future, the darkness that lay ahead. What would become of Aquila and Penny? They had both survived the loss of Rebecca. Essie's own impending death would devastate them. She wished she had Hazel or Celia to comfort her. Celia remained in Cromwell, and Hazel was secretly working for the enemy.

Essie hadn't even been granted the opportunity to see Aquila. She imagined staring into the crowd from the hangman's platform, her eyes pleading for mercy. She yearned to tell those she loved how she felt. Essie's stomach soured, and her forehead broke out in a cold sweat. She propped herself up against the damp stone prison wall and let herself cry. The acrid stench of mildew, coupled with her tears, caused her nose to become stuffy. She coughed, using her ragged sleeve to wipe the spittle from her mouth. She placed her head between her knees and tried to breathe. With not a glimmer of hope left in her shattered existence, Essie broke down again. Her wrenching sobs almost prevented her from hearing the voice of her beloved and the squeaky sound of the prison door opening. Through red, swollen eyes, Essie saw Aquila enter with two men carrying a long object wrapped in a burlap tarp. Aquila held a leather satchel.

Startled, Essie wondered if she was imagining the scene. She cleared her throat. "Aquila, are . . . are you really here? What is happening?"

"It is I, my love. We haven't any time to talk. Do as I say and be quiet."

Essie watched as the two men set the tarp on the floor and Aquila extracted a dress from the satchel. "These men will turn their backs. Put this dress on and leave your clothes on the floor. You must hurry!"

Not understanding why but having faith in Aquila, Essie did as she was told. Aquila took her hand after she dressed and said, "Quickly, a carriage outside is waiting to take you to Cromwell. I'll explain shortly."

Essie looked back and glimpsed the two men unfurling the tarp. She could make out the body of a woman, close to her age and size, now deceased. A black hood covered the head. "Who is that?" she asked her husband.

With a finger on his lips, he begged her to stay quiet. When they hit the street, Essie shielded her eyes from the bright sunshine. With her arm over her face, Aquila whisked her into the carriage, climbed in behind her, and ordered the coachman to proceed with haste. Once they were on their way, Aquila enfolded Essie in a long embrace. His muscular arms around her were like a caterpillar being enveloped in a protective cocoon.

"What just happened?" Essie asked through a throaty voice that sounded nothing like herself. "Who was that woman?"

Aquila stared into her eyes. He spoke slowly. "I failed in my attempt to get you released. An alternative plan was needed. Laurens was determined to hang you."

He took her hand and squeezed gently. "This won't be easy to hear."

Essie nodded. She couldn't imagine what Aquila had done to rescue her. She listened intently.

"As a condemned woman, they could hang you without the public seeing your face. All that would be visible is your body and a black hood. I entered this request on your behalf."

"I understand. So you swapped me for a dead woman who was approximately my size and build? Laurens is unaware that he is hanging a woman who had already been executed. Ingenious. But where did you get the body?"

"That's the hard part." Aquila paused, trying to find the right words to break the difficult news. "The British caught Hazel and hanged her in the town square.

We recovered her body after the British retreated from Philadelphia. I handed the guards one pound of silver each for their cooperation."

And with that news, Essie let out a shriek and sobbed like she hadn't sobbed in years. "They killed Hazel?" Then she shuddered with realization. "It's my fault. I asked Hazel to fulfill the mission. I killed my best friend." Suddenly, surprised by her errant thought, Essie asked, "How will a dead woman walk to the gallows?"

Aquila placed his hand on her leg and squeezed gently. "The guards will drag the body, pretending that the prisoner passed out."

She nestled close to her husband and cried until her stomach, wrenched in a knot, made her sit up and look him in the eye. Aquila offered her his foulard, remaining silent. He held her. He let her cry it all out. They rode in silence for close to an hour.

"It's all my fault. How will I ever find peace?"

"You mustn't blame yourself. Hazel understood the risks. She was a brave soul in the Agents of Liberty. Her service was fruitful and helped stop the spread of smallpox through the colonies. She was a genuine hero, and I will make sure she is remembered thusly."

Essie couldn't respond. She leaned her head against Aquila's broad chest and struggled to collect her emotions. Then, her thoughts transformed into a state of panic. "Laurens will believe that I am dead. How can I live and work as normal?"

"For a spell, you will need to hide. Charles owns a cabin in the eastern part of Virginia. It's a small town called Mecklenburg, and it resides along the Potowmack River. Penny will accompany you, as will Clement. You will have everything you need, and I will visit as often as I can."

"But for how long?"

"I am unsure. I know this isn't desirable, but you must keep in mind: You are alive, and the future is ours. Once the war concludes, we can make Congress aware of your escape and petition for clemency."

Essie shivered. "It all seems so horrific, a lonely existence on the outskirts awaiting the taste of true freedom. Perhaps I should change my appearance and become your 'third' wife."

Aquila caressed her shoulders. It eased her burden. Then he said, "I'm sure you suggest this in jest. There are no straightforward solutions. Tonight, you shall rest comfortably in your own bed. Tomorrow, you shall journey to the cabin."

"Are you not accompanying me to Mecklenburg?"

"Yes, but then I must return to the war."

CHAPTER 56

New York, New York

André sat in a pub favored by British officers and loyalists. He threw back his second shot of whiskey and stood to leave, wanting to avail himself of the nearest privy. While relieving himself, a man came from behind, making himself nearly invisible. He tucked a small scroll inside André's pocket, stating in an unfamiliar, gravelly American voice, "For your reading pleasure, Major. In private, of course."

The man left before André could turn around. He was like a shadow, here then gone in an instant. André inserted his right hand into the pocket of his bright red uniform and felt the scroll, not daring to remove it until it was safe. Attempting to look casual, André strolled lazily out the pub door and meandered down a cobblestone street, seeking a remote hamlet in which to read the correspondence. Finally, seeing nowhere else, André veered into the Church of England four blocks south. Given the time of day in the middle of the week, the church was empty. He entered and took a seat on the back pew. After another glance to confirm his solitude, the scroll was unfurled and read:

To Major John André:

You are cordially invited to meet with General Benedict Arnold at 7:00 p.m. on 21 September at the home of Joshua Hett Smith along the Hudson River one mile south of West Point.

André smiled and silently thanked Peggy for getting word to Arnold. Things were in motion, and soon, he was sure, he would hold the proof that General Clinton required to accept Arnold. This would be the event people would talk about for generations to come. The instant when the entire momentum of the war would change. The moment when John André was hailed as the conquering hero of Britain's illustrious victory over the upstart rebels.

CHAPTER 57

Mecklenburg, Virginia

With Penny in tow, Essie nestled in. Charles Greene's "cabin" was anything but the envisioned tiny, wooded outlet buried deep in a forest. In fact, the house proved quite large. It was made of stone, not wood, so in Essie's mind, the cabin moniker seemed a misnomer. The blue, gray, and white river stones provided the house with a charm accented by the forested surroundings and the fresh smell of the Potowmack River flowing nearby. It reminded Essie of her first trip to Cromwell right after arriving in Annapolis. She traveled with Aquila and Penny, and as they got closer to Cromwell's Passage, the Bush River was their temporary companion, and that, in and of itself, reminded her of rural England she once called home.

The house styling resembled Europe—more German, Essie thought, than British. As Aquila had explained on the journey south, Charles had purchased the home from the descendants of the von Friedburg family. People said Johann von Friedburg came to eastern Virginia in the early 1730s and made his fortune in mining. After he passed, his widow succumbed to illness, and his two daughters, by then married with children and homes of their own, could not pay the taxes or afford the upkeep. So Aquila had explained that Charles tells friends he got a bargain. The home had a large, picturesque fireplace, a separate kitchen building, and a formal parlor for entertainment. The rear of the home sat on a bluff overlooking the peaceful flow of the Potowmack. Essie wondered how a home this grand could sit idle. Celia had never mentioned this place, and Essie wondered if she had been here or if she were even aware of its existence. Men like Charles, despite being kindhearted, kept things to themselves. In their minds, women, even their devoted wives, were not worthy of knowledge concerning the family's finances. Essie's first husband, Thomas, in his chivalrous manner, shielded her from the burden of their debts for his medical practice. Had she been aware all along, she might have helped him plan his way through. Instead, she wound up in the London Debtor's Prison, suffering in the aftermath of her ignorance. Shouldn't a loving husband wish to have his wife cared for properly if he were to pass? Essie often thought Thomas would have been mortified if he had known what happened to her after his death. Shaking the terrible memories from her mind, she sidled up to Penny at the dining table. From behind, Essie heard the unmistakable yap of a puppy. Clement entered the room holding a saucer of tiny bite-sized beef cutlets. Before Essie could say a word, the cream-colored puppy was next to her, licking her ankle and then moving toward Clement, who lowered the bowl to the floor and allowed the dog to eat.

"I found her along the river. She seemed scared and alone, so I brought her home," Penny said.

Essie kneeled and gently caressed the soft fluff on the back of the dog's neck. To the puppy's delight, Essie scratched behind its floppy ears. "There isn't another home around here for miles. I wonder where she could have come from?" Essie hadn't had a dog since she was a girl. She and the terrier had been inseparable. It seemed like another lifetime. Essie sighed. "I suppose we can hold on to her until we find out where she belongs."

Penny's smile stretched from ear to ear.

Essie silently admired that old Clement, who never showed a trace of emotion, had burst into something that must have resembled a pleasant childhood memory.

"What shall we call her?" asked Essie.

"Fanny, I think," stated Penny.

Essie chuckled while still petting the puppy, who had just finished her saucer of cutlets. "And why Fanny?" she asked.

Penny, a voracious reader of fiction, replied, "Fanny Goodwill was a favorite character of mine from a Fielding novel. She was innocent and pure as the driven snow. Like this little one." Penny picked up Fanny, who promptly began licking her face. "What breed do you suppose she is?"

Essie patted the puppy's head and contemplated the wavy, cream-colored fur and the spotted nose with the bent corner ears. The enchanting eyes captivated her. "A spaniel of some sort, although I don't think she's purebred."

Penny cradled the puppy to her face, delighting in the affection. "I love you, Fanny," she said.

Essie sat down at the table. Clement had brought out a bowl of rolled oats and some fresh berries and tea. Essie nibbled and contemplated the sudden presence of the dog. Fear overtook her. The small appetite she had before vanished in an instant. *To the outside world, I am dead. I wait here. Hiding. Another cannot see me outside this house.* The puppy meant people were likely nearby. They would come looking. Had she made a grievous error in allowing Penny to act as the animal's temporary custodian? She, Penny, and Clement had agreed to stay in the house. If they remained in isolation, no one could raise questions in town. But what, pray tell, would she do if someone meandered up the front path looking for a lost puppy? Clement! She would have him answer the door and profess to being Charles Greene's caretaker for the riverbank home. Essie and Penny would remain out of sight. Clement could even go into town and seek food and other necessities without fear of being questioned.

Essie relaxed and contemplated the day ahead. It had been forever since she had made a quilt. With nothing but time on her hands, that was the plan for the day. As was her custom, she enjoyed crafting elaborate scenes of beautiful landscapes, and the Potowmack River was a natural source of inspiration. The great room in this stone marvel overlooked the river. The morning sun shone brightly through the window. It glistened on the babbling waters, which splashed off rocks and pitched against the muddy riverbank. Essie wondered how long she could remain here, idle in terms of meaningful activity. Once upon a time, back in Wickhamshire, a day of quilting was a treasured luxury. But she had come so far since then. She missed the hustle and bustle of the hospital and planning for the army's medical needs in the field. She even missed assisting her husband's Agents of Liberty.

With that notion, her thoughts turned to Hazel. Essie's self-indulgence in her dual role as an Agent of Liberty and director general for the Medical

Department of the Continental army compelled her to employ Hazel to spy on General Willard. Hazel had done so reluctantly. Her demise was Essie's doing. Her stomach knotted at the thought. Had she erred in her judgment? Was Aquila correct when he said Hazel understood and accepted the risk of her assignment? Was her husband trying to placate her, knowing full well how emotion might overwhelm her ability to process logic? Nevertheless, Essie felt the pain of losing her best friend. They had endured so much together. Hazel was the sister she never had. In retrospect, Essie reassured herself that her plan to have Hazel spy on Willard was the correct tactical decision. But as long as she drew breath, she would never forgive herself.

Much like her decision to write to Prime Minister North, the choice she made with Hazel proved nothing short of disastrous. It had all led to this moment. To her exile. Essie supposed she was where she deserved to be. Cast aside in the wooded reserve of an isolated part of Virginia, perhaps never to be heard from again, waiting for an ambiguous reprieve from the same government that sentenced her to death.

Is this house, lovely as it is, to be my last hurrah? The place where my life concludes? Or may God grant me the strength and resolve to emerge from the ruins of my life somehow once more to aid my family and the country I thought I loved?

Essie stared out the window, watching the rolling waters of the Potowmack. Instinctively, her hands began quilting while her mind continued to turn.

CHAPTER 58

West Haverstraw, New York

John André dismounted and tied his horse to the hitching post. He straightened his red military coat and brushed the journey's dust off his white pants. His black boots were unsightly, but there was nothing to be done about it; he was already late for the meeting. Smoke curled from the chimney into the early evening sky, resplendent in its gray and orange hues. André inhaled the cool air before approaching the front door and knocking. This was the moment. *His moment.* The meeting that would fulfill his every dream of personal success while helping to end the war in Britain's favor. Placing his left hand across his abdomen, he rapped with his right. A man with gentle features greeted him.

"Major André, I am Joshua Hett Smith, the proprietor. We are expecting you. General Arnold is waiting in the parlor. Please follow me."

André delivered his most humble smile and trailed Smith through the narrow hallway. Smith's long, powdered wig draped down his shoulders, and André couldn't help but wonder if Smith, not much older than he, was bald. With each step through the house, the floorboards creaked. The walls bore a distinct odor, as if they had just been whitewashed. When they arrived at the parlor, Benedict Arnold approached and extended his hand. His embrace was firm. Important, thought André. His father had always taught him never to trust a man with a limp handshake.

"Would you like some tea?" offered Smith.

André politely declined. Smith left him and Arnold to speak in private. The two men sat by the crackling fire in overstuffed, high-back chairs.

Arnold lit a pipe and turned his head, blowing the initial burst of smoke away from André. André appreciated this. He never embraced the habit. He preferred drinking to tobacco, and beautiful women above all else.

"Has General Clinton agreed to my terms?" inquired Arnold.

To answer in a way that conveyed the upper hand, André said, "Not completely. Our agreement hinges on the depth and breadth of intelligence you provide."

Arnold smirked. André thought him a man who possessed an air of conceit. He had encountered many of this type before. Feeding their egos usually got him where he needed to go.

Arnold reached for the documents on a nearby table. One was a sheaf of parchment, and the other a long, rolled-up paper secured by a small blue ribbon. "I believe these will satisfy your 'depth and breadth' requirements."

André read the parchment first. His eyes darted across the first page until he comprehended the magnitude of what he held in his hand. Attempting to keep his voice even, he said, "These are minutes from Washington's war council meeting."

"Precisely," Arnold stated proudly. "And there is more where that came from."

After taking the ribbon from the rolled paper, André grasped its contents. "And these drawings . . . the builder's plans for West Point. Remarkable."

"With these plans and the war council minutes, your army will have no difficulty securing West Point." He paused and then added, "Especially when I order the gates to be opened and unguarded."

"So that's your definitive plan?" André inquired.

"Yes. On a day to be agreed upon, I shall do exactly as I have stated. Your navy will provide me with a rendezvous point along the Hudson where I can board. Once I am safely away, I will deliver the remaining war council minutes in exchange for my commission as a general in the British army and twenty thousand pounds. Is this agreeable?"

André had always been proud of his ability to negotiate. But in this case, Arnold had handed him everything he could have wanted on a silver platter. "Agreed," he said while extending his hand. Then, out of pure curiosity, perhaps driven by his affections, he asked, "What of your fiancée?"

"Peggy and I will marry next week. Once we win the war, she will join me in London."

"I see," was all André could muster. His errant thought of Peggy Shippen marrying him and not Arnold shriveled like a prune in the noonday sun.

"The handover of West Point will occur in ten days' time," said Arnold. He puffed his pipe for a moment and then continued. "I know for a fact that patriot soldiers and militia roam these parts in great numbers. That red coat would doom you to capture. You will need to travel to your nearest ship incognito. Mr. Smith has clothes for you befitting a man of this area. You shall carry this to ensure your safe passage."

Taking the paper from Arnold, André read:

This man, John Anderson, is an authorized courier for the United States of America and may pass freely by order of General Benedict Arnold.

Below the note were Arnold's signature and his seal. "Thank you," André replied. "I have experience as a thespian. I shall endeavor to fulfill my role as John Anderson, patriot courier."

CHAPTER 59

Mecklenburg, Virginia

Perhaps it was paranoia. Or the icy cold shivers of fear that invaded Essie's woodland peace. Even with chamomile tea in hand, amid the sanctuary of Charles Greene's isolated hideaway in the wee hours of the morning, she couldn't fight the nagging feeling she was being watched. *Should I share my suspicions with Penny? Or Clement?* No, she concluded. Why worry them with a concern that had no obvious bearing?

She had been in Mecklenburg only a short time. It felt like an eternity. Other than walks around the grounds and an occasional trek to the river, Essie had barely left the house. But now, the walls of this scenic home were closing in. The overstuffed chair she had favored since her arrival now enveloped her, as if she were held in a vise. Nowhere in the spacious home offered freedom. Essie's chest heaved. She coughed. It was a dry, heavy expectoration. The sort that brought no relief when one suffered the ills of a chest cold. She tried to control her breathing. *Slow everything down,* she told herself. Let your brain rule your body. Essie reminded herself that the world thought her dead. Back home, people believed they had hanged her for treason. No one would give the slightest thought to the possibility of her still being alive. Penny was presumably visiting relatives with Clement as chaperone. Cromwell remained blissfully ignorant.

Her breathing settled into a soothing rhythm. Essie sipped, inhaled the earthy aroma of the tea, and closed her eyes. *Control your breathing,* she urged herself. *In. Out. In. Out.*

Essie's eyes remained closed. A cool, gentle breeze entered from a nearby window. The light perspiration across the bridge of her nose abated. Her heartbeat returned to its normal state, and she slowly opened her eyes. When she did, Hazel, her best friend, appeared before her. Was it an apparition? Essie still believed the woman she had sent into danger was haunting her. There was no means to reconcile the guilt. Rationalizing what she had done to Hazel was an impossible endeavor. Essie would have to live with Hazel's death and the disrespectful manner in which they used her body. *But how could she?* Hazel! Sweet Hazel, who always said what she thought and had a heart big enough to run through brick walls for those she loved. Essie told herself that Hazel had acted in service to her country. But the deep-hardened truth slapped Essie across the face with an open hand. She was to blame. Essie found no other worthy explanation. She closed her eyes once more and returned to her earlier salve. *Control your breathing,* she urged herself. *In. Out. In. Out.*

Essie thought to rise and walk down to the river where the sound of the water rushing over the polished rocks would calm her. She would take Aquila's recent letter received via an Agents of Liberty drop. Reading it brought solace amid the longing for his touch. Essie rose from the large blue velvet chair. Teacup in hand, she ambled to the kitchen to prepare her basket. But before she made it to her destination, an icy dagger of fear tore through her chest, and she let out a bloodcurdling scream.

A stranger with a peculiar owlish face stood immobile by the window.

Essie blanched. Not knowing what else to do, she dropped, making herself level with the floor. The intruder might have a gun. During her time in America, Essie had developed a keen sense of expected danger. There might be others. She dared not scream again. Perhaps they surrounded the house. Essie didn't wish to alarm Penny or Clement. But what if, at that moment, the scoundrel outside the window shot one of them as they walked downstairs? If that happened, she would never forgive herself. Essie slithered like a snake to the parlor, inching her way to a long, narrow table and its accompanying drawer. There she had hidden one of several pistols Aquila insisted she keep around for safety reasons. Staying low, she reached up and, feeling around with her right hand, found the weapon. She strained to lift it and seized the handle. She raised herself into a low crouch and proceeded to the front door.

Opening it cautiously for fear of making a ruckus, Essie went outside, standing and looking left and right. The man was nowhere to be found. Essie relaxed. Perhaps he had been just a wayward beggar, a vagabond seeking food, and she had scared him away. *No*. She thought the clothing he wore was not that of a drifter. Pistol raised, her hand trembling, Essie walked the expanse of the house's perimeter. She found no trace of the stranger. Her instincts told her the immediate danger had passed, to return to the house, lock the door, and alert Penny and Clement. But something made her keep going. She entered the woods and followed the path leading to the river, keeping the pistol at the ready. Then she heard the shuffling of leaves behind her. It could be the intruder, or maybe a coyote or bear. Essie became rigid. A stiff wind kicked up the dark orange and brown leaves from the forest floor and whipped them toward her face.

Turning her body to evade the sudden onslaught of wind, she saw him. The owlish man with the round spectacles. He was short and stocky in build. His clothes represented a man who had a trade, a respected man of the community. He did not appear to be a threatening sort. She reverted to her prior thinking that this was a man who had fallen on hard times and needed a helping hand. After all, very few people knew she was alive or, for that matter, where she was. She lowered the pistol and stepped toward the man, intending to offer hospitality and a hot meal. She would introduce herself with a different name and urge Penny and Clement to play along. The thought of turning away someone in need was too much to bear. After all, how many times had she needed a random act of kindness from a stranger? Resolved in her approach, Essie glanced at the morning sky. Dark clouds appeared, and the wind brought a gathering storm ever so close.

Essie took a step toward the stranger, ready to offer her services, when he said, "That's far enough, Mrs. Wright. Drop the gun."

Shocked and stymied by her foolish thinking, Essie saw the man brandishing his own pistol. In that moment, she recalled the words of Isaiah Trumbull as he handed her a pistol during the Battle of Cromwell: *Shoot first, ask questions later.* Without further deliberation, Essie raised her pistol, aiming for the man's chest. Her trembling hand betrayed her, and a bullet sailed low, striking the man in the right knee.

He screamed, dropped his gun, and fell to the ground, writhing in pain as he placed his hands over his bloody limb.

Essie stood shaking in the icy wind.

Fanny barreled down from the house, barking protectively. Penny followed and grasped what had happened. She grabbed the gun and ran to Essie, embracing her before asking, "Who is this man?"

Through a throaty voice she did not recognize, Essie replied, "I don't know. I assumed he was a vagabond in need of food and shelter." Then, hesitating and fighting the lump in her throat, she added, "And he knows who I am."

Essie watched as her stepdaughter, transcending the end of her teenage years into a strong young woman, returned to the owlish man squirming on the ground. Penny held the man's own pistol to his head, and in a cold, hard voice Essie did not recognize, she asked, "Who are you? What is your business here?"

The man blanched, still reeling from his sudden reversal of fortune. He said, "I am Louis Pembery, an agent of His Majesty's government."

Essie gasped. "Pembery? You were Washington's aide-de-camp. And now you come here as a spy? To what end?"

"George Washington is a trusting man. He never knew my family name, Wilkinson. We are loyalists. I assumed the name Louis Pembery to aid King George."

"You are a charlatan, to say the least," Essie replied. "Why come here?"

"I deserted my post in the Continental army. Staying near the perimeter of General Washington's camp, I overheard him say that your death was improvised and you took refuge here. I thought capturing the woman who was bold enough to write to Prime Minister North might restore my name to good standing."

To Essie's surprise, Penny was the first to reply. "Well, think again," she said coldly. And before Essie could stop her, Penny pulled the trigger, sending a bullet through the brain of Louis Pembery.

CHAPTER 60

Haverstraw, New York

With the documents tucked in the bottom of his boot, John André made his way on foot through the woods near Haverstraw Bay. There, he would reboard the *Vulture,* the ship that had ferried him north along the Hudson for the meeting with Arnold. Somehow, André considered, he felt lucky. Circumstances always seemed to favor him. With the war council minutes and West Point plans in his possession, and the takeover of the fort all but assured, André allowed himself to fantasize about his upcoming promotion. Maybe one day, he thought, the prime minister's office in Whitehall would be his. John André, an advisor to the king of England, and the architect of his country's future. In his mind's eye, he envisioned it all as he pitched forward toward the bay.

Disrupting his placid consideration of the future were the abrupt, thundering sounds of cannon fire. He was close enough to the water to see the smoke and inhale its unwanted presence. Close to his rendezvous point, André watched in horror as the nearby American fort bombarded the *Vulture.* André stood listlessly as the ship that was to return him to New York City began its retreat southward on the Hudson. There was no way to signal the ship safely. The captain would not have reversed course. No one man stood above the collective needs of the military. André understood this. He leaned against a towering northern red oak tree, collected his thoughts, and considered his options. There was only one. He must make his way to West Point as John Anderson, patriot courier, and meet with Arnold. There, they could pivot, enabling André to plan his return to the command post in New York City. If luck favored him, he could walk the fifteen miles in six hours.

Stopping to rest, André emptied his bladder. Two hours into an unexpected sojourn, his stomach was crying for food. He hadn't eaten all day and was famished. He tried to be as quiet as he could, using his arm to wave overgrowth away from a mulberry bush. The season waned. The berries that remained had spoiled. André didn't care. Any nourishment would be better than none. He didn't wish to take the time to hunt and cook. So he plucked what he could from the wilting bush and ate.

"You there in the bush. Toss out your weapon and come out with your hands up."

André offered his pistol and a knife he had tucked in his boot. He raised his hands and reminded himself to speak without a trace of his British accent. He was John Anderson, patriot courier. Delivering his most engaging smile, he said, "Gentlemen, good afternoon. I was just looking for something to eat."

Three men looked down from their horses. The lead man said, "You are American. What are you doing in these woods? It is not safe. Redcoats and their spies are roaming about."

Trying to remain at ease, André calmy replied, "I wouldn't want to run into the likes of them."

"Who are you?" asked the lead man—still a little too aggressively, thought André.

"My name is John Anderson. I am on a diplomatic courier mission for General Benedict Arnold. I have a pass signed by the general himself."

He took from his inner breast pocket the document that would now serve as his lifeline. He handed it to the lead man and waited while he read it.

"And how do we know this is General Arnold's actual signature?" The lead man showed it to one of his compatriots, who replied, "Looks fake to me."

André pondered the simplistic minds of these American militiamen. Actually, it surprised him they could read. "Do you not see the general's seal?"

"Also looks fake," the lead man said. Then, glancing over to the third man, he said, "Dismount and search him. He may have other weapons."

André delivered his most disarming smile. "I assure you, gentlemen, that I have already relieved myself of the only weapons I possessed."

The third militiaman got to his feet and patted down André before anyone else could speak. "He's okay," the man said to his leader.

The leader glowered in a distrustful manner. "There's something about him I just don't trust. Take off your boots. Let's make sure you ain't hiding anything in there."

The documents lay flat at the bottom of his right boot. André contemplated how he might remove the boot, show off his stockinged foot, and not have the man on the ground look inside. It was a long shot. He sat down on a nearby stump and pulled off his boots. Rolling back, he hoisted his stockinged feet in the air to demonstrate the silliness of the exercise, hoping that would end the intrusion.

"Take a look inside," the lead man commanded.

André watched the man as he looked inside the left boot, finding nothing. Then, his heart sank as he did the same with the right. "What have we got here?" The militiaman turned the boot over, and the folded documents tumbled onto the forest floor. The lead man aimed his rifle at André's chest.

André needed to remain calm. He had no weapon and could not take on three men by force.

Reading the documents, the militiaman's eyes went wide. He looked up to his mounted leader and stated, "This man is a British spy. We need to take him to General Wright."

CHAPTER 61

West Point, New York

Benedict Arnold has fled, Your Excellency," Aquila proclaimed in a state of disbelief.

George Washington shook his head. "Secure the fort. Be sure there are no more traitors among us."

Aquila felt for his commander in chief. The war had made everyone tougher, not by choice but through the trials and tribulations of ambition, greed, and fear. None of them would ever be the same, Aquila thought. War had a way of changing one's perspective. The dark remnants of death and destruction stuck to a man's mind like molasses. Some men, Aquila knew, never broke free from the demons.

"General Wright," said a young intelligence officer he had been training. "I have an urgent dispatch from Colonel Greene in Virginia. They sent it through our New York dead drop."

Aquila knew the spot. A Liberty Tree near where he had saved a young boy from a burning hotel. The trunk of the massive poplar had a secret, hollowed spot on the storefront side. A master carpenter concealed it. It was all but invisible, like the words on the parchment he held in his hand. In his fine penmanship, Charles had written a letter to a friend speaking of mundane topics that wouldn't arouse anyone's suspicion. But Charles made sure the courier knew to convey urgency. Once the fort was secure, he would sit in private and apply the acidic liquid that would reveal Charles's true message.

Aquila scrambled around the fort, finding the other members of Washington's inner circle. He huddled with Lafayette and Hamilton, the aide-de-camp.

"Do we have any idea where Arnold may have fled?" asked Aquila.

Hamilton shook his head. "No, but personally, I can't wait to apprehend the traitorous leech and hang him for all to see."

The young Frenchman snickered. "In my country, they publicly torture traitors of this magnitude before death."

"Somewhat barbaric, don't you think?" asked Aquila.

"Perhaps," replied Lafayette. "But the slim hope of survival yields revelations, confessions, accomplices, and other plans not yet implemented."

"I'll settle for catching the miscreant and watching him hang," Hamilton declared.

"General Washington has ordered that all exits be sealed and each man stationed at this fort be interviewed. The two of you shall conduct the investigation, and we shall meet this evening to discuss your findings," said Aquila.

The young soldier who had delivered the dispatch from Charles Greene interrupted. "General Wright, there is a commotion at the main gate. Three militiamen have arrived with a prisoner. Shall we let them enter?"

Looking at Lafayette and Hamilton, he said, "I'll handle this. The two of you have your orders." Then to the young soldier, "Come with me."

At the gate, Aquila saw the four men—three armed militia on horseback in soiled, ragged outfits and a man on foot with a rope encircling his waist and his hands bound behind his back. Upon seeing Aquila, the lead man proclaimed, "General Wright, sir. I am Horatio Parker. We are Agents of Liberty. We apprehended this British spy in the woods near Haverstraw Bay."

"You may enter. Bring him to the guardhouse. My aide will show you the way. I will be there forthwith."

Aquila walked through the camp, inspecting each aspect of the operation to secure the fort. Guards armed themselves at each entrance, and Lafayette and Hamilton questioned soldiers. His next move was to converse with the three Agents of Liberty and inspect the documents they presented upon arriving at West Point.

Horatio Parker had a mop of black curly hair and a beard grown mid-chest. He was a man whose gnarled cheeks told the story of a hard life. The dark eyes bore commitment to his cause, and for this, Aquila was grateful. Men like Parker were the unsung heroes of the war. Without their dedication, strategic advances would be far more difficult.

"When you discovered the fort's plans and war council minutes, did the spy say anything that might reveal accomplices or his true identity?"

"Nah," replied Parker in a gruff tone. "He handed us this," he said as he produced the pass from Benedict Arnold.

Aquila studied it. The name John Anderson was fake, but the document possessed what Aquila believed to be Arnold's legitimate seal. "Thank you, Mr. Parker. You and your men have done America a great service."

Aquila turned and proceeded to the guardhouse. Upon arrival, he ordered the armed guards to stand outside the door so he might interrogate the prisoner in private. Initially, this man looked like any merchant or tradesman in the area. His jacket was a light buckskin, and his black trousers and muddy boots gave him proper cover. He was otherwise well-groomed and clean-shaven with his hair affixed in a ponytail just over the neckline of his white collarless shirt.

"Who are you?" demanded Aquila, glaring downward at the bound prisoner resting on the floor, his back propped against the wooden boards of the far wall.

The prisoner stood. "I'd offer my hand," he said, referring to the bound state of his hands. "Forgive my inability to be polite. If you would be so kind . . ."

With his small blade, Aquila obliged, and the two men sat opposite each other at the long oak table in the center of the room.

"Thank you," the prisoner said. "I am Major John André of His Majesty's Royal Army."

Aquila's right eyebrow rose in disbelief. "André? You are the British spymaster."

André grinned. "Yes, although that is not my official title. I am responsible for intelligence in the British colonies."

"I presume you aided the traitor Benedict Arnold?" Aquila inquired.

"We were working together. I will tell you everything. I am experienced enough to understand the peril of my situation. In exchange for answers to your questions, I ask only to be executed by a firing squad, as is befitting an officer."

"First, tell me. Where is Benedict Arnold?" Aquila demanded.

André hesitated and then spoke slowly. "I suspect by now he is safely aboard the HMS *Vulture*, sailing south on the Hudson. Now, about my request for an honorable death . . ."

"I shall confer with General Washington. The decision will be his. You will remain here in the meantime. I will have porridge brought in."

And with that, Aquila left to find Washington. He found the commander in chief, Lafayette, and Hamilton in Arnold's former command office, reviewing the details of everything they had discovered. After Aquila stated what he had learned from André and conveyed the request of death by firing squad, he saw a cold side of George Washington he had yet to witness.

"Debrief him without agreeing to his demand. Then hang him."

"It shall be done, Your Excellency," Aquila replied.

That evening, they hanged John André. By sunset, he was dangling in the wind. With André's last breath, Aquila hoped, went the remainder of the British intelligence effort.

The huge orange sun set slowly on the horizon, melting into the treetops. Aquila was exhausted. The act of treason uncovered at West Point was one of the most egregious events of this never-ending war. Tired, hungry, and battle-worn, Aquila retired for the evening with a half loaf of bread, a pitcher of ale, and the urgent dispatch from Charles Greene. He took a bite of the loaf, chewed, and drank the ale. Then, he brushed the clear acidic solution between the lines of Charles's pleasantness and revealed the true message.

Aquila,

Penny shot and killed Washington's former aide-de-camp, Louis Pembery, on the grounds of my cabin in Mecklenburg. Essie, Penny, and Clement are unharmed. I don't believe Pembery was working with anyone. As a measure of extreme caution, I have arranged for the three of them to be moved. Penny and Clement can return to Cromwell's Passage, while Essie will live in the home of my second-in-command in Richmond.

Aquila bristled at the thought of his wife and daughter in such grave danger. How had Pembery discovered Essie was alive? Or, for that matter, her location?

And the bravery of Penny, to confront and kill the man threatening their safety. Oh, how he longed to wrap his arms around them both.

Aquila exhaled, rose, and went to seek an audience with George Washington. With the commander in chief's permission, Aquila would take leave and return home to Cromwell.

CHAPTER 62

Richmond, Virginia

How does one emerge from death? This was the central thought in Essie's mind as she acclimated to her new hideaway. The home of Captain and Mrs. Robert Barlow was a quaint two-story home. It reminded Essie of the cottage she had once shared with her first husband in Wickhamshire, not in the manner of its design but in the modestly appointed abode shared by a childless couple without relatives in the vicinity. Essie had yet to meet the man of the house. He was at war. But Essie was told her presence in Captain Barlow's home was arranged with the proprietor by Charles Greene. The experience in Mecklenburg left her rattled. Her current plight was frightful, albeit in a different sort of way than prior tribulations. Being taken to debtor's prison in London was harrowing. Her exile from Cromwell after Penny's run-in with a black bear and twice being sentenced to be hanged all felt different from her current plight. In the prior debacles, there seemed to be only one escape: death. In hanging or melancholy, death seemed like the only way to bring an end to the suffering. Trapped in the filth and deprivation of the London Debtor's Prison, Essie recalled praying for death as a release from her living hell. Now, within the confines of the Barlows' modest home, she was already deemed expired. Essie worried she was to live out her remaining days on the run as a nameless, faceless person who had forfeited her home, her family, and her purpose. There was no escape. There was no one to break her free from the shackles of her predicament. Sweat ran down to the small of her back as she brushed a finger across the smooth, freshly painted platform of the bay window in which she sat. Atop a plush velvet cushion, Essie sat stymied, crippled by her dilemma. How, she wondered again, does one escape faking one's own death?

The Barlows had no servants. The house was quiet and rested in the burgeoning city of Richmond, Virginia's new capital and a key to the fruitful south. Essie had lived in isolation in Mecklenburg. In Richmond, she was hiding in plain sight. Essie's stomach knotted at the thought of going outside, meeting people, and becoming part of the Richmond community. She shook off a sudden chill. Essie wrapped her arms around her knees and lowered her head. A tear rolled down her cheek. In Mecklenburg, she had Penny, and even Clement, to comfort her and offer a sense of normalcy. Here in Richmond, she knew not a soul. She was like a ghost floating in and out of varying scenes that haunted her ability to possess the strongest of human needs . . . hope.

CHAPTER 63

New York, New York

General Clinton wore a scowl. His lower back screamed, and the knife in his leg reminded him of the sciatica accompanying the onset of his twilight years. Clinton, having been educated on Long Island as a youth combined with his time during the war, had simply had his fill of New York. He yearned for his aristocratic, comfortable life in London and a return to his service in Parliament, despite his nostalgic affection. Sipping his tea from a porcelain cup he deemed inferior to the fine service maintained in a proper British home, Henry Clinton was bound and determined to bring the war to a swift conclusion. As the commander in chief, he now had that power. There would be no pussyfooting. Swift, decisive action was the medicine to be prescribed.

A servant brought his breakfast: a poached egg, bacon, and two slices of toast with apple butter. Clinton had a sweet tooth and enjoyed the scent of the topping. He licked his lips in anticipation of the first bite. As he closed his eyes to savor the taste, his momentary bliss was ruined by Charles Cornwallis, the general he believed was the key to ending the war and sending all loyal Britons home victorious.

Clinton dabbed the corner of his mouth with the white linen that had lain against his chest and rose to greet his subordinate.

Cornwallis saluted. Clinton instructed the younger man to stand at ease. Then he offered a smile and embraced Cornwallis, who had just returned from an unscheduled trip to England.

"I'm glad you have returned, Charles. I am so deeply sorry for the loss of your wife. Hopefully, she died peacefully," said Clinton.

"Thank you, Sir. Jemma withstood a long illness and died two months after I returned to Culford. Her last days were . . ."—Cornwallis hesitated, and Clinton thought he might break down—"painstakingly difficult for us both. Beyond her illness, I believe my time away left her downtrodden, overwrought with grief."

Clinton felt for the man. Cornwallis always proclaimed his deep love of family. He could think of nothing else to say except, "At last, she is at peace in her final resting place."

Cornwallis shrugged. "I hope you are right. Jemma asked to be buried with a thorn tree over her heart. I reluctantly honored her last wish."

Clinton watched as Cornwallis's eyes lowered. This man was broken. But, as Clinton had witnessed many times over the course of his illustrious military career, a return to battle, despite its overtones of blood and death, restored a man's resolve for living. Clinton concluded he must engage Cornwallis in the war's planning.

"Down to business, then. We have moderate positions of strength in New York and points north. To end the conflict, we must envelop the south. We have more men, more armament, the world's best naval force, and far more experience in military maneuvers. There is no reason we should not recapture the entirety of the British colonies and end the conflict within the year."

"Yes, sir. I concur in your assessment. We must be bold and strike where the enemy is weakest. What are my orders?" Cornwallis asked.

"Capturing the south is the key to ending the war. You will lead the southern forces. Report to Charleston. Work your way back north through Virginia. Make us proud," Clinton stated in a manner designed to lift the ruptured spirits of a proven field leader.

"For king and country," Cornwallis declared. "I shall leave today."

Clinton sat down at the well-appointed dining table and growled for the servant. "My breakfast has turned cold. Take this away. Bring me another. Now!"

CHAPTER 64

Cromwell, Maryland

Aquila had never ridden a horse at such a furious pace. With nary a rest for him or his horse, Aquila returned from New York in record time. His sprawling family estate seemed worn, like himself. Weary of war and the fight for freedom, Aquila dismounted. The smell of burning firewood brought calmness to his troubled mind. He watched the chimney's smoke swirl into the night sky as he ascended the stairs to the front door. His stomach rattled with the wind as it whistled by his ears, muffling the sounds of the early evening. Aquila barely heard the door opening before he reached the top.

"Father!" Penny cried in delight. Throwing herself at him and holding on tight, she proclaimed, "I've missed you so."

Aquila said nothing. Standing in the doorway, he held his daughter and cherished her presence, her safety, and her love. He took solace in the simple act of human touch. When they finally separated, Aquila smiled at his beautiful daughter, whose brown hair cascaded down her back. He gently kissed her on the forehead.

War paid no heed to the needs of people. It had a mind of its own. For Aquila, it had aged him rapidly. The lines in his face, the white at his temples, and the creakiness of his bones were all the proof he needed. For Penny, it was different. The war years had seen her bloom from a young girl to a beautiful woman. Her experience caused her to grow up too fast. Aquila felt for his daughter. Life had deprived her of a normal childhood. With Essie in hiding, she no longer had a mother to learn from. In their absence, Penny was in effect overseeing one of the largest homes in Harford County.

Despite his exhaustion, Aquila beamed at Penny. It was as if he had witnessed the beauty of a rose from seedling to flower. "I thought you'd be staying with Celia," he stated.

Penny smiled. "I did for the first week, but then I told her I was no longer a child in need of a guardian. Besides, I have Isaiah who checks on me, and Celia visits every day."

Aquila's instinct was to protest. Penny's safety was what he valued. He remained mute but committed to placing additional guards on the grounds. The redcoats couldn't be trusted.

Their butler arrived promptly behind Penny. "Welcome home, General. May I get you something to eat or perhaps draw you a hot bath?"

Three days of pounding a hard path left him smelling of sweat and dirt. "Yes, a bath is in order. Then I shall like a quiet supper with my daughter."

Then, to Penny, he said lovingly, "You have been through quite an ordeal. I wish to hear everything."

—∽—

The next morning, as was his custom, Aquila arose at dawn, dressed, and walked to the mill where he would speak with his trusted foreman, Isaiah. He found him doing what he did best, giving men instruction on the proper operation of the mill. The two old friends embraced and receded into the privacy of Isaiah's small office inside the main building.

"Essie is well?" inquired Isaiah.

"Yes, Charles has seen to that. Once the war is over, I will figure out some way to return her name to good standing."

"Do you see the war ending anytime soon?"

Aquila sighed. "I wish I could say I did. We have decent positions in the north and are working to fortify the south. Washington expects an assault on South Carolina. The British are enlisting slaves to fight for their cause with the promise of freedom if they win."

Isaiah winced. "Perhaps the British are wise in this regard. They are playing to the known discourse among American philosophies. Divide and conquer, as they say."

"Unfortunately, you are right. Washington has not yet forged a response. He knows keenly that enlisting slaves to fight for America will alienate southern plantation owners." Aquila paused and then added, "We could increase our numbers dramatically if Congress would adopt abolition."

"Look at what we accomplish here without holding slaves," Isaiah remarked. "We pay men a fair wage for a day's work and have one of the most productive and profitable mills in the region."

"I couldn't agree more," Aquila stated stoically. "But as a slaveholder himself, Washington faces a strategic and moral dilemma not easily solved." Then, turning his mind to the business of war, Aquila added, "I must return to the army within the coming days. I plan to visit Essie." Placing a hand on Isaiah's shoulder, Aquila looked him steadily in the eye and said, "I don't know when I can return to Cromwell's Passage."

"You needn't worry. I look in on Penny every day. As do Celia and the house staff. The redcoats have a modest presence in town, but I don't see them as the threat they once were in these parts."

"How can a father not worry?" Aquila wondered aloud.

The two men embraced once more.

Considering his friend and employer, Isaiah said, "You know I would give my life to defend your family."

Celia wore an emerald-colored day dress with simple white lace along the wrists and a string of modest pearls.

Aquila thought about how elegant she looked, even when she had nowhere in particular to go. They sat in the Greenes' parlor, sipping tea and discussing their shared longing to reunite with their spouses. After expressing his heartfelt gratitude for her care of Penny in his and Essie's absence, Aquila broached the subject of his journey south.

"Painful as it may be, you mustn't go see her," Celia decried in a surprisingly authoritative manner. "She is living under a new identity and, as well as I know Essie, she will not wish to compound her current plight by having to relocate once more."

Crestfallen, Aquila sank lower in the overstuffed chair by the fireplace. "What am I to do? Return to war and forget my wife?"

"No, Aquila. You must continue writing. The Agents of Liberty can deliver your letters through clandestine channels. When the time is right, Charles and I will do whatever we can to help you and Essie to reunite and clear her name."

"You are too kind. Time and again, you and Charles have been by my side with aid and comfort. I don't know how I will ever repay you."

"There is no repayment required. We love you as family, and family looks after one another. No questions asked."

"May I borrow paper and ink? I wish to write Essie a letter. I will leave it here for you to deliver."

"Certainly. I will show you to my writing desk in the next room. Take your time."

He scarcely knew where to start. What does one say to a wife who is forced to hide for attempting to serve her country? The quill twitched in Aquila's hand. Essie would not even recognize his own script if he weren't able to steady his nerves. He put the quill down, leaned back in the chair, and closed his eyes, trying to imagine what words might help heal Essie's empty days and longing for him and Penny. He understood the perils of war required him to communicate cryptically. Then, he wrote.

Aquila folded the letter in thirds and handed it to Celia. He watched her slip the letter beneath the red and white checkered lining of a small wicker basket filled with food.

Then she looked up at Aquila and said, "Charles will get this letter to Essie. Don't you worry."

CHAPTER 65

Richmond, Virginia

Essie's eyes went wide at the sight of the oversized scissors. Wincing, she tried to remain still as Stella Barlow hacked away at hair cultivated from childhood. Essie watched in horror as the chestnut locks drifted to the wooden floor. She could feel the cool air of the room on the nape of her neck. Without the benefit of a mirror, she knew her hair was now shorter than many of the men she associated with, even Aquila.

Stella maneuvered Essie across the room and sat her in a hard chair over a large washbasin. Warm water spilled over her head from a pitcher Stella had retrieved from her cupboard. Essie's neck strained as Stella kneaded her fingers roughly through her scalp. The woman's fingernails scratched at her like an angry cat.

"We must transform you into a convincing black-haired maiden," declared Stella. "I know it's uncomfortable, but it's the only way to penetrate your natural brown roots."

Essie tried her best to remain still. The stench was overwhelming. Still, she felt herself squirm with each movement of Stella's fingers.

"Stay still," Stella commanded. "You don't want the dye to stain your face or neck."

When the discomfort finally subsided, Essie breathed a sigh of relief until she saw Stella dipping a small rag into the jar of homemade dye.

"Finally, the eyebrows must match the hair on your head."

Essie groaned, perhaps a bit too loudly. "That smell. What is in the dye?"

Stella toiled, never taking her eyes off the job at hand. "It is a mix of sage, rosemary, and charcoal."

"How dreadful," Essie stated. "If I were an older woman, I think I'd prefer to be gray."

Stella removed her hands from Essie's face and stood back two paces. "There, you look different already." She handed Essie a mirror.

Essie gasped aloud as she saw her beautiful chestnut hair had been ruined. Essie thought she resembled a demon from the old campfire stories her father once told. *What would Aquila think?* She loathed the thought of her beloved's face as he laid eyes on the horrid sight. She was repugnant. How could Aquila still find her attractive?

"You will get used to it," Stella said. "But don't worry, we don't have to apply the dye again for at least a week."

Aghast, Essie quipped, "We have to do this again?"

Stella replied, "Why, of course," while she cleaned up the dye and the rags. "You must maintain the dye to preserve your cover." Stella added, "You will get used to it," taking the mirror from Essie's hand. "Now, let's wash it. You will find it more to your liking once your head is dry and you can brush out your hair."

Essie groaned in acknowledgement. *What remains of my hair,* she thought. In her heart, she knew she was acting like a schoolgirl being chastised for speaking out in class. She had withstood hardships before, for sure. Imprisonment had made her thin and worn, but on this occasion, her looks were changing willingly. And she detested it.

Stella interrupted her internal tantrum with further instructions. "My family name is Ross. I grew up in Staunton, in the Shenandoah Valley. My grandfather came to Virginia from Aberdeen. You will pose as my cousin, Mairl. We will say that you are the daughter of my mother's youngest brother, and you are here to keep me company while Robert is off to war."

"Mairl Ross," Essie said aloud. It was a strong name, and Essie couldn't help but wonder what history the name possessed in Stella's Scottish ancestry.

"Oh, and one more thing. That English accent will not do. Are you proficient in Gaelic?"

The blood drained from Essie's face. "No, I haven't a clue how to speak with a Scottish dialect."

"No matter," Stella replied. "We shall say my uncle, your father, settled in London to work as a banker. You were born in London and moved to Virginia when you were just a girl."

Essie marveled at how quickly Stella spun a tale. At least she thought, Stella's deviousness was being used for good.

Hours passed. Essie was afraid to leave the Barlow house. While she looked different, she felt the same. How could she pretend to be another? What if she slipped up? She faced the reality that she was likely to be apprehended by both loyalists and patriots. Her senses heightened with a knock at the front door.

"Stay here," commanded her hostess. Stella returned with a basket. Holding it by the handle, she laid it on the table. "It's for you. From Colonel Greene," she stated with little emotion.

Opening the lid, Essie peered inside. Two jars of apple butter and two jars of spiced peaches were accompanied by a rolled-up note tied with a blue ribbon. The paper bore Charles Greene's hand.

Essie's sense of wonder heightened. The note read:

Enjoy these fruits of your labor. Remember to always look deep within when contemplating your actions.

Essie thought that the rush of intrigue had vanished from her soul forever.

"The scissors," Essie cried. "Get them now!" She hadn't intended to sound like a plantation overseer, but her excitement overcame decorum.

Essie cut away the red and white checkered lining of the basket and quickly found the folded paper resting quietly at the bottom of the basket. It was from Aquila! The mere sight of his written words lifted her spirits before she began reading. She grabbed the letter and retreated to the cushion in the bay window, where she savored every word.

My Dearest Essie,

Penny arrived home with Fanny, whom I grew to love as much as our daughter does. She may be the most affectionate dog I've ever encountered. I pray you are settled comfortably. But for friends' insistence and the war, I would have visited. I will work tirelessly to ensure our reunification as quickly as possible.

All my love,

Aquila

PS: I have been in touch with Cousin Heather, and she sends her regards.

Cousin Heather! Essie recalled her training for the Agents of Liberty and the identity of Heather Walters, who, along with her husband's former gang, had become instrumental forces in Charles's recruitment efforts. While Essie had never met the Baltimore tavern owner, she knew of her and understood Aquila's cryptic note to send further communications to him via Heather. Essie smiled and pondered how to write to her husband as Mairl Ross, an identity he knew nothing about.

CHAPTER 66

Charleston, South Carolina

Cornwallis huffed. His relationship with General Clinton had all but dried up. They spoke of military strategy but little else. Cornwallis knew that Clinton's sympathy for his wife's recent passing expired in deference to the war. Without proper time to grieve, Cornwallis turned inward. His zest for organization, strategy, and war tactics had dissipated. He was going through the motions.

The solidification of Georgia had succeeded. Their overarching plans to engage Southern loyalists and promises of freedom to slaves were proving most effective. Now, as discussed in broad terms, Cornwallis must continue his siege of the South. With Georgia under control, the Carolinas were next, and finally Virginia. Willard had made such a mess of things in the north. Cornwallis and Clinton found it more difficult to gain standing in the region. The South was the key. He was sure of it. And the place to strike hard and fast was Charleston. General Benjamin Lincoln and five thousand troops protected the largest Southern port, which the rebels held. They were in for a surprise. By sunrise, Charleston would be under the magnificent flag of Britain.

Cornwallis took a swig of the port he had brought from his furlough. He was drinking more. Alone, he gazed out his window and up at the yellow corn moon, fighting the lump in his throat that preceded unwanted tears. His uniform sagged on his frame. With little appetite, he was losing weight. He was listless. The melancholy consumed him. Cornwallis took another deep pull from a metal flask and stripped down. In his nightshirt, he lay down on the cot in his field quarters and submitted to his grief.

—∞—

Cornwallis hardly slept. He rose well before sunrise, dressed in his white trousers and red coat, and rousted the men out of their bunks. "Up," he yelled. With each breath of humid South Carolina air, Cornwallis's head throbbed. Lack of sleep and too much port had done him in. He trudged forward in the muddy ground upon which they camped and continued to bark orders: "Fall in, fall in. The siege begins in three-quarters of an hour."

Cornwallis urged himself to fulfill his duties. The British navy, along with three times the number of men as the rebels, would quickly capture the city. He would personally lead a regiment of five thousand men, the equivalent of the entire American force in Charleston. The one thing that bothered Cornwallis was the number of loyalist militia he had inherited in the South. They supported the cause but proved to be undisciplined and often insubordinate. Many didn't grasp that warfare demanded a controlled approach. He would make do with what he had.

On schedule, his troops set out. They were to take the western flank, protected by only fifteen hundred men. From the sea and the efforts of the men he now led, Cornwallis knew they would emerge victorious. Cannons rolled and infantrymen set up along the perimeter of the city. Advance scouts rode out to provide intelligence about the exact location of the enemy. When the sentries came back, they reported the Americans were just rising and did not suspect the imminent attack. Cornwallis gave the order to go forward.

They encountered the enemy moving about camp in the early morn on the edge of the forest. Although people considered him a statesman, a competent military leader, and a gentleman, Cornwallis disliked killing. Still, dozens of men fell in the first blitz of the British army. Cornwallis, atop his able-bodied chestnut horse, watched as the remaining rebels armed themselves and prepared to hold ground. Cornwallis gave them no quarter.

"Fire the cannon," he ordered. Then to his ground troops, "Charge!"

He witnessed the smoke from the cannon rising from the bloodshed as his men executed their orders with precision and speed. Cornwallis rode forward to inspect the spoils of war from the wave's first attack and estimated they had killed at least one hundred men without a single British casualty. He ordered his men to press forward. They would plow over the rebels until they reached the city's perimeter.

Four hours later, they arrived at their destination. The men were tired but ecstatic in their victory. Cornwallis urged them to remain quiet. "We don't know what lies over the hills ahead. Remain vigilant."

As he prepared his men for the battle's final stage, Cornwallis witnessed the navy bombarding the city with cannon. The artillery attack was too much for the undermanned and unsuspecting enemy. They had done it. They had crushed the rebels. The army sealed escape routes and supply lines. Surrender was inevitable.

CHAPTER 67

New York, New York

"This codebook is phenomenal," Aquila gleefully remarked as he and Major Tallmadge sat alone in the cellar of the younger man's quarters.

"It contains false identities and seven hundred and sixty-three numbers. The numbers can represent a person, a place, or even a pertinent word."

"Extraordinary," said Aquila.

"Everyone who is part of the northern department intelligence effort is represented in some manner." He paused and added, "Even you and General Washington."

Tallmadge rose from his seat and paced, appearing more at ease to speak while in motion. "Lifelong friends of mine have been recruited to carry intelligence through circuitous routes, over many drop points and handoffs, between Setauket and New York City. The operation is ready to commence."

"You have done well, Major. Your efforts may be just what the Continental army needs to finally get British troops off our northern shores. I do, however, have a few questions."

"Of course," replied Tallmadge respectfully.

"These friends of yours ... are they in the Continental army?"

"No, sir. All are just citizens living and working at pedestrian jobs —farmer, fisherman, barkeep, et cetera. Not being directly in service to the government allows them to move about clandestinely," Tallmadge explained.

Aquila nodded his approval and once again began staring at Tallmadge's codebook. His right index finger drifted over the page and chose one entry. "Agent 355. What can you tell me about him?"

Tallmadge hesitated. Aquila thought he had discovered a crack in the visage of the young man's ingenuity. Tallmadge, in a plain state of nervousness, bumped into the chair upon which he had been sitting. He paced before declaring, "General, ignorance is preferable. Only those who create messages and adhere to the codebook will know who these people are."

Aquila scoffed. He was indignant. "How, pray tell, am I to decipher coded messages I receive if you don't teach me how to decode them?"

Tallmadge was sweating. "You misunderstand, General. You will master the decoding process. It's just the identities of the agents we wish to preserve. These people are not military personnel. They are embarking at enormous risk to their personal safety and that of their families. The fewer people that know, the better."

Aquila collected himself. Anger would not serve his purpose. And truth be told, Tallmadge's logic was sound. Still, Aquila persisted. "I am your superior officer, answering directly to General George Washington, the commander in chief of the Continental army. You will tell me the identity of the man who is Agent 355."

Tallmadge stared back at him, not answering before proffering a vague reply to Aquila's direct order. "General, I didn't say Agent 355 was a man. A number denotes each person in the book. Mostly, they know only their own assigned agent number. A select few possess knowledge of other agents' numbers, and many have false identities. I have gone to great lengths to draw a compromise between ensuring the agents' safety and advancing the needs of our country's intelligence requirements. I assure you this will succeed."

Aquila arched an eyebrow. It was as if the dark clouds of the conversation broke in favor of the first ray of sunshine after a downpour. "I understand. For now, keep these identities to yourself. Let's see how things unfold."

"Thank you, General Wright. There is another urgent matter we must discuss."

"Certainly. What is it?"

"Oliver De Lancey," stated Tallmadge. "He is the loyalist appointed to continue the work of John André. You may be familiar with him. He raised a band of fifteen hundred Tories and rose to the position of general in the British army. De Lancey is here in the city. One of my agents overheard a conversation he held with a subordinate in a local tavern."

Tallmadge again appeared nervous. Aquila braced himself for unpleasant news.

"It has to do with your late wife," said Tallmadge.

"Essie?" Aquila asked incredulously. Before speaking, he had to check himself. He didn't wish to accidentally reveal that his "late" wife was very much alive. "Please, Major. Enlighten me."

"Apparently, the general and his men were well into their fourth pitcher of ale. De Lancey boasted aloud that Mrs. Wright's letter to Prime Minister North gave the British an opportunity to frame her for treason."

"Frame her? This is preposterous," Aquila replied.

"How did Henry Laurens and George Washington discover the news about Mrs. Wright's letter to the prime minister?" Tallmadge asked.

Aquila stared at the far wall. The thoughts in his head ran faster than a jackrabbit in the throes of a hunt. "We . . . we never knew. Ever since they accused Essie, I have deliberated that exact question."

"As De Lancey tells it. North was going to sack General Willard anyway, despite the revelations exposed in Mrs. Wright's letter. Willard was Germain's man. North held Germain in low regard because of the length of the war and the inroads we had made. The British already knew of Mrs. Wright and her accolades. I suspect they also knew of her role in the Agents of Liberty. They saw it as a way to take out a key player."

Aquila looked up at Tallmadge while running his right hand through his rich brown hair. "And so they sent an anonymous letter to Laurens."

"Yes, sir. In all likelihood, that is exactly what happened."

Aquila was beside himself. The information was startling. He pushed back from the wooden table, bid Major Tallmadge good day, and ascended the steps of the cellar, unsure how to use what he had just learned. The one thing he was sure of was that somehow, he would free his beloved from purgatory.

CHAPTER 68

Richmond, Virginia

Essie awoke in unfamiliar quarters at the Barlow residence. The nightmare left her quivering in the early morning chill of the strange chamber. She ran a hand through her hair, but all she felt was the short rasp of her once beautiful locks. It was an ugly reminder of the lonely circumstances in which she found herself embroiled—the crushing sacrifice she made for the love of her country and its quest for freedom. Essie folded her arms across her chest to quell goosebumps. She held fast to her memories and the people she loved. It was the only way she might survive an undetermined period of isolation, where she contributed nothing. She merely existed.

Then, lingering remnants struck her soul. The dream! Oh, how she wished she could forget. So many mornings, the prior night's dreams evaporated or hung in faintly recalled fragments. Not this one. She was in a room with the young nation's dignitaries. Washington, Laurens, Adams, and even her old friend Benjamin Franklin were there. Aquila was by her side. They were discussing important matters. How to win the war. How to frame the new government. Essie struggled to share her thoughts. With each attempt to speak, no sound left her mouth. The men looked at her as if she were some sort of sideshow act. It angered her, and she attempted to berate them, to scream at the top of her lungs. This time, a sound came out. Not her voice, but the sound of a wounded animal crying for help. Then she awakened. The sound of a boar's pained squeal rising from her throat was all that Essie could think of. At last, her state of fear was disrupted by Stella entering the room.

"Dress and come downstairs. I will make breakfast and then we shall venture out," she said with little feeling. Essie hadn't been in Stella's company for very long but, so far, she found this woman's presence very discomforting. Certainly, she was an able hostess and had made every effort to protect Essie's identity and provide material comfort, but Essie did not see them becoming friends. Stella did not embrace her, nor did she share insights into her own life. She went about her business and conveyed nothing, not even an occasional wayward facial expression. Essie would need to break through Stella's armor-like exterior. Essie's own state of disarray left her needing a confidant. She knew herself well enough to understand that feelings bottled like a jar of pickled beets led to greater unrest.

An hour later, dressed in a simple brown dress and a plain white bonnet, Essie stood at the front door behind Stella, who already had her hand on the knob. Essie was paralyzed.

"Let's go," Stella commanded. It reminded Essie of the manner in which the guards once addressed her at the London Debtor's Prison. She tried to move one foot forward toward the door. But she couldn't. Her right foot felt as if it weighed twice as much as the left. Moving ahead would prove challenging, like trudging through quicksand.

"Are you coming?" asked Stella.

Essie sensed Stella's growing displeasure. Yet Essie couldn't bring herself to move. What if someone recognized her? Would they cart her away to face another farcical jury, sentencing her to be imprisoned again, or rehang her?

"You go," she said to Stella. Her voice was unsteady. "I'll stay here. I will work on an idea for a new quilt while you complete your errands."

Stella snatched Essie's arm, jerking her body forward and said, "My sole errand is to get you into town so that you may live a normal existence for however long you are here."

Nodding, Essie allowed herself to be pulled through the doorway and followed Stella outside.

They strolled down Main Street toward the center of town. "Do you remember your cover?" Stella asked.

"Mairl. Mairl Ross. I am your cousin from Staunton."

Stella nodded in approval. "I will introduce you to people in town. Smile and say as little as possible."

Through the next hour, Essie fought the butterflies in her stomach as she cautiously met everyone Stella knew in town, from the butcher to the local architect. Her inhibitions thawed ever so slightly.

"Over there," Stella said, pointing to a small storefront across the street. "Our last stop. The town doctor."

Essie glanced at the glass-front building with a modest sign showing the name of Dr. David DeBusschere.

"Is the doctor from Holland?" Essie inquired, thinking of Henrik and wondering if the two might know one another.

"No, Dr. DeBusschere came here years ago from the Austrian Netherlands. He shows deep dedication to the people of Richmond." Stella paused and added, "I saved him for last for a reason. He is one of us."

"An Agent of Liberty?" Essie whispered excitedly.

"Yes. But please, I urge you. Do not show emotion. You are simply making an acquaintance."

Essie nodded. Before they could cross the street, she saw two men carrying a patient into Dr. DeBusschere's office on a stretcher. Then, as if a bolt of lightning struck her, Essie's mind cleared. She remembered what Isaiah had said right before they had arrested her and taken her to Philadelphia. The stretcher was a means of conveying intelligence. Before they crossed the street, Essie grabbed Stella's hand, bringing her to a stop.

"We've met so many people today. So many tradesmen. But we didn't meet a carpenter. Do you know one?" And off they went before Essie could meet the town doctor.

CHAPTER 69

Camden, South Carolina

Cornwallis's back ached. The pounding of hooves on rough patches of the Charleston battlefield had taken its toll. But they had secured victory. That was all that mattered. Now, as he rested and regrouped further north, he treated himself to a pipe with his favorite tobacco, an earthy blend with a trace of cherry. His new southern headquarters, Kershaw House, provided a place to billet and to strategize with his officers. Joseph Kershaw, the town's founder, built the Georgian-style home. Cornwallis relieved him of it with little resistance. The grounds held barracks and a stone barricade wall, as well as a large grass field. The Kershaw House provided an excellent foothold for his plans. Here, he could practice military maneuvers and offer the twenty-five hundred elite troops he commanded a decent place to reside. The home's proximity to the Wateree River and the Great Wagon Road was ideal. With access to each, Cornwallis could marshal men and supplies to aid his mission. Camden was an important point in the southern theater.

Slouching in his high-back chair, Cornwallis straightened his posture to ease pressure on his lower back. He blew smoke toward the ceiling and allowed himself a period of melancholy with which to reminisce about Jemma. Soon, the war would be over. He would return home to England, and then what? Settle down? With whom? Cornwallis could not imagine his life without Jemma. In his thoughts of the future, he had always seen himself dying bravely in battle with Jemma surviving and carrying on as the matriarch of the family. He ran his hand along the crushed velvet of what must have been Kershaw's favorite chair. A wayward tack used to fasten the velvet to the chair was loose and pricked his finger. He placed it in his mouth and sucked the dot of blood. Then, he wrapped the finger in a handkerchief he pulled from the pocket of his breeches.

His thoughts returned to Camden. A decisive blow would clear the path for a British takeover of North Carolina. Feelings about home would have to wait. Defeating the rebels was his sole priority. Although he was tired, sleep was elusive. He would remain awake and lead the march scheduled for five o'clock in the morning.

—~—

With his men and field commanders in tow, Cornwallis trotted forward on his favorite horse, a seventeen-hand palomino. The sight of the horse's cream-colored mane eased the shards of bile rising through his chest. This, Cornwallis presumed, was normal for any general leading men into battle. The sun peeked over the nearby tree line. Progress in his quest to end the war would come with the new day. In the semidarkness of the early morn, the smell of the forest, fresh and clean, brought a sense of calm and confidence. As his men pressed forward, Cornwallis took comfort in his choice to bring the best of the troops from the victory in Charleston. It never proved wise to underestimate the enemy—an error he knew his predecessors had made with regularity.

Much to his surprise, they encountered the enemy within the first hour of their march. The Americans were coming to greet them! With daybreak in full bloom, Cornwallis could now see that the opposition force was in disarray. Scores of ragged soldiers with disparate artillery and broken looks approached without the vim and vigor expected of a well-trained battle force. Cornwallis shook his head at the sight. It defied belief. That the rebel forces had deteriorated to this extent gave him hope. The left flank was nothing more than a band of tawdry militiamen. Cornwallis gave the order to charge. His elite redcoats pressed forward. The battalion in the center ran forward with bayonets extended and slaughtered the ragged enemy troops in a matter of minutes. From his vantage point, Cornwallis saw the alarm on the enemy militia's faces as the entire left flank turned and fled.

The best the enemy had to offer fought on under the command of Baron Johann De Kalb. Cornwallis knew De Kalb by reputation. He was one of the French commanders brought to the colonies by Lafayette. He heard De Kalb order his battalions to continue fighting. The onslaught of bullets and bayonets proved too much for De Kalb's bravest. The rebels fell in rapid succession, and finally, British soldiers toppled and stabbed De Kalb himself. By Cornwallis's count, at least a dozen bayonets ran through the body of Johann De Kalb. A rifleman shot him in the shoulder. Despite his wounds, De Kalb urged his remaining men to continue fighting. Cornwallis respected the courage and condemned the stupidity.

In under two hours, the British had soundly thrashed the enemy. Cornwallis looked over the bloody battlefield, satisfied that his men had earned a hearty win for king and country. He looked over his shoulder and called out, "Where is Gates?" Apprehending the esteemed American general commanding the south was critical. His capture would be a mortal blow to the rebellion. A voice called out from the simmering smoke of the melee, "He has fled north."

Cornwallis nodded. "Fine, fine. Outstanding effort today, men. Let's go back to headquarters. Another battle soon awaits."

CHAPTER 70

Richmond, Virginia

Emboldened, Essie discovered she could wander incognito in the city. She looked different, and with Stella's aid, she dressed in a manner more appropriate to the mountain frontier life of Staunton. She was even becoming accustomed to greeting townsfolk and using her new name, Mairl Ross. Essie thought it was a beautiful name. Upon questioning Stella about why she chose *Mairl,* Stella had simply replied that it was the name of a childhood friend. Despite her best efforts, Essie struggled to forge a bond with Stella. She questioned whether her presence in Stella's life was an obligatory nuisance, a favor granted by the husband she seldom saw.

Essie shivered on the chilly January morning. Her cloak did not protect her from the cold north wind. As she folded her arms across her chest to shield her body from the chill, Essie reproached herself. Who was she to criticize Stella for her behavior in the face of extreme loneliness? Essie understood that sorrow manifested itself differently from one person to the next. Since her staged death, Essie had gone months without seeing Aquila. When she was younger, the absence of her husband would have broken her. Now battle-hardened, Essie found strength and comfort in knowing she had weathered far worse.

She stepped onto the porch of Dr. DeBusschere's office and surveyed the quaint town. It lacked both the commerce of Philadelphia and the charm of Baltimore, yet it dwarfed Cromwell. She wondered why Richmond hadn't yet formed a hospital. Stella told her the nearest one was in Williamsburg, at least a day's carriage ride away. Next to the doctor's office was an apothecary, and across the street, a cobbler, a dressmaker, a butcher, and a brand-new post office. Essie smiled. The post office made her remember her friend Benjamin Franklin, who served as the first American postmaster general. How proud he must be of what he accomplished! Essie imagined Benjamin at their dinner table at Cromwell's Passage. The memory calmed her.

Sidling up to her was a man accompanying a woman in distress. She was pregnant, clearly in the final stages and nearing delivery. Essie rushed forward, wanting to help. Then, she checked herself. As much as she wished to provide aid, she could not reveal her skills as a midwife. She observed as Dr. DeBusschere, a tall, strongly built man with rugged looks and wavy black hair, burst through the door to help the woman inside. Essie exhaled. The distressed woman was in good hands. Essie's cover was almost shattered, a frightening reality. Had the doctor not arrived when he did, Essie very well might have chucked it all to ensure the woman's health.

Essie stepped away from the doctor's office. She wished to survey the apothecary to see if it held the plant-based remedies she had grown in the garden behind the Cromwell hospital. As she stepped into the street, she heard the pounding of hooves and the whooping and hollering of a band of rowdies. The horses kicked up dust from the main road, and when it settled, Essie could see the redcoats and the British flag hoisted by one of the lead men. Before Essie could blink, one soldier tossed a glass bottle into the street. The bottle shattered on the road, and a small fire erupted. Essie saw the other men stuffing dirty white rags into bottles of liquid and striking the steel of their swords with flint to ignite the bottles, likely filled with turpentine. The men hoisted flaming bottles into the general store and the post office. Fearing for her life, Essie retreated to the doctor's office, breaking into the lobby and screaming, "It's a raid. The British are burning the city down!"

The startled doctor, his nurse, and the couple with the baby boy just born bolted toward the back of the building when the doctor screamed, "I have a covered wagon. Follow me."

Without being invited, Essie followed, and they piled into the wagon. Dr. DeBusschere quickly affixed blinders to the two horses, climbed into the seat, grabbed the reins, and guided the wagon from the building's rear to the main street. From the back of the wagon, Essie saw the city as it burned. Dark smoke plumes swirled skyward, and hot embers flittered in the breeze, creating a scene Essie thought resembled an orange snowstorm.

The infant was crying. "My baby!" the new mother said. "The smoke. How do I protect him?"

The husband struggled to shield his wife and new son with his body and coat. The young nurse was inexperienced. Essie thought she looked as frightened as the mother. With the doctor guiding them to safety, Essie had to act. In the wagon, she noticed a large jug. She removed the cork and smelled the contents, wanting to ensure it held fresh water. Satisfied, Essie reached into her coat pocket for the lace-edged handkerchief she had made and soaked it with water from the jug. Handing it to the young mother, she said, "Take this and cradle it over the baby's nose and mouth. It will shield him from the smoke."

The woman did as instructed. The baby calmed, and the wagon rolled toward a forested road outside of town. As Dr. DeBusschere steered the wagon up the road, the noise and smoke from the British raid faded in the distance. Essie relaxed and straightened her legs across the wooden slats of the wagon floor. The doctor came around the back and assisted all of them in getting down from the wagon. When she was back on her feet, Essie saw the grand, two-story, colonial red brick house and felt safe. The surrounding forest might burn, but the majestic beauty of Dr. DeBusschere's house would not.

Dr. DeBusschere took Essie's hand and introduced himself. "And you are?" he inquired in his Dutch accent.

"I am Es—" and she stopped herself. The excitement of the raid had caused her to forget her new identity. "Mairl Ross," she said, collecting herself. "I am staying in town with my cousin, Stella Barlow. Pleased to meet you."

In a scratchy voice, the young mother, shaky on her feet as she held her new babe, said, "You saved my son's life."

Essie demurred. "Well, I just helped him to avoid breathing in smoke and soot."

With the moist cloth continuing to hang from the mother's hand, Dr. DeBusschere remarked, "That was quick thinking, Mairl."

"It was fortunate that you had a jug of fresh water in the wagon," Essie replied.

The doctor smiled. "I get thirsty on long runs visiting patients in the region."

And then Essie thought that Dr. DeBusschere was Richmond's equivalent of old Doc Bradley, who traveled the expanse of Harford County before the hospital opened. Essie desperately wanted to discuss the formation of a hospital but knew the time wasn't right.

"Let's all go in and warm ourselves by the fire. My wife will prepare tea and biscuits." Then to the nurse, "I will direct you to a guest room where you can care for our new mother."

Essie admired Dr. DeBusschere. Faced with grave danger, he rushed them to safety and opened his home to strangers in the name of healing and compassion.

Hours later, a soldier in the blue coat of the Continental army pounded on the front door. Dr. DeBusschere let him in, and Essie could see the black smudge on his face from the fire's remnants. His uniform was in tatters, and he smelled of smoke and sweat.

"Doctor, you must come with me. The traitor, Benedict Arnold, and his battalion of redcoat militia have burned the city to the ground. People are dead in the street. Our military storage shed has been destroyed. The wounded are everywhere."

Dr. DeBusschere took command of the situation. "My wife will watch over the newborn."

To the nurse and Essie, he directed, "The two of you come with me. We will need every pair of hands we can find."

The scene of the city from which they had just escaped was chaotic. A raid no one expected had largely obliterated Richmond in a matter of hours. The British presence in Richmond heretofore was scant. Now, it seemed the carnage was everywhere. Buildings smoldered as men threw buckets of water from wooden troughs. Panicked people ran through the ruins looking for loved ones. Essie's heart sank as she questioned how much of her medical knowledge she could put into use without questions being asked.

"Fan out," Dr. DeBusschere ordered to Essie and the nurse. "Take one of the spare medical bags in the wagon. Do what you can. Call for me if you need help. We can't save them all. Tend to those you think can survive."

The fire had burned the first man Essie found so badly that no one could recognize him. Yet he was still breathing. Reluctantly, Essie ran to the next body. A man lay in the dirt with a footlong shard of glass protruding from his shoulder. It made her remember when someone brought Aquila home after he was impaled in a bridge collapse. The shard was thin enough and in a part of the body where Essie felt comfortable removing it. With a cloth taken from the medical bag, she treated the injury as best she could and gave the man laudanum to drink for his discomfort.

Then, she moved on, encountering a woman lying on her side with her knees bent. She rolled the woman onto her back and gasped. It was Stella! Essie quickly examined her and found no outward wounds. But she was not breathing. Essie checked for a pulse and found none. Stella must have died of smoke inhalation. Her face was slightly contorted, and it resembled the ashen remains of choking victims she had seen before. The horrific thought that Stella's death was her fault raced through her mind. Essie had risen early and gone to town while Stella was still asleep. When the raid broke out, Stella must have taken to the streets in search of her. *Stella died looking for me,* Essie thought. *Oh, how dreadful.* She forced herself to keep moving. The wounded lay writhing in agony everywhere she looked. She would pontificate later. Essie took two steps from Stella's body and encountered an elegant-looking black man wearing the coat of the enemy. He was flat on his back. Essie had heard that the British were enlisting slaves with the promise of freedom. It was the first time she had seen it in practice. She questioned whether she should help him or move on to someone who wasn't the enemy. Human kindness took precedence. The man was unconscious but seemed otherwise unharmed. Essie took a glass vial out of the medical bag and put the bottle beneath the soldier's nose.

Gradually, his head moved back and forth, and his eyes popped open. "What is that awful smell?" he asked, looking up at Essie.

"Spirit of hartshorn. A fainting remedy. Are you all right? I must tend to others."

The man sat up. "I think I'm okay. Thank you. It is kind of you to give aid and comfort to the enemy."

Essie stared at the man a bit too long. He had kind eyes. She would have liked to learn more about him and how he had come to fight for the British. Despite his uniform, Essie sensed a strange feeling of attachment to the man, something of a kindred spirit. "You are welcome. We are all people, sir, equal in the eyes of God, despite our political differences."

She rose to leave, seeking the next person she might aid. The soldier grabbed her skirt.

"Unhand me," Essie demanded.

The man smiled. "I am sorry. I meant no harm. My name is James Armistead. I need to get a message to General Washington."

With a curious eye, Essie stared at this man a bit too long, not sure she should trust him. Why would a former slave fighting for the British want to get a message to the leader of the Continental army? And why, pray tell, should she aid such a request? "Who are you?" she asked. "Really?"

"As I stated, my name is James Armistead. I was a slave of a patriot plantation owner. He allowed me to join the redcoats, worm my way into their good graces, and convey intelligence back to the Continental army."

Essie stood flabbergasted. This man faced the same situation that she had asked Hazel to undertake. Her stomach clenched as she thought of her best friend and how Essie's zeal to help America cost Hazel her life. How could she aid Armistead in a similar venture? How could she carry the guilt of getting another person killed? And then the worst thought of all: Did this man somehow know her true identity? The notion sickened her.

With great hesitation, Essie asked slowly, "Why me? What makes you think I can help you get a message to the commander in chief of the Continental army?"

Armistead replied in a scratchy voice, revealing the weariness of battle. "My conduit was killed in battle a week ago. Currently, I can't convey any vital information. I chose you because you extended me a kindness. I trust you can find a way."

Essie blanched at the explanation. She was supposed to be hiding, lying low, and definitely not getting involved with her former responsibilities. Still, her allegiance was not to herself, or her instinct to merely survive, but to America and its promise of a brighter future. Essie took Armistead's hand, squeezing it, and said, "Tell me what you wish to convey."

CHAPTER 71

Guilford County, North Carolina

The march north proved tiresome. Despite the weariness of the twenty-five hundred men he now commanded, Cornwallis held steady in his pursuit. His light infantrymen reported that his counterpart, General Nathanael Greene, was employing a zoned strategy to protect the Guilford Courthouse perimeter. The light infantry assessed that the Americans had almost five thousand men. The North Carolina militia held the front line, the Virginia militia was in the middle, and in the back, toward the takeover target, were the Continental army troops.

Cornwallis accepted the news with poise, as befitting his stature as a wartime British field general. After all, how could he lead men into battle if he did not exhibit outward confidence? Inside, however, Cornwallis was unsure. He was outmanned two-to-one, his troops were weary, and he could not employ an element of surprise. The British had won the Battle of Camden quickly. Capturing Guilford Courthouse would be a much greater feat.

Cornwallis dismissed the scout and went to the privy. Pulling down the stark white breeches, he sat and relieved himself, thinking only of how to overcome the current odds. Rising, Cornwallis returned to his temporary headquarters and assembled his officers. They would win the battle at any cost. A victory in Guilford County would show the commander in chief that he was correct in his assertion. Rampaging through the South was the path to ending the revolution. Strangling the economic boon of the region's rich natural resources was instrumental. Engaging the slaves and the large faction of loyalists was a master stroke. He would recommend to General Clinton that they march to Yorktown after winning this battle. The location in Virginia was perfect for onboarding fresh troops and resupply. And once Yorktown fell, the South would be under control of the British Army. After dismissing his officers, Cornwallis sat down and penned these exact thoughts in an encrypted letter to Clinton.

Early the next morning, Cornwallis began what he expected would be the pivotal turning point of the war in the south. After removing what Cornwallis thought of as nuisance troops at the New Garden Meeting House, he then ordered his infantry to march to the open field where the first line of rebel defenses was stationed. General Greene would not position his best troops on the front line, and therefore, he ordered a steady rifle volley at short range. The effect was crushing. Soldiers gunned down the North Carolina militia in short order. The rest retreated, abandoning weapons in the open field guarding the densely wooded area holding the second line of rebel defenses. Cornwallis was pleased. Thus far, his forces had sustained few casualties. The second phase of the battle would be far more difficult. Battle in the open was one thing; dispatching the enemy in the forest was another. Cornwallis's men moved forward, about three hundred yards by his estimation, at the ready with rifles, bayonets, and cannon. The Virginia militia was far more organized. The fighting was close at hand. Men fighting other men with the butts of their rifles and fisticuffs. Greene's layered defense negated the British's disadvantage in troop numbers. The fighting continued for an hour before the Virginians retreated.

Now, Cornwallis thought, came the toughest part of the mission: seizing the ground near Guilford Courthouse. Here, they would encounter the best of the American forces. Cornwallis gave the order for an advance and commencement of steady artillery rounds. The rebels on this final front were undismayed. From his vantage point atop the palomino, Cornwallis became concerned when a band of dragoons entered the fighting in the open ground near the courthouse. The dragoons attacked his men on the flank and in the rear. The enemy halted the advance. This was a defining moment in the battle. Once again, his men were engaged in hand-to-hand combat.

Cornwallis inhaled deeply. He had to make what was perhaps the toughest call of his military career. Dying would be his only alternative to holding the ground. Cornwallis glanced behind him toward the cannon brigade major and issued the order, hoping he wouldn't regret it. Moments later, the cannon ignited and a burst of grapeshot fell over the fighting, striking members of both sides. His stomach soured at the sight of his own men falling, clutching their bodies and writhing in pain on the blood-drenched battleground. Many would die. Others would be wounded, preventing them from joining his planned march to Virginia. Still, when Cornwallis spotted the Americans in similar disarray and in the throes of retreat, he knew he had made the right decision. Sacrifices had to be made. The ruin of the prolonged anarchy must take precedence over the lives of the individual soldiers. Cornwallis trusted that his men understood this.

When the field cleared, Cornwallis led the advance through the early morning haze and its battle remnant smoke. He perched his aching back against the breakaway bark of an old sycamore tree in front of the Guilford Courthouse. Exhaling, Cornwallis stepped away from the tree, raised a fist in triumph, and yelled, "For king and country!" Then, he turned his head, taking in the panoramic scene of the battle, and took solace. The war would soon be over.

CHAPTER 72

New Windsor, New York

Even though Dr. Bond had taken over Essie's responsibilities as director general for the Medical Department of the Continental army, Aquila still felt obliged to visit the mobile hospitals his wife created. In his own role, Aquila relied upon the system of clandestine intelligence exchange envisioned by George Washington when he accepted Essie's idea for the mobile hospitals. Some of these operations were extremely difficult to visit. Doctors and nurses with bloody garments, often with insufficient medical supplies, ran like chickens in a coop, to and fro, barking orders at anyone in the vicinity they could enlist to help. People stationed at a mobile army hospital received a crash course in medical support, despite their backgrounds. A fresh pair of hands and a strong constitution were the only tools required for the job. Doctors were in short supply. Dr. Bond's medical training school in Philadelphia was not churning out graduates at a pace to keep up with mounting casualties, especially in the South. The facility he now found himself in was northwest of West Point, a few miles from George Washington's current headquarters.

Aquila roamed the battlefield hospital and found it in an aberrant state of temporary tranquility. The British had shifted resources and focus to the south, and fighting in this region was scant. Aquila located the doctor in charge, a grizzled colonel and surgeon with an unkept beard hailing from Boston. He looked as if he had seen it all. Aquila greeted the doctor and explained his role as chief of intelligence.

"I know who you are," the doctor stated. "Your operation is part of the training we receive before being deployed to take over a mobile medical unit."

"Of course," replied Aquila. "And how is that aspect of your unit performing?"

The man shook his head. "I suppose you could say okay. Truth be told, our unit is so near the army headquarters that most intelligence goes directly there."

"I see. That makes sense. In fact, that is where I am heading next."

Before another word was spoken, Aquila saw two soldiers carrying a rack of six stretchers, with one stacked upon the other. The men placed their load on the ground and began pulling on the tips of the stretcher poles.

"What are those men doing?" Aquila inquired.

The older man harrumphed. "They are checking for intelligence. A system I am told that was conceived by your late wife."

Aquila felt foolish. How could he not know? Essie must have placed the system in play prior to her arrest. He returned his attention to the scene in front of him. The barrels of the stretcher handles had been hollowed out. One by one, they inspected the innards of the stretcher handles but found no messages. When they got to the bottom of the stack, Aquila saw one of the young men extract a rolled-up piece of paper secured by a thin blue ribbon. He ran with the rolled-up scroll and handed it to the colonel.

The doctor removed the ribbon and began reading, getting no farther than the salutation before stating, "It's addressed to you, General Wright. How fortuitous that you were here when it arrived."

Aquila thought the same. The communique was likely headed to Washington's headquarters in hope members of that camp could locate the letter's intended recipient. He took the letter and began reading.

To General Aquila Wright,

My name is Mairl Ross of Richmond. I learned from a reliable source that Cornwallis is planning to mobilize forces in and around Yorktown, Virginia. They are advancing from Guilford County, North Carolina.

You should also know that General Arnold has burned our city to the ground. The fire claimed the life of my cousin. Our circumstances here are dire.

Aquila's heart raced. The penmanship was unmistakable. And the butterfly! It resembled the pendant he had given her before they were married. Essie! His beloved. Aquila marveled that she never stopped fighting in service to her country. God, how he loved her. Aquila's heart beat faster as he read the letter again. It gave him chills, and he fought back the welling emotions desirous of an exit from his tired eyes. Essie was in trouble. Alone and in need of aid. Aquila was all too familiar with Benedict Arnold and his zeal for besting America.

"Is everything all right?" asked the doctor.

Aquila nodded. "Yes, quite. The message contains urgent news. I must leave at once for headquarters." Then, Aquila swore to himself, he would ride for Richmond, faster than the strongest wind could carry him, to rescue his beloved.

CHAPTER 73

Richmond, Virginia

Essie felt strange being in the Barlow house while Stella lay dead on the street. The feeling was even more absurd when she considered the circumstance of how she had a double agent spy in the parlor, recuperating from battle. And a slave at that! What on earth would happen if someone knocked on the door? Surely, Essie could pass off her assumed identity as Stella's cousin from Staunton. But if a visitor should see James Armistead, a presumed runaway slave and a traitor to America, no explanation would suffice. They would cart her away and try her for aiding and abetting the enemy. Oh, how Essie wished she could seek counsel from Aquila. Then, she thought of Pastor Vinson. So many times, he had calmed her with his words of wisdom.

Essie placed a kettle on the fire. Tea would ease her frayed nerves. She recalled enough sentiment from Aquila and Pastor Vinson to reconcile her anxiety with the fact that she was doing the right thing. Pastor Vinson had said that all men were children of God. America's Declaration of Independence said God endows all men with unalienable rights such as life, liberty, and the pursuit of happiness, because all men are created equally by God. Cherishing these ideals, Essie undertook the mission to help James Armistead. After all, was it not he who was risking his own life to aid America in secret? Why, then, should she not perform in kind? The prospect of lying low under an assumed name would have to be placed to the side. The water boiled, and Essie removed the kettle from the fire. A knock befell the door, startling Essie, who almost dropped the kettle. She strode to the parlor, where her guest slept fitfully on the striped settee.

"Mr. Armistead, wake up!" Essie implored gently.

The man stirred and then opened his eyes. "What's wrong?" he asked.

"There is someone at the door. You must hide in the root cellar. Out the back door. There is a hatch. Go quickly and be quiet."

Essie straightened her apron and tucked a lock of stray hair behind her left ear as she approached the door. There stood two men, members of the Continental army. Essie coaxed herself to breathe. "May I help you?" she asked.

One man, with a tricorn hat and sergeant's white epaulettes, spoke first. His voice was deep, a baritone. Shadows cast about from the afternoon sun blurred his facial features. "Mrs. Barlow?" he inquired.

"No, I am her cousin, Mairl. They killed Mrs. Barlow in the raid today." Essie attempted to feign a look of sorrow she didn't feel for a faux relation she didn't know.

"You have my deepest condolences, ma'am," replied the sergeant. "I am afraid I am the bearer of more bad news," the man stated. He paused, took a breath, and continued, "Captain Robert Barlow died in North Carolina during the Battle of Guilford Courthouse. You have my deepest sympathy."

Essie wished she could summon tears at a moment's notice. Instead of her terrible thespian attributes, Essie bowed her head and whispered, "Oh my God. The world is so cruel. I don't know what I shall do."

The sergeant and his private expressed their sympathies once more, and Essie closed the door. Now, what would she do? The people whose home she inhabited were now gone. How long could she stay here? What if the British stage another raid? Essie stopped her frantic rumination. *Think*, she urged herself. Stella said they had no relatives left, either here in Richmond or in Staunton. It reminded Essie of her situation with her first husband, Thomas, back in Wickhamshire. No one would come to claim ownership of the house. She reasoned she could stay indefinitely. Then, quick as a gunpowder flash, Essie remembered that James Armistead was hiding in the cellar.

She eased down the cellar stairs. The opening benefitted only from the remaining daylight. Essie found Armistead sitting on an old wooden stool with a lit candle, squinting to take in the cramped space. In her short time in the Barlow house, Essie had yet to explore the root cellar, and now she knew why. It looked as if no one had been down there for centuries. Apart from the old stool, numerous glass bottles, covered in dust, rested on two shelves. The contents were indiscernible, but Essie assumed they once contained food since turned rotten.

Armistead handed Essie a candle and lit it with his own.

"Tell me how you came to work as a double agent?" Essie asked.

Armstead stiffened and declared, "General Lafayette proposed the idea."

Stunned, Essie stammered out, "The Marquis de Lafayette?"

"The same," Armistead said proudly. "My master, William Armistead, he taught me to read and write. Then he agreed to let me enlist in the Continental army as the general's personal assistant. After the general came to learn of my literacy, he conceived the idea of having me pose as a runaway slave in search of Benedict Arnold's battalion. The British are promising freedom to slaves who enlist."

Flabbergasted, Essie shook her head in disbelief. This man was a wonder. "General Lafayette knows my husband, General Aquila Wright." She paused, knowing the information would startle Armistead on two counts. She was not disappointed.

Armistead's mouth formed an *O*. "But you said your name was Mairl Ross and you were Mrs. Barlow's cousin from Staunton."

"I did at that, sir. And you claimed to be a soldier in the British army."

Armistead smiled. Essie was now confident that they could form an alliance. "My real name is Essie Wright from Cromwell in Maryland."

"Do you know Colonel Charles Greene?" asked Armistead.

Essie lit up. "Why yes, he and his wife Celia are dear friends. You've met?"

Armistead stood and moved closer. Essie was no longer concerned about his intentions. She could see that Armistead had a good heart.

"After Lafayette suggested my dual role as a spy, Colonel Greene came to train me on the rudiments of spycraft. He told me I am now an Agent of Liberty."

"A movement created by my husband and Charles," Essie replied. "We will help each other. We need to work out a method of communication. You must continue to refer to me as Mairl Ross. No one here knows my true identity.

The leaders of our country sentenced me to death, and they believe that is what happened."

"What did happen?" Armistead asked gently. He seemed unsure of his freedom to intrude into the details of her life.

Essie held Armistead's hand in hers and took him further into her confidence. The sense of relief in unburdening herself to a kindred spirit was intoxicating. Essie wanted to pour her heart out but knew time nor circumstance permitted such a luxury.

"I will fix you a hot meal. Then you must return to where the British expect you."

"That would be back at camp with General Arnold. Lafayette is presently on his way back to Virginia with sufficient numbers to defeat Arnold. Once that occurs, I would like to abandon my dual role and serve the Continental army in whatever manner I am able."

Essie was so impressed with this fine man. She hesitated to make promises she couldn't fulfill, but she vowed to liberate Armistead after the war.

After agreeing on drop locations and potential clandestine meetup spots, they moved toward the stairs to escape the dingy remains of the ancient cellar. Essie, leading the way, stumbled and extended her right hand along the poorly illuminated wall to break her fall. The surface was rough. A jagged edge of broken glass sliced through Essie's palm, and she screamed at the sudden excruciating pain.

Rushing over with his candle, Armistead said, "That's a nasty cut. I have a fogle somewhere." Digging through his pockets, he produced a large tan cloth. While wrapping it around Essie's hand, he wondered, "Why would broken glass be sticking out of a cellar wall?"

"Bring the candle closer," Essie said. After scrutinizing the bottle's remnants and the burned parchment, she declared, "Something is within! Someone buried the bottle in the wall. If I had a pair of forceps, I could extract the paper."

In his search through the root cellar for anything to use, Armistead discovered an old long-handled axe. "Stand back," he commanded. Essie retreated to the rear while Armistead hammered the wall above the embedded glass bottle. After a dozen solid blows, the portion of the wall holding the bottle fell to the floor.

The remaining glass shattered, and the old parchment stared at them, begging to be free of a long-kept secret.

Essie walked over to the rubble and reached for the parchment.

"Be careful," warned Armistead. "Glass shards are everywhere."

Essie bent over and secured the corner of the weathered document between her thumb and index finger, raising it toward her body. Then, she returned to the back wall and unrolled the parchment on a soiled tabletop.

"Look at the date," Armistead remarked. "Sixteen seventy-two." He whistled in surprise.

"It appears to be some sort of map," Essie said. Underneath the year, in writing almost too small to read without a magnifying glass, was the word "de Groot."

CHAPTER 74

New Windsor, New York

"The intelligence is extraordinary," proclaimed George Washington. "And to think Essie risked her life in service to her country. This is something I won't forget."

Aquila tried to suppress his smile but found it difficult. The pride he felt burst through his stoic facade. The grin was short-lived, for Aquila, in a flash, regained the sense of danger his wife was in. Arnold had raided the city. Stella Barlow was dead. Essie was on her own in a hostile environment.

Seeing the worry that now consumed Aquila's face, Washington set out to relieve it. "A week ago, I received a letter from Lafayette. He was in Head of Elk, en route with twelve hundred men to confront Arnold in Virginia." Washington cleared his throat, which Aquila surmised was strained from the never-ending meetings and counsel required of his position. "By my calculations, he should be there anytime."

"I shall leave at once to join Lafayette and to tend to Essie. Perhaps it is time to remove the shroud from our charade. Essie belongs at Cromwell's Passage with Penny. She needn't hide forever because of a misinterpretation of a good-hearted deed."

Washington did not immediately respond. He weighed his words before speaking. With one finger on his chin, emphasizing his concentration, he proclaimed, "We mustn't let haste dominate common sense."

"Sir?" Aquila responded. "How can we not come to Essie's aid?"

Washington, the brilliant war strategist, broke into an amiable smile, revealing his rotting teeth. In the years he had served under Washington, Aquila rarely saw Washington smile fully. When the commander in chief showed teeth, Aquila's experience taught him that a plan had formed. Usually, it was something beyond the pale, a formula for success. Aquila waited in silence for Washington to speak.

"When you arrive in Richmond, assess the possibility of Essie remaining in place and continuing her work as an Agent of Liberty using her pseudonym. The intelligence is unprecedented. She clearly has a source on the inside. We must preserve and cultivate the stream of information. It could turn the tide of the entire war."

Aquila's stomach knotted. While he couldn't argue with the wisdom of Washington's order, Aquila believed he could further the efforts of the Agents of Liberty without placing his wife in harm's way. Like Washington, he paused, deliberating before uttering words that might reveal emotion over logic. "Sir, I believe Essie might be of greater service to America if we extract and debrief her."

"Nonsense," replied Washington. His calm manner had deteriorated like the dew on a sunny spring morn. "You have my orders, General Wright. You also have my word that when the war is over, I will personally see to the reinstatement of Essie's good name."

Aquila was defiant. If Essie died before the war ended, Washington's pledge would be worthless. He had to pursue the opportunity to free her now or he would regret it for the rest of his life. "But sir . . ."

Washington cut him to the quick. "That is all, General Wright. Dismissed."

CHAPTER 75

Richmond, Virginia

"My husband's letters never revealed the magnitude of your charm," Essie said to Lafayette. "How kind of you to pay me a visit."

"Oui, madame. General Washington sent me an urgent dispatch. You are a valuable asset of the Continental army." Lafayette proffered a muffled giggle and then said, "Even though I thought you were dead. General Washington surprised me when I learned the truth."

"Asset?" Essie remarked. "Is that all I am?" Essie's stomach turned. Somehow, her letter to Aquila had reached the commander in chief. At least no one had abandoned her and left her for dead. Washington continued to hold a measure of respect for her prior service. Still, being called an asset was irritating, especially as she languished alone in Richmond.

"Mon Dieu," replied Lafayette, horrified at the notion he had offended Essie. "I know your husband, and he must miss you terribly." Embarrassment flushed Lafayette's face.

Essie was enjoying the repartee with Lafayette, whose youthful appearance belied his otherwise polished demeanor. She estimated she was at least a decade older than the baby-faced Frenchman. It was hard to imagine being significantly older than a decorated leader in the Continental army. How quickly life was passing by.

"And I miss him more than you could know," Essie replied.

In the parlor of the Barlow house, Essie briefed Lafayette on recent events and the discovery of the map.

"It is fascinating to consider how the confluence of events has brought us together," exclaimed Lafayette. "I served America alongside your husband, and you encountered James Armistead during a raid by the man I was sent to defeat."

"*Armistead* is fascinating," Essie said, borrowing the description of events just used by Lafayette. "He is intelligent and compassionate, and he works tirelessly in service to our country. He places his life at risk, as much or more than the infantrymen you lead."

"Oui, James is remarkable. I have promised I would petition Congress for his freedom when the war is over," Lafayette stated.

"I vowed to do likewise," replied Essie.

"So, madame, we are united in a common goal." Then, Lafayette moved his lean frame on the settee and gazed toward the dining table in the next room. "Is that the map you and James discovered?"

Nodding, Essie moved to the end of the table opposite Lafayette. "It is over one hundred years old," stated Lafayette in amazement. Then, noting the burned edge, he said, "And it appears to have survived an encounter with a flame."

"As if someone started to burn the map, and another saved it," added Essie.

"Or . . ." replied Lafayette, "someone changed their mind and blew the flame out."

"I guess there is no way to know," said Essie. "There are so many strange symbols. Do you know what they mean?"

Lafayette studied the details of the map, tracing his long index finger along the snake line denoting the James River. "I believe this is a map of where we are today." Moving his finger to points on either side of the river, he said, "These triangles are likely denoting Indians who lived on this land before Europeans arrived."

"And at the top, in a strange handwritten manner, was the word *Henrico*," Essie said. "That is the name of the county in which Richmond is situated."

"Oui, look at this," Lafayette pointed to a small, curved *x* encircled with a set of numbers, *37N, 77W*.

"What on earth could it mean?" asked Essie.

Lafayette smiled. "Latitude and longitude. These numbers are coordinates representing the location of this area." Lafayette furrowed his brow. "This circled *x*, it seems to indicate a more precise location within the framework of the land."

"The cartographer spent an enormous amount of time depicting the topography of the area," Essie proclaimed.

"And since I have spent considerable time in these parts, I can tell you that whatever secret this map holds is likely under our feet, literally."

"In the Barlow root cellar," asked Essie.

"That is my guess. The root cellar predates the house. Someone buried the map in the wall of the root cellar. I suspect the Barlows never knew of its existence."

"How do we solve this mystery?" Essie inquired. "Is it even worth solving?"

Lafayette smiled in his boyish manner, intrigued by the hunt for answers. "Oui. We need a local historian."

—∾—

That evening, under the cover of darkness, Lafayette returned to the Barlow house with a tall man in a black cloak. Essie was surprised to see Dr. DeBusschere. Employing her alias, Lafayette greeted Essie at the entrance.

"Bonjour, Madame Ross. I believe you know Dr. DeBusschere." Lafayette stated in his elegant manner that he had discreetly asked to be referred to the local historian when inquiring about the town. His voice was so suave. The words, no matter what their meaning or intent, flowed from his tongue like butterflies dancing atop wildflowers. Maybe it was the French way. Or perhaps it was just *his* way.

"Of course. Welcome, Doctor. Let's sit in the dining room where we can properly examine the map."

Dr. De Busschere's eyes went wide. His voice rose an octave when he proclaimed, "de Groot."

"Was this perhaps the original name given to this area?" asked Lafayette.

DeBusschere rebounded from his state of momentary surprise. He stood erect and wiped the sweat from his brow with a monogrammed foulard. "de Groot was not a place. It was the name of a Dutch explorer, Frans de Groot. People believed he was one of the earliest sailors to inhabit the land we now know as Richmond. This map is a significant find. de Groot was said to have brought riches from Holland that today would be worth millions."

Lafayette's eyes also went wide. Essie herself felt short of breath. The intrigue of this discovery had far-reaching ramifications.

"Might this fortune be buried beneath the house we're in?" asked Essie. Her heart raced with anticipation of the answer.

DeBusschere crinkled his bushy brows and inhaled slowly as if he were about to pass on an ancient secret handed down across the generations. "It is possible," he conceded. "But digging too much in the root cellar would likely cause this house to collapse. And that would raise unwanted suspicions, especially amongst the British who occupy our city."

"But, Doctor, we have exact coordinates," Lafayette stated emphatically.

Reconsidering his assessment, DeBusschere once more examined the map. "Yes, General. We need to determine where this is." Pointing to a symbol just south of the James River, he added, "And this strange symbol. I don't know what to make of it."

Essie moved in closer to see the ambiguous symbol. It stood below the topographical demarcation of the forest. Three squares with rounded edges formed a stack, with two on the bottom and one on top. There was a shaded space between the bottom two figures. Around the strange symbol was a spray of crooked lines draping down across the top.

"Early Dutch explorers did not use any standardized system of cartography," DeBusschere stated. "They simply made things up to suit their own purposes."

"You mean to conceal something of value," Lafayette surmised aloud.

"Most likely," DeBusschere answered.

"I don't understand how we will find the exact spot," Essie said, her frustration evident. Pointing to the map's latitude and longitude, she said, "These numbers are meaningless."

"Au contraire, Madame," Lafayette said excitedly. "With the use of a sextant at high noon, we can fix the precise north–south position. The latitude. Then, a marine chronometer will help determine the east–west position, or the longitude."

"But where do you find such instruments, and do we know how to use them?" Essie asked. The discouragement shone through in her strained voice. What had they stumbled on? This map she discovered that might hold the key to some buried treasure chest was likely sheer folly. Was it even worth the effort? Then she remembered the words of Dr. DeBusschere, ". . . that today would be worth millions." Essie reassessed her emotions. Conversations with Aquila about the war years were fraught with concern over a dearth of financial resources, uniforms, and supplies. What if she could unearth a fortune to aid the United States government? This, she determined, would be the genuine statement of independence enabling the fledgling government to retire its debts to France, Holland, and Spain. Aquila denounced the extent of the domestic borrowing through the issuance of bonds. A necessary evil, he asserted. Even though it was the longest of long shots, Essie felt her excitement build. This was the way, she thought. Her way of serving the country she loved and reclaiming her true identity and the life she longed for at Cromwell's Passage. Essie thought her heart might leap out of her chest. Then, just as quickly as the excitement built, Dr. DeBusschere's words acted as a lightning bolt splitting apart a majestic oak.

"My best guess is that de Groot used his own interpretation to conceal the location of something he didn't want known to the casual observer. I contend the symbol to be a cave or a rock formation, hidden behind foliage or a waterfall. Clearly along the James River in an area presently occupied by Benedict Arnold's camp."

CHAPTER 76

Guilford County, North Carolina

Cornwallis said nothing. But he heard the grumbling of his battle-weary troops. "He fired on his own men," he heard one say around the evening campfire. While in the privy, he heard voices echoing similar sentiments. "Next time, it will be us. Does he expect us to trust him? The bugger must be mad. I don't want to be in battle to find grapeshot raining down from our own bloody cannon." Cornwallis was unsure how to address the despondency. Surely, the men comprehended the gravity of their situation. Any of them would have made the same decision.

Standing alongside his cot in the command tent, Cornwallis removed his general's hat. The dark material with its gold fringe sat heavy on his head of thinning hair. He let his oversized hat dangle in his right hand by his knee. Bile rose from the pit of his stomach, and for a moment, Cornwallis thought he might be sick. He heaved. Cold sweat broke out on his back, soaking the white linen shirt under his red coat. Vertigo made him light on his feet, so he sat on the edge of the cot because he feared the men now despised him and he did not want them to find him in a weakened state. Gathering himself, Cornwallis reached for the jug of water resting on the small bedside table. He pulled the cork and chugged. Then, he poured the remainder of the jug's contents into his right hand and splashed his face. The cool water felt good. It wiped away the fear he could never divulge to another living soul. After a few moments, he rose, placed the hat on his head, and resolved to repair the morale of his troops with a pep talk.

Before he could exit the tent, the major of the cannon brigade poked his head inside and requested permission to enter.

Granting the request, Cornwallis spoke matter-of-factly to his subordinate, attempting to appear nonchalant. "Major, have we received a dispatch from General Clinton?"

"No, sir. But I need to make you aware of the presence of a few dozen rogue Americans spotted in and around the woods."

"Take the men you need. Rifles and bayonets, I should think. Eliminate any threat," Cornwallis responded before sending the major on his way.

Alone in his tent, Cornwallis paced back and forth, forming the words in his mind of the speech he would soon deliver to the troops. He was unsure what to say. Then, he shook his head in disgust when considering that Clinton had not yet seen fit to bless his plan for advancement into Virginia. Cornwallis stretched his arms wide, and, finding his resolve, he decided. His worn-down forces and dwindling supplies made time a luxury they could ill-afford to waste. He must get his men back on their feet. Waiting for Clinton's approval was no longer an option. They would leave at once. Cornwallis set Yorktown squarely in his sights.

CHAPTER 77

New Windsor, New York

Hours passed after Washington had issued his orders. Aquila should have already departed for Virginia. Yet he rested on a tree stump near the edge of camp. His dilemma consumed him: defy George Washington's order to have his wife remain in place and aid the Agents of Liberty, or preserve her safety. Did the needs of the country outweigh his own? Logically, Aquila knew the answer. Therefore, he risked his life repeatedly for America's independence. His commitment to his country was unwavering. But what other man was being asked to sacrifice his beloved? Aquila spied his horse tied to a nearby tree, rested and ready to ride. He shook his head in despair. He rose, disengaged the horse, and prepared to mount when the commander in chief called him.

"I thought you had left. I've been deliberating about the intelligence you conveyed and have scheduled a strategy meeting in ten minutes. Your presence is required."

"Yes, sir," Aquila replied sullenly.

"Buck up, General," Washington quipped. "Perhaps you are not as troubled as you believe," Washington said.

Stymied by Washington's words, Aquila nodded, wondering all the while if this man could read his thoughts. Then, he remembered Essie telling him he always wore his emotions on his sleeve. Washington saw right through his attempt to shield the raging conflict churning inside his head.

Aquila trudged into the tent that Washington used as his command center, as if his feet were made of stone. Aquila saw Generals St. Clair, Knox, and Lincoln. Along the back wall of the tent stood Washington's current aide-de-camp, Colonel Tench Tilghman. The men stood, none daring to speak before George Washington did. The commander in chief approached the rectangular table holding a dog-eared map of Virginia.

"I have given a great deal of thought to the intelligence brought forth by General Wright," said Washington. "I believe a historic opportunity lies at our feet. If Cornwallis is bound and determined to establish a foothold in Yorktown, we shall meet him with everything we've got."

"With the whole of our powder," quipped Arthur St. Clair in his Scottish brogue.

Aquila never took St. Clair to be a man with a sense of humor. His face was stonelike, connoting a constant air of seriousness.

"And then some," Washington replied with a toothless grin. "As soon as we are prepared, I want every available soldier on the march to Yorktown."

Benjamin Lincoln wiped a hand across his prominent forehead and said, "We can move troops in from New Jersey, Pennsylvania, and Maryland. All in, I estimate seven or eight thousand men."

Washington glared at Lincoln. "Think bigger, General. What about Rochambeau and other forces here in New York?"

Tilghman approached the table. "The French have seven thousand troops we can deploy. Here in New Windsor and at West Point, there are another three thousand or so."

That seemed to please the commander in chief, Aquila noticed. Washington confirmed it when he responded to Tilghman's assessment.

"Very well, at least seventeen thousand men. Plan the march south." Looking at St. Clair, Knox, and Aquila, Washington ordered, "Gather Rochambeau and the four of you all ride south. I want Yorktown under American control within a fortnight."

No one said a word in reply until Henry Knox, the artillery chief, chimed in as the men prepared to disperse. "Your Excellency, I should point out that a brief pause to the march will be required for resupply."

"Of course," replied Washington. "Where do you plan to stop?"

"Philadelphia, sir," replied Knox.

"Very well. I trust the interlude will be brief," Washington said. "Dismissed." And before Washington turned away from his wartime commanders, he glanced at Aquila and winked.

Aquila understood. Washington foresaw the capture of Yorktown as the event upon which victory would be secured. Washington's earlier order to leave Essie in Richmond would be void. Aquila breathed easier. The end of the war was in sight. He would soon restore his life with Essie and Penny. But first, a battle had to be fought.

CHAPTER 78

Richmond, Virginia

Essie was emphatic. She would accompany Lafayette and a handful of his most trusted men, along with Dr. DeBusschere, to the banks of the James River.

"No, madame. I cannot permit it. Should any harm come to you, I would never forgive myself," Lafayette said. Collecting his thoughts, he continued, "Until our men defeat Benedict Arnold and rid the city of the redcoats, no one will chase the secrets held by de Groot's map."

Essie sighed. She knew she had no choice. She had been fortunate to survive the last British raid that burned down most of the city and killed Stella Barlow. Parading around the occupied riverbanks with a band of soldiers in broad daylight was not a prescription for keeping a low profile under an assumed identity. "Very well," she stated with resignation.

Gunshots and hollering stole their attention. Lafayette moved to a window and drew back the drape to get a look at the commotion.

"Our men flood the street. Mon Dieu. The reinforcements have arrived from the north. I must gather my men and join the battle. Stay here. I will send two men to protect you."

Before Essie could acknowledge Lafayette's instruction, he was out the door. Essie moved to the window, kneeling while sneaking a peek. A swarm of Continental army soldiers charged down the street amid the debris and remnants of the burned-out buildings. A small band of redcoats was visible down the street where the post office once stood. They were on their heels, outmanned. Essie could see the Continental army soldiers picking them off one by one with pistols.

Minutes passed. They felt like hours. Although Essie was relieved the Americans seemed in control of the battle, fear gripped her. She slid to the floor, wrapping her arms around her knees and lowering her head. Tears welled and ran down her cheeks like rain rolling down a pane of glass. *Enough!* Years of fighting and sacrifice. Her banishment to Virginia. The time away from her family. And all the men who died fighting for America's independence. It was enough already. Would life ever return to normal? She tried to pray, but the noise from the battle outside prevented her from concentrating. All Essie could think of was embracing Aquila and feeling safe in his arms.

A rapid succession of knocks on the door caused Essie to gasp. Did redcoats break from the fight, arriving here to cause her harm? She could feel her cheeks turn crimson. Cautiously, Essie rose from her crouched position and looked out the window toward the front door. Two soldiers in blue remained tranquil. She walked to the door, unlatched it, and revealed only the smallest part of her face.

"General Lafayette sent us to guard you," one soldier stated. "We shall remain outside the house. Do not fear, Miss Ross. We will be right here if you need us."

Essie thanked the soldiers, closed the door, and retreated to the dining area where the map still lay on the table. Essie feared the redcoats would kill her and claim the map if they overtook the two soldiers, so she rolled the ancient paper as she had found it and slipped it under a loose kitchen floorboard. Consumed with worry, her stomach remained in knots. She couldn't sit. She couldn't eat or drink. Reading and sewing were out of the question. So Essie paced. From the kitchen to the parlor and toward the foyer. Back and forth. The expenditure of energy held her emotions at bay. This day had no end. Essie paced for an hour. Her feet hurt, and she panted. All she wanted was to sit and cry. Her strength was gone. Her courage was exhausted. She blew her nose into a linen napkin from the dining room and realized the noise from the battle had subsided. Returning to the window, she glanced at the area near the front door and saw one soldier still camping out. The other man must have gone around back.

But the fighting had stopped. Redcoats lay dead in the street. The Continental army was gone. They had left the city. Was anyone coming back for her? Essie reached under her bonnet and yanked at her hair. She coughed. All the crying left her nose congested and her throat raw. Deep within, she urged herself to find courage. She couldn't afford to remain locked in the Barlow house, playing the victim. She must do something!

—⁂—

Wondering and waiting was taking its toll. Despite the silence outside, Essie could not summon the nerve to leave the house. She cracked the door and inquired of the soldiers by her front door.

"We have no information, Miss Ross. But do not worry, we will not leave. You are safe."

While that offered a measure of comfort, the silence outside was deafening. How long could she remain cooped up waiting for answers? Essie considered asking the soldiers to escort her to Dr. DeBusschere's home, but that seemed presumptuous and dangerous. *He is one of us.* Stella's words about Dr. DeBusschere came back to her. *An Agent of Liberty.* This war had taught her that detached troops from the enemy could still roam these parts, eager for retribution against anything or anyone American. No, as much as it hurt her, Essie concluded she must stay put. She retreated to the kitchen, rifling through Stella's cabinets seeking anything that might settle her. She discovered nothing that satisfied her desires. Essie grabbed a dusty bottle with a handwritten label, *Corn Beere.* The liquid was clear and didn't look suitable for consumption. But desperate to soothe her frayed nerves, Essie removed the cork, lifted the bottle to her nose, and took a whiff. To Essie, it smelled of compost. But she had seen Stella take a swig from the bottle when she was at her worst. Perhaps it would help. Essie placed the mouth of the bottle on her lips, closed her eyes, and gulped three times. The liquid was vile. She spat it out onto the kitchen floor and choked. Her eyes watered as she swallowed the leftover corn beere in her mouth. She found a jug of water and began drinking at a furious pace. Anything to remove the taste. How could anyone drink this? For any reason? Essie crunched up her face and fought back a sneeze. Then she dropped to her knees with a rag to clean up the horrid concoction she spat onto the floor. Before she finished, the front door burst open, and Essie heard what she had been dreaming of. She questioned whether it was real or a manifestation of the detestable corn beere.

"Mairl Ross, you are safe. The Continental army is at your beck and call."

Aquila! Her beloved used her alias to maintain the deception. Before Essie could rise from the kitchen floor, he stood before her. How long had it been? Months, she thought. No matter the time, Essie would never get used to it. She thought she must be a sight to her war-weary husband. Her eyes were bloodshot. She could feel the bags under her eyelids from lack of sleep. He approached and helped her to her feet.

And then, just like in a dream, he pulled her close, and without saying a word, kissed her passionately. It evoked memories of their first kiss. He pulled away, and with his hands on her shoulders, he mused, "You taste of moonshine. And that short dark hair. Are you sure you are my wife?"

Essie didn't speak. She nodded, fighting back tears of joy. And she threw her arms back around her husband, proclaiming, "I never want to let go."

"You don't have to," her husband replied softly. "I shall see to it."

Lafayette interrupted their embrace when he entered the house with James Armistead. Lafayette inquired about Essie's safety and then introduced Armistead to Aquila.

"We have driven the British from Richmond!" exclaimed Lafayette excitedly.

Armistead, who had shed his redcoat but still wore the remainder of the British uniform, stated. "General Arnold retreated on the James River to Portsmouth. I hope that means I never have to don this uniform again."

"I should hope not," replied Aquila. "The United States notes your meritorious service. I will petition for your freedom when the war is over."

"I am grateful for your support, General Wright," Armistead humbly replied.

"It's a shame Arnold fled before we arrived. I was hoping to capture the scoundrel and return him to General Washington for questioning," stated Aquila.

"Questioning?" asked Lafayette. "I think you mean hanging."

"Yes, I am sure that would be his ultimate demise," Aquila said.

Essie, perched next to Aquila and clinging to his arm, laid her head against his bicep. "I just want the war to be over."

"We shall head home tomorrow. The devil with your isolation. I shall argue before Congress for your freedom to be yourself. They should know the sacrifices you've made on behalf of our country."

Essie squeezed his arm in a gentle show of affection. "But first, my love, with the British gone from the banks of the James River, we can pursue the secret of the de Groot map."

CHAPTER 79

Wilmington, North Carolina

Cornwallis reached over his shoulder to alleviate an itch. The profuse sweating in the late summer heat caused a rash. He poured water into a tin cup and sipped. Inhaling, he committed to resupply while in Wilmington and taking it easy on the men. As a port city, Wilmington gave them the enjoyment of taverns—and the pleasure houses he would never enter. Such trivialities were for infantrymen and those with low moral character. Cornwallis had no use for the noise, the smell, or the pox. After all, he was a gentleman.

Two days' liberty for the men and then the march over the Virginia border would begin. Studying the map spread across his bunk, Cornwallis chose Petersburg as the first destination. From there, they would proceed to Williamsburg, and finally to Yorktown. It was a perfect plan. Yorktown afforded him every strategic opportunity to succeed in Virginia. Access to the sea for resupply and fresh troops was strategically important. The location also enabled the British to avail themselves of the naval superiority they so cherished. The Americans with their fledgling navy were a joke. Even with support from the hapless French, they stood no chance. The French were driven by emotion. The British dominated through might and mind. What, he wondered, was Clinton involved in that was so important he couldn't take time to respond to his recommended course of action? Cornwallis found his patience worn as an old hand-me-down sweater. He would take matters of strategy into his own hands. Capture Virginia. End the war. Return to England to mourn Jemma in the manner she deserved.

CHAPTER 80

Richmond, Virginia

The sun blazed at high noon. Even though fall was around the corner, Richmond remained hot and humid. Essie, with help from Aquila, dismounted her horse and secured him to a nearby oak. Lafayette, Armistead, Dr. DeBusschere, and a host of Lafayette's men soon followed.

DeBusschere believed that what they sought was worth a fortune and that the river concealed it with foliage or a waterfall. Lafayette and his nautical instruments would erase any shard of ambiguity. Employing a sextant and marine chronometer, a French sea captain pinpointed the precise latitude and longitude noted on de Groot's map. When the group reached the location, there was no waterfall. Essie spied a wild overgrowth of plants. Thorned weeds and wildflowers sprayed a tangled menagerie of greens and browns across a ten-foot area. The thick mess obscured everything. It reminded Essie of a fairy tale in which the growth symbolized an ancient evil gatekeeper assigned to protect treasures placed by the gods, intended only for the person with the proper credentials to penetrate the fortress of overgrowth. DeBusschere's Flemish dialect shook her back into the moment.

"Legend has it that de Groot left Holland in the aftermath of the *Rampjaar*, otherwise known as 'the disaster year.' France, England, Münster, and Cologne invaded Holland—simultaneously. After the lynching of Grand Pensionary Johan de Witt, de Groot, a wealthy shipbuilder, fled the country with as much treasure as he could carry."

"Fascinating," replied Aquila. "And you believe that de Groot's treasure is here? Along the riverbank?"

DeBusschere nodded. "I have always believed it. But until your wife discovered the hidden map in the Barlow root cellar, it was just a tale handed down through the generations."

Lafayette instructed his men to clear the overgrowth. Six men using a combination of fascine knives and billhooks attacked the growth with fervor. Two of the men wore heavy gloves to remove the chopped vines, not wishing to be poked by the thorns. It took almost an hour, but when the men completed their task it revealed exactly what de Groot had drawn on his map. A small cave surrounded by three ancient boulders. The soldiers removed the last of the brush. The group stood, peering into a cave opening so small, they wondered how de Groot could have concealed anything of extreme value inside.

Essie blanched as a black snake slithered out from the cave opening. She hated snakes. When she was a little girl growing up in England, a snake was hiding in her father's rowboat and gave her a terrible fright. Papa came to her rescue and whisked it away with his bare hands, hurling it into the lake. The memory caused Essie to tremble.

"None of us is small enough to go into the cave," exclaimed Lafayette.

"I might be," Essie replied while trying not to reveal her trepidation.

"Have you taken leave of your senses?" Aquila exclaimed. "There has to be another way."

"What if we could rope the boulders and then some of us could pull them away from the cave opening?" Armistead said.

"It is worth a try," answered Lafayette. And Essie watched as Armistead tied a thick rope around the top boulder. Then, he and three of Lafayette's soldiers stood in a line, each holding the rope. Essie watched as Armistead bellowed, "Heave!" To her amazement, the first boulder toppled down. And so they repeated the process until they moved all three boulders far enough to reveal . . . nothing. Just darkened ground, drenched with moisture from the shade of the rocks.

"What do we do now?" asked Essie.

"We dig," proclaimed DeBusschere. "The secret of the map must lie beneath this spot."

CHAPTER 81

Yorktown, Virginia

The Franco-American forces totaled seventeen thousand. Conferring with General Benjamin Lincoln, Aquila questioned Knox on where and how to set up stores of artillery. The Americans had never had the luxury of so much firepower to prepare for a single battle. Knox had an impressive mind. His talent for the strategic placement of men and supplies was invaluable. Satisfied with the shrewdness of Knox's recommendations, Aquila and Lincoln turned their attention to the Comte de Rochambeau, the French general who would fortify the northwestern flank. He would be supported by the men brought to Yorktown by Brigadier General Peter Muhlenberg, the minister who led the Virginia troops. The men they aggregated on the march from New York would accompany Lafayette to complete the envelopment of the area, trapping the British and strangling their plans to advance north.

Aquila stood tall. He clapped one hand on the backs of Lafayette and Lincoln and smiled. The Franco-American troops outnumbered the British by a significant margin; they were well-supplied and held advantages by land and sea. The troops would rest for two days. Many had marched at a furious pace from New York, New Jersey, Pennsylvania, and Maryland.

"The chances of success are far greater if the men are fresh," Aquila had stated to his military brain-trust.

"I couldn't agree more," chirped a familiar voice.

Aquila turned and greeted George Washington. "Your Excellency! We were not expecting you. Please allow me to review our plan for your approval."

"You already have it," Washington smiled as he stood proudly near the flap of the command tent. "I was here the entire time. My counsel wasn't required. I couldn't have crafted a better plan."

"Thank you, sir. That's very kind of you to say," Aquila replied.

Becoming stoic, Washington walked toward his leaders and proclaimed, "This battle may be the defining moment of the war. I could not imagine missing it."

The first sounds of battle were explosions in the dead of night. The first line of siege rained artillery down on unsuspecting British troops, who were unaware of the extent of the enemy's advances. Smoke streaked across the black sky, obliterating Aquila's view of the moon. The cover of darkness would serve them well. The initial bursts of cannon and mortar hit the redcoats hard. Aquila watched from his position on a rear hill, waiting to charge. When the smoke cleared, British casualties lay strewn across the battlefield, never knowing what hit them. Aquila waved his right arm and yelled, "Attack!" to the second line. The Maryland regiment ran forward, bayonets and rifles at the ready, trampling the dead and the wounded men wearing red. The fighting continued for hours.

When no more British troops were visible, Aquila called for his men to halt and begin collecting weapons and valuables from the defeated enemy sites. As planned, he would make camp along the river one mile from Gloucester Point, and tonight, his men would move into the Yorktown settlement Cornwallis had been constructing for months. Just like the British had done in Richmond, Aquila would burn every structure to the ground.

The Continental army's light dragoons crept into the makeshift town. Essie had told Aquila how Arnold's men used turpentine and flint to create fire in glass bottles when they leveled Richmond. Aquila decided they deserved exact payback.

He rode with the dragoons and gave the order to begin the operation. Two dozen men, each armed with three glass bottles, rags, and small decanters of turpentine, struck the flint against the steel of their swords and lit the fires, tossing bottles with reckless abandon in every building they encountered. British soldiers ran out into the street, most in their nightshirts, choking from smoke inhalation. Aquila waved in the second battalion, Pennsylvania riflemen, who took aim and shot the fleeing enemy soldiers dead in the street.

"Where is Cornwallis?" Aquila spoke aloud to no one in particular. One of his men rode up next to him, stopping so suddenly that the horse's hooves kicked up an inordinate amount of dust from the road. Aquila rubbed his irritated eyes. The smoke and dirt were taking a toll.

"Our men have inspected Cornwallis's quarters. He has fled," replied the leader of the dragoons.

The city was surrounded. Access to the sea was cut off by Admiral de Grasse of the French navy. Finding Cornwallis was only a matter of time.

CHAPTER 82

Yorktown, Virginia

Cornwallis was almost there. He could hear the rushing water of the nearby river. The now-distant smell of smoke still invaded his nostrils. To think how close he had come to being captured in his quarters. Once the fires broke out and the gunshots wailed, he had thrown a black cloak over his head and proceeded on foot to the forested paths he had come to know. The past three months in Virginia had afforded him many solitary walks in the woods near the camp they had built. Although he never imagined it would be necessary, Cornwallis had asked his men to position a small rowboat on the banks of the York River. He told his men that the boat was a contingency for resupply in case the main port was cut off by the enemy. But his true purpose was escape. He had done everything he could think of to bring glory to His Majesty's government. Cornwallis made all major decisions with little help from his superior. Capture the south, proceed to the north. Take advantage of the British naval superiority. It all seemed so plausible. Now, his only instinct was survival.

Cornwallis questioned where to go. The French naval forces overwhelmed Admiral Graves's fleet. The French controlled the Chesapeake Bay. Though he reached the rowboat, the sea presented no safe exit. The rebels had Yorktown surrounded. There was nowhere to run. Cornwallis sighed. He placed his hand on the pistol affixed to his belt and considered ending his life. No, he admonished himself. *You are a British officer and a gentleman. Do not succumb to the coward's way out.* Then, he heard feet shuffling through the fallen leaves on the forest floor. And a voice.

"You there. On your knees. We have you surrounded and will not hesitate to fire."

Cornwallis gazed up. The Continental army general looked as if he meant business. Slowly, Cornwallis lowered himself to the ground and raised his hands in the air. His breeches absorbed the moisture where his knees pressed into the ground. Cornwallis was done. His attempt to convince himself he was up to the chore of leading England to victory was over, the folly concluded.

"I am General Aquila Wright of the Continental army. Identify yourself," the leader of the enemy brigade said.

"I am General Charles Cornwallis," he said with as much dignity as he could manage. "I wish to negotiate a surrender."

CHAPTER 83

Richmond, Virginia

Three months earlier, Essie had thought she and Aquila were on the precipice of normalcy. But it had taken time to assemble the troops and bring the plans for Yorktown to fruition. Now, with the American victory in hand, her dreams were closer to reality. Aquila had suggested that Essie assist Dr. DeBusschere in formulating plans to start Richmond's first hospital. She began by writing. To pass the hours, she wrote every instructive word she could think of about how to begin the process. From architectural design suggestions to staffing. She even detailed the planting of a medical garden to ensure the supply of needed elixir ingredients. Finally, she included ideas on housekeeping standards and procuring surgical supplies. When she was done, Essie handed the journal to Dr. DeBusschere at his home, following one of the many dinners she had been honored to attend.

"What is this?" DeBusschere asked when taking the journal from Essie's hands.

"This is your way forward," she replied affectionately.

DeBusschere began skimming the pages, and once he realized what he was holding, his heart swelled with glee and he said, "I don't know how I can ever repay you for this generous undertaking."

Essie beamed. "You already have. In more ways than you will ever know."

The doctor's mood shifted as he grasped the lack of funds for a hospital.

Essie read his expression and decided now was as good a time as any to allay his concerns. "One of de Groot's treasure chests will provide you with the funds you need."

"And then some," DeBusschere stated happily. "But you told me you planned to give the treasure to the United States government."

"Yes, and I will honor that intention. We discovered six chests. Five remain. Keep the fact that someone bequeathed one to you a secret."

"You, Essie, are a gift from God."

"And I couldn't agree more," interjected Aquila, who had just entered the DeBusschere's hilltop home.

Essie rose from the table and ran to her husband, embracing him as tightly as she ever had. "Is it really over?" she asked.

"Yes, Cornwallis officially surrendered today. He handed his sword to General Lincoln. The war is finally over."

Essie stood on her toes and kissed her husband passionately. She glanced at DeBusschere, who blushed at the display. But then, in an act of inspiration, he moved to his wife and draped an arm around her shoulder, pulling her close.

"I must return with George Washington to Philadelphia. I will accompany you to Cromwell's Passage and return to you within a fortnight," stated Aquila.

"Why must you go to Philadelphia?" Essie asked.

"To report the news of the British surrender and to deliver the six chests of de Groot's treasure."

Essie took a step back and stared her husband in the eye. "It's five chests, and I shall accompany you to Philadelphia. I wish to confront Congress and petition for my freedom. America is free, and so I shall be."

Aquila shook his head in resignation. "Okay, okay. You win—wait. Five chests?"

"Yes, it will be our little secret. I have designated one chest of de Groot's treasure to Dr. DeBusschere's care for the construction and operation of the new Richmond hospital."

"Perhaps we will name it after you," DeBusschere said proudly.

Essie approached the tall man, stood on her tippy-toes, and hugged him around the neck. "I believe the man who has dedicated decades of his life to treating the citizens of Richmond should receive that honor."

CHAPTER 84

Philadelphia, Pennsylvania

Essie was there to regain her identity, but until that opportunity arrived, she stood at the back of the hall, dressed in a wide-brimmed hat she pulled down to hide as much of her face as possible. Her dress was plain, a shade of dark blue. She didn't aspire to be recognized. It would ruin everything. Should events not unfold in the manner she hoped, Essie would need to make a clean break from Philadelphia without being noticed. Would she remain dead to the world, hiding as Mairl Ross in some faraway place? With all she had been through, Essie was prepared for anything. Aquila, on the other hand, was adamant. Regardless of whether the men of Congress approved her pardon, they, along with Penny, would stay together. If need be, they would place Cromwell's Passage under custodial possession of Charles and Celia Greene and allow Isaiah Trumbull to run the mill. Aquila's plan was to go to Paris. Then, to other parts of Europe. After that, who knew? They may never return, Aquila had said. They knew nothing would separate them again—not war, and certainly not politics.

Essie was content with whatever unfolded. Aquila secured the entire top floor of a boardinghouse on the outskirts of the city. He registered them as Mr. and Mrs. John Corruthers, a made-up name. No one asked questions. Her body still felt the warmth of the fire's glow from the rented room they shared the prior evening. Their rapture had them naked on a bearskin rug by the fire, making love as if they had never made love before.

Her attention sprang back to the meeting of Congress in the compact hall. George Washington was at the lectern addressing the assembly.

"Through unquestionably long odds borne of too few men, inadequate artillery, the lack of a proper naval force, and insufficient clothing for our troops, we have emerged victorious. I take great pride in informing this Congress that, with the surrender of General Charles Cornwallis subsequent to the battle of Yorktown, America has won the war."

Congress stood and cheered in unison. Hands clapped relentlessly until Washington held up his arms in a gesture seeking quiet.

He continued. "Without the help of the French, who provided men, money, ammunition, supplies, and their naval might, this victory would not have been possible. Loans from Spain and Holland were also instrumental. Our debt to these nations is staggering. One might argue that the amounts we owe are insurmountable and will leave us beholden to our allies for generations."

Essie's nose twitched in the manner it always did when she became excited. Washington was about to intercede on her behalf. She backed against the wall as her knees buckled.

Washington spoke with a subtly rising voice, stating, ". . . our nation is blessed. During our foray into Virginia, a dedicated citizen discovered a map tucked away in the wall of a root cellar. This map led to the discovery of five treasure chests carried to the New World in 1672 from Holland by a wealthy shipbuilder named Frans de Groot. General Lafayette, with help from his troops and a local historian, extracted the treasure. The woman who found the map—the rightful owner of this fortune—has donated its entire contents to retire the debts of the United States government."

Again, the room erupted with raucous applause. Henry Laurens. the president of Congress, yelled out, "May we know the identity of the woman who so generously saved our young nation from financial ruin?"

Washington waited for the hall to settle before answering. Stoically, he said, "The woman you inquire of, sir, is Mrs. Esther Wright."

Gasps rippled through the room. Essie bristled, wondering if she was about to be apprehended and thrown in the very same jail she had once escaped.

Henry Laurens rose and thundered, "You are mistaken, General. We hanged Mrs. Wright for treason."

Washington again raised his arms high to gain the attention of the stunned assemblage. "I regret to inform you that, with my aid, Mrs. Wright evaded her sentence and was whisked away to Virginia to live in anonymity."

Laurens became incensed. "My God, General! You openly admit to aiding a woman convicted of treason? Do you realize the consequences of your declaration, sir?"

From the rear of the hall, Essie could see how the anger turned Lauren's pale cheeks bright red. "And besides," he bellowed, "I saw her hanged with my own two eyes."

Washington, however, was cool as a cucumber. "No, Mr. Laurens. You saw a decoy with a black hood over her head. The decoy was of similar size and proportions to Mrs. Wright, someone the British had just hanged."

Laurens didn't reply. He stood fuming.

Washington, however, had not concluded his remarks. "This assembly may prosecute me if it wishes. I understood the actions I undertook and did so willingly, and if presented with the same choice once more, I would enthusiastically do so again. Mrs. Wright's action of writing a letter to British Prime Minister North resulted in the punishment for treason. Her sole aim was to notify him of General Willard's actions in the intentional spread of smallpox to our citizens and our troops. His plan was to eviscerate the country, reclaim the land, and recolonize it. Granted, Mrs. Wright had no authority to evade diplomatic channels and communicate directly with Prime Minister North, but I put forth that without her actions, our country would not exist today. I realize the failings of my inaction. I should have inoculated the troops sooner. Mrs. Wright's forward thinking overturned my error and ensured the continuity of health for all. For her troubles, we sentenced her to die. I hope you will agree with me that we, the United States of America, have made a grievous error in misjudging the intentions of a true national heroine."

While Laurens stood fuming, Essie lifted the brim of her hat to get a better look at the cheering men who, with Washington's wisdom and patient delivery of well-crafted remarks, had saved her.

"And now . . ." Washington waited for the noise to settle. "And now, Mrs. Wright, without being asked, and in the aftermath of our horrendous wrongdoing against her, has donated tens of millions to help secure our financial independence. I ask you, should we not restore her good name and offer our extreme gratitude?"

Aquila swiftly approached and took Essie by the arm. He escorted her to the front of the room where George Washington announced, "I give you Mrs. Esther Wright."

Washington stepped away from the lectern, and Essie ascended. She watched over Congress as the body cheered her presence. Butterflies danced in her stomach, and pinpricks ran through her toes. *Signs of anxiety*. She urged herself. *Speak up! Speak up and fight for those who still need your help.*

"Thank you. Your forgiveness of my well-intentioned actions means more to me than you know. I merely wish to return to my husband and daughter and the quiet life at Cromwell's Passage. But first, I would like to read a letter from the Marquis de Lafayette, cosigned by my husband, General Aquila Wright, and endorsed by His Excellency, George Washington. The letter tells the story of a heroic man named James Armistead."

Essie completed her remarks. Had she needed to flee, Lafayette's letter would have been read aloud by George Washington. But the commander in chief was confident in his assessment of the day. Washington thought it more impactful for Essie to read the letter to Congress, and Essie had agreed with enthusiasm. Washington, master strategist that he was, understood that after reclaiming her name, America would owe Essie a favor, to say the least. Congress ratified Armistead's petition for freedom. Essie couldn't wait to convey the good news. She and Aquila promised James the use of the cottage on Cromwell's Passage as a place to start out. To live and work in whatever manner his newfound freedom prescribed.

Essie and Aquila strode arm in arm down the aisle. They exited the hall where old Clement waited with the Wrights' finest carriage. They climbed in, cuddled up on the crushed velvet bench, and vowed never to be apart again.

EPILOGUE

Cromwell, Maryland

Mairl Ross was dead. *Thank God,* thought Essie. Existing as someone else was a struggle. Most people find it difficult just to be themselves. Essie could appreciate that sentiment more than most, for, with a grateful heart, she wished for nothing else. Be yourself, people often say. Essie would never again take for granted the freedom to be herself. The view from her porch relaxed her. The holidays were near, and the air was growing cold. She was now where she aspired to be, home at Cromwell's Passage with her family and the knowledge that her husband no longer had to place his life at risk. They had earned this! The fight for freedom was always about the country and the individual liberties all people deserved. But Essie knew more than most that freedom came at a heavy price. The loss of life. The destruction of land and property. The sacrifice. Her experience proved one thing. The circumstances would get worse, much worse, before they improved when a war for independence was waged. She sighed. Now, they could start a new chapter. Thanks to the efforts of men like George Washington, Lafayette, and her own husband, they could begin anew. That's what America was all about. Opportunity to pursue one's dreams. Essie's mind wandered back to her early days as a young wife in Wickhamshire. How idealistic she was! How far she had come.

Penny wandered up the path while holding hands with her new beau, the young Dr. Robinson, who had been working with Henrik and Timothy at the

Cromwell hospital. The time away had afforded her daughter the opportunity to blossom even more, finding love in the throes of war.

"Is Father about?" inquired Penny.

"I believe he is reading a book in the parlor. He so rarely gets to relax," Essie said. "Can it wait?"

Penny beamed. "Well . . . I suppose so, but John really wants to speak with Father."

"Oh!" Essie said, understanding Penny's meaning. "Let's see if we can find him."

They all walked into the house. Fanny, the spaniel rescued from the woods of Mecklenburg, bounded across the foyer and leaped to her hind legs to greet Penny. They found Aquila where Essie predicted, sitting by the fire, puffing on a pipe and reading a book. Penny led her beau into the parlor, and she and Essie retreated to the front porch, resting comfortably on the rockers they had shared over the years for all the heart-to-heart talks.

"Will Father give his blessing?" Penny asked.

Essie took Penny's hand and squeezed. A fresh breeze blew in from the edge of the tree line. The scent of pine filled the air. "Of course he will. You and John will have an incredible journey together."

AUTHOR'S NOTE

When I began writing the Essie Lassiter Trilogy, it occurred to me that my first knowledge of the American Revolution came from junior high school, fifty years earlier. Like many people, I maintained an interest over the years and visited the occasional museum. But when I thought about it, I did not have the requisite knowledge to create a period drama. Consequently, an abundance of research has been done. Along the way, there were a lot of "Oh yeah" moments when my research revealed a key detail from 250 years earlier. That was enjoyable! But if I am being completely honest, the fun was not in remembering the detailed account of the war and its many players; it was in placing them in fictionalized accounts with made-up characters. That enabled me to feel like I was living the history—as if I had traveled back in time! I hope you experienced the same.

Words cannot express my appreciation for my wife, Denise, who once again patiently put up with my countless hours at the computer, researching, writing, and revising. Her point of view on all things Essie is invaluable. She is my first reader and best friend. The field trips we took to historical sites and museums, and the watching of documentaries, were so much fun. Thank you, Denise, for your enduring love and support.

After I complete a manuscript, I also depend on a group of wonderful people to give a frank assessment. Sincere thanks go out to Tom Brunner, Greg Harmis, Anne Hicks, Dave Jennings, Becca Mitchell, my son, Ryan Polakoff, Bruce

Savadkin, and Greg Tutino. Your keen insights helped to make this installment of the trilogy worthy of the first.

And as usual, my ace-in-the-hole, five-star proofreaders, Jeanne Brooks and my mother, Sheila Weinstock, did an outstanding job helping to perfect the final product. Thank you both for your meticulous work and attention to the minutest details.

All six of my novels have benefitted from the dynamic duo of Gwyn Flowers from GKS Creative and Kim Bookless, an expert copyeditor. Gwyn's magic creates eye-catching covers and the interior design and layout. Gwyn fashions the words into a book rivaling those produced by the big publishing houses. Kim's relentless efforts are the final polish on the finished product. From word choice suggestions to punctuation, and everything in between, she is a superstar. I am proud to have you both as part of my publishing team.

Heather Walters was the winner of a drawing to have a character named after her. The character first appears in chapter 18 and is the Baltimore tavern owner who helped facilitate the Agents of Liberty.

Thank you for purchasing this novel. It is gratifying to see that someone who longed to write since childhood would someday craft a series of novels desired by seasoned readers. I am truly humbled.

The writing of the last installment of the Essie Lassiter Trilogy awaits. Until then . . .

Sam Polakoff
January 1, 2026

PLEASE LEAVE A REVIEW

THANK YOU FOR READING

Freedom's Lonely Cry

Your honest reviews on Amazon and Goodreads
are greatly appreciated.

Tell a friend!

STAY IN TOUCH

Join our mailing list for updates on future releases.

FOLLOW

Facebook @sampolakoffauthor

Instagram @sampolakoffauthor

X @spolakoffauthor

YouTube @sampolakoff4320

KOMODO DRAGON BOOKS

Komodo Dragon Books, LLC

Forest Hill, Maryland
https://komodokdragonbooks.com

www.ingramcontent.com/pod-product-compliance
Lightning Source LLC
LaVergne TN
LVHW091118080826
845145LV00008B/1962

* 9 7 8 1 7 3 3 8 8 9 8 8 9 *